CHRISTMAS ANGELS

CHRISTMAS ANGELS

A MERCY ALLCUTT MYSTERY
BOOK 7

ALICE DUNCAN

ALSO BY ALICE DUNCAN

The Mercy Allcutt Mystery Series

Lost Among the Angels

Angels Flight

Fallen Angels

Angels of Mercy

Thanksgiving Angels

Angels Adrift

Christmas Angels

Hollywood Angels

The Daisy Gumm Majesty Mystery Series

Strong Spirits

Fine Spirits

High Spirits

Hungry Spirits

Genteel Spirits

Ancient Spirits

Spirits Revived

Dark Spirits

Spirits Onstage

Unsettled Spirits

Bruised Spirits

Spirits United

Spirits Unearthed

Shaken Spirits

Scarlet Spirits

Book and cover design by eBook Prep
www.ebookprep.com

October 2022
ISBN: 978-1-64457-278-8

ePublishing Works!
644 Shrewsbury Commons Ave
Ste 249
Shrewsbury PA 17361
United States of America

www.epublishingworks.com
Phone: 866-846-5123

ACKNOWLEDGMENTS

Diana Jackson has become the hero of my life. She's my plot partner, editor, and overall best influence over my writing life I've ever had. Thank you, Diana! I'll never be able to thank you enough. By the way, Diana lives in the U.K., and I live in the U.S.A., but that hasn't mattered so far.

Thank you, too, to Sue Krekeler and Margaret Cronk for their excellent beta reading. I don't know why they want to do this, but I'm *so* glad they do!

The Chinatown depicted in my Mercy Allcutt books isn't the one that was there in Mercy's day; however, I know and love it so well that I use it. Today's Chinatown wasn't around until the late 1930s. So I cheat occasionally. I do *so much* research for these books, I figure a cheat every now and then is fair.

If you enjoy this book, please tell people and leave a review somewhere online. Thank you! Authors rely on word-of-mouth. We can't survive without readers!

ONE

By Saturday morning at Mercy's Manor—the name Lulu LaBelle had christened my boarding house—I still felt a trifle shaky when I went downstairs to partake of one of Mrs. Buck's delicious breakfasts. Mrs. Buck, my cook-housekeeper, served an informal meal on Saturday mornings, setting things on the sideboard for us to pick at as we chose. She generally went to the Grand Central Market to do her main weekly shopping as we lazy sleepers-inners dined.

I lifted the lid on one of the bowls sitting on a hot plate on the sideboard. "Oatmeal." I sighed, the notion of oatmeal not having lifted my spirits one teensy bit. Not that there is anything innately wrong with oatmeal; it's only that my mother had forced my sister and me to eat it every morning of our childhoods. It had made me sick to my stomach.

"Don't you like oatmeal?" Lulu asked, dolloping several big spoonfuls into her own bowl.

After quickly scanning the area to make sure Mrs. Buck was nowhere within hearing distance, I whispered, "I think it's awful. My mother used to make us eat it, and it actually turned my stomach."

Lulu squinted at me, holding her bowl in one hand as she reached for a butter knife with the other. "Well, it would probably make me sick if your mother made me eat it, too."

Appreciating Lulu's loyalty more than I could say, I started to pass by the oatmeal bowl and head to the bacon, sausages and toast.

"But," said Lulu, stopping me in my headlong retreat from oatmeal, "I'll bet you'd like it if you knew how to eat it."

It was my turn to squint, so I squinted at Lulu. "You spoon it into your mouth, chew once if you can stand to, and then swallow it and hope it doesn't come back up, don't you?"

"Fah," said Lulu, making me blink. "Here's what you do with oatmeal." She explained as she demonstrated. "First you put a bunch in your bowl, then you put a big pat of butter on it."

"So *that's* why you were holding the knife," I muttered.

"Exactly. Did you think I was going to stab you with it? And then you spoon lots of brown sugar on it." She put two heaping spoonfuls of brown sugar into her buttery bowl. "And *then* you pour cream on it. After that, you take it to your place at the table, mix it all up, and chow down."

"My goodness. Mother allowed us one skimpy spoonful of white sugar and a splash of milk on ours. She told us we should be grateful for the luxury because people in Scotland had to eat their oatmeal with salt."

Mixing the contents of her bowl with anticipation, Lulu grimaced. "Who cares what people in Scotland do with anything? Besides your mother, of course."

Because I didn't know anything at all about people in Scotland, I shrugged. Deciding my mother would probably faint dead away— if she ever found out and did such things as faint—I followed Lulu's example and plopped butter, brown sugar and cream onto my own tiny scoop of oatmeal and took it to the table.

My mother was the reason for my tentative, shaky feelings that Saturday morning. I'd defied her on Friday night. Unless you have a death wish, especially if you were one of her daughters, you didn't defy my mother. I feared consequences and the anticipation of what they might entail made me nervous.

Nevertheless, I sat, stirred my itsy-bitsy helping of oatmeal, said a silent prayer that I wouldn't do anything embarrassing at the breakfast table, shut my eyes, took a bite of doctored cereal, and chewed.

When my eyes popped open, they saw Lulu grinning at me. "See? Told you so."

I got up for more oatmeal, saying as I did so, "I might have known my mother would spoil even oatmeal for me."

"You don't have to worry about your mother anymore, Mercy. You told her so last night."

"True. And now I'm petrified. She's going to retaliate, Lulu. I know she will."

"Nuts. She can't do anything to you," said Lulu, a true friend if ever there was one.

My mother, whom everyone in Boston, Massachusetts, called Honoria (or Mrs. Allcutt), and whom her two daughters call the Wrath of God, is a formidable woman. She'd telephoned the night before demanding I spend Christmas week with her and my father in Pasadena, where they'd bought a lovely new winter home. Taking all my courage—not to mention my life—in my hands, I'd rejected her command.

Heck, I'd barely survived Thanksgiving with my parents in Pasadena! No way was I going to attempt Christmas, especially now that I had a lovely home of my own and lots of friends *and* my wonderful sister, Chloe. I'd bought my grand home on Bunker Hill (the one in Los Angeles) when Chloe and her husband Harvey had moved to Beverly Hills. They'd wanted to be closer to Harvey's studio. Harvey Nash was a big-time motion-picture...well, something or other. Producer? Director? He was some kind of movie mogul, at any rate.

"You don't need to be scared of that old bag," said Lulu, brave with twenty-two miles separating her from my overbearing mother. "You've got your friends to rely on! Heck, I'm not going to be able to go home for Christmas. I was sort of hoping you'd have Christmas here. Maybe one or two of the other girls will be here, too."

Soon after I'd bought my home, I'd decided to let rooms to other working women. I'd come to Los Angeles from the thin air of Boston's elite society in order to become a member of the worker proletariat, and I wanted to help other working women. Preferably women who, unlike me, actually had to live on their incomes. I kind of cheated every now and then, having been left a sizeable annuity by my late Great-Aunt Agatha, who'd been a wonderfully eccentric woman. My mother had hated her. Yet one more reason to love Great-Aunt Aggie.

"And Ernie," said Lulu with enthusiasm. "I don't think Ernie's got any kin in the L.A. area."

Mr. Ernest Templeton, Private Investigator, was my employer. At present, I acted as his confidential secretary, but I hoped one day to learn enough about private snoopery to become his assistant. At least his right-hand girl. I'd actually helped him with quite a few of his cases since I'd first stepped foot into his office in June of 1926, if anyone's keeping track. Ernie himself might not acknowledge the truth of my assertion, but truth it was, darn it.

"I think you're right. I think he has family in the Chicago area. But he has Phil and Pauline Bigelow. They probably invite him over for holiday meals and so forth."

"Huh," said Lulu, who wasn't a fan of Phil Bigelow, mainly because he'd arrested Lulu's brother, Rupert, for suspected murder not long back. I kind of didn't blame Lulu for her attitude. "Well, if you want to have Christmas here, Rupe and I will join you."

"Thanks, Lulu." I carried my almost-overflowing oatmeal bowl back to the table and began stirring the gooey mixture.

My other two tenants, Caroline Terry, who worked at the hosiery counter at the Broadway Department store; and Sue Krekeler, who worked as a receptionist in a dentist's office near where Lulu and I worked, straggled into the breakfast room.

"Morning," said Lulu brightly.

Lulu wasn't generally bright in the morning. She was probably looking forward to our planned Saturday Christmas shopping expedition. I was too when I wasn't worried about my blankety-blank mother.

"Good morning," said Caroline, a serene and proper young woman whose parents lived in Alhambra.

"What's for chow?" asked Sue, hurrying up to the sideboard to look for herself.

"Lots of good stuff," said Lulu.

Sue gave a moue of distaste. "Oatmeal. Well, I guess it's good for you." She grabbed a bowl and headed for the brown sugar and cream. I noticed she bypassed the butter. But heck, if Mother had allowed Chloe and me brown sugar and cream, I probably wouldn't have considered oatmeal a dish from hell. I shook my head, thinking my mother could spoil darned near anything.

"Oatmeal is a fine, filling breakfast," Caroline opined as she filled her own bowl. She, I observed, plopped a pat of butter into her own bowl.

"How come everybody knew how to make oatmeal palatable except me for my whole life?" I asked no one in particular.

Caroline, who was adding cream to her bowl, glanced at me, perplexed.

Sue giggled. "Not everyone loves oatmeal. I'm not all that fond of it, but I don't hate it."

"But hurry up, Mercy," urged Lulu. "We've got to hit Chinatown."

"Anybody else want to go Christmas shopping with us?" I asked my tenants.

"Gotta work this morning," said Sue. I hadn't noticed before, but now I saw she wore her white nurse's uniform. She wasn't a nurse, but her dentist liked his staff to look professional.

"I'm taking the bus to Alhambra," said Caroline, smiling sweetly. "I'll spend the night at my parents' house. We'll decorate the place for Christmas." She gave a tiny shiver of pleasure. "I love this time of year."

"I do now that I live in Southern California," said Lulu. "It was too blasted cold in Oklahoma this time of year."

"Michigan, too," said Sue. A little wistfully, she added, "I kind of miss a white Christmas."

"Is your family still in Michigan, Sue?" I asked, never having considered her circumstances before.

"Oh, no. They're here in California. My dad is head of an orange-packing firm. They live in San Bernardino."

"How'd you end up in Los Angeles?" asked Lulu.

With a shrug, Sue said, "I just wanted to see what it was like. Los Angeles is a lot more interesting than San Bernardino. There's nothing but orange trees there." With a little grin, she added, "Smells great in the springtime, when all those trees are blooming. But there's not a lot of work there for a girl, and I didn't feel like standing in a packing line and sorting oranges into boxes."

"I never even thought about how oranges got from the trees to our tables," I said, probably not telling anyone anything they didn't already know.

Shoot, I was a rich kid from Boston. I didn't know how anything in the world worked. In my family, you asked your maid or the cook for what you wanted, and it would be delivered unto you. Most people in the world didn't live that way, and I wanted to be one of those people who could and did fend for themselves.

Yes, I know most people would love to trade places with me. My philosophy—I'd actually only thought of it that morning, and I liked it—is that you never know what will happen in the world. It's good to be able to cope with whatever comes one's way. If my father's financial universe went blooey, my mother and father would be at a total loss. I, however, had honed certain skills, and I had used them to acquire a job!

Very well, so perhaps being a secretary to a private eye isn't everyone's ambition. I was proud of having achieved my position. And not merely because I could support myself on my own dime—enhanced occasionally by my late great-aunt—but I was learning about *life*. Life as it is lived by real people in real circumstances; those who didn't live in Boston's rarified air.

And I guess that's enough about that.

After we'd all finished our breakfasts, we toted our dirty dishes to the kitchen, rinsed them off, and stacked them neatly in the sink. I'd once washed our Saturday breakfast dishes and had been soundly scolded by Mrs. Buck, who said washing dishes was *her* job. All right by me.

As Sue left for work and Caroline vanished to her room, I guess to pack for her trip to Alhambra, Lulu and I dressed for our jaunt onto the mean streets of Los Angeles, there to shop for Christmas presents. I knew *just* what I wanted to get for Chloe.

The chilly air nipped our noses, but the rest of our bodies were all snuggled up in scarves, coats and hats as Lulu and I made our way to Angels Flight, the tiny, almost vertical funicular railroad a couple of blocks away from my home. In a minute flat, it would take the two of us—and everyone else riding the car we occupied—from Bunker Hill to Hill Street. From paradise to…well, downtown L.A. That morning we gave the engineer our nickels and made the quick trip on the car called Olivet. The other car was called Sinai. I'm sure there's a reason for the names, probably having to do with the Bible and the fact that the railroad existed in the City of Angels, but I hadn't bothered to look it up yet.

"What's on your list?" I asked Lulu as we took seats on the wooden benches.

"I already sent Mom and Dad their presents. I wanted to make sure they got to Oklahoma in time for Christmas. What about you? I guess you don't have presents to send now that your folks are here in California."

Mom and Dad? Lulu called her parents *Mom and Dad*. My eyes got all misty for a second as I contemplated a family occupied by children who felt safe and happy enough to call their parents Mom and Dad. How lovely the pronouns sounded.

"Mercy? Mercy! What's wrong?"

"What?" I jerked out of my reverie and realized I hadn't answered Lulu's question. I'd lost track of what she'd said after the "Mom and Dad" references.

"What's the matter with you? All of a sudden you drifted off somewhere. Daydreaming about a certain fellow, perhaps?"

"What? No!" It irked me that both Lulu and my sister thought I was fonder of my boss than I actually was. "I was…" My voice kind of trailed off. Lulu would think I was being silly. On the other hand, she'd met my mother. "I was thinking about how nice it would be to belong to a family in which the kids called their parents Mom and Dad. That sounds stupid, doesn't it?"

Cocking her head to one side, Lulu contemplated my words for a second or two. Then she said, "Naw. If I had parents like yours, I'd run away, too. I wouldn't call your mother 'Mom' on a bet."

With a sigh, I said, "Nor would I. Anyway, I think I know what I'm going to get for Chloe. I want to see if they have some of those embroidered silk Chinese pajama sets for kids. You know. Wouldn't it be darling to see a wee baby dressed in a pair of red silk pajamas embroidered all over with dragons? Or maybe butterflies."

"That would be cute. When's the baby due?"

"Chloe and Harvey think it will be born in February."

"Two months from now," Lulu mused. "I guess you could get tiny pajamas in green or yellow since you don't know if it'll be a boy or a girl."

"I think red is considered a lucky color for the Chinese." I wrinkled my nose, trying to remember where I'd learned this tidbit of information. Maybe I'd made it up, but I didn't think so.

"Yeah," said Lulu thoughtfully. "I think I read that somewhere. Maybe you should get some of those paper Chinese lanterns in red and hang them in your house."

"Where in the house would I hang paper Chinese lanterns?"

With a shrug, Lulu said, "I dunno. In the entryway? They'd be pretty with those black and white tiles. You have the prettiest house, Mercy. You know that, don't you?"

"Yes." I smiled. "I'm so lucky! Very well, red lanterns and red silk embroidered pajamas. If they have baby sizes."

"Get some for yourself. Heck, I'll get some, too! We can all wear red and usher in the new year in a lucky color."

"Sounds good to me."

Olivet landed at the small station on Hill Street, and Lulu and I clambered out. Chinatown was a short walk from the station, and it was our primary goal for shopping that day. Plus, we could have lunch in Chinatown. Lulu and I both loved Chinese food.

"What are you going to get for Rupert?" I asked Lulu as we walked.

"Think I'll get him a hat. Maybe one of those men's hats. You know, a fedora."

"That sounds nice," I said, recalling Lulu's wisp of a brother. I'd only ever seen him in one of those flat newsboys' caps. A fedora might spruce him up a trifle.

"I'll probably get it at the hat shop down the hill from the Figueroa Building."

"Ah, yes. That's where Mr. Buck and I took Ernie's fedora when Phil Bigelow stepped on it."

"That Bigelow chump *stepped* on Ernie's *hat?*" cried Lulu, indignant on Ernie's behalf.

"He didn't mean to," I told her. "It was an accident."

"Hmph."

With a slight shudder, I decided to drop the subject. I'd seen a murderer in that hat shop and had been quite frightened at the time. The owner of the shop was perfectly harmless, but I didn't know it then.

"I don't know what I'll get for Ernie," I mused.

"A bottle of bourbon would be good, probably," said Lulu.

"Lulu! Where in the world would I get a bottle of bourbon? And *why* would I? That's illegal!"

"Yeah, yeah," said Lulu, who might have mentioned bourbon just to get a rise out of me. Unfortunately, it was an easy thing for people to do. "Just kidding."

I sighed heavily. "Well, I'll think of something to give him, I hope."

"I'll help you find him a gift."

"Thanks, Lulu. Actually, Ernie could use a new fedora hat himself, but I don't think that's an appropriate gift for a secretary to give her boss."

"Appropriate, fiddlesticks," said Lulu.

We'd been walking on the west side of Hill Street, but the shop I wanted was on the east side, so we scurried across the street, dodging automobiles and people on bicycles and pedestrians and generally taking our lives into our hands. Or maybe our feet. Anyway, Chinatown was a crowded place.

Most of the shops on both sides of Hill Street in Chinatown sold similar merchandise, but some carried goods of a generally higher quality than most. I headed to a shop where I'd found a lovely dress once. I knew the shop sold clothes, so I hoped they'd have some baby things.

By the way, Chinatown in Los Angeles wasn't really much of a place. I only knew about it because Ernie liked to dine at a little dive called Charley's. In fact, he'd taken me there on the very first day I'd gone to his office to ask for an interview. Still, it was where a lot of Chinese people had gathered, and they had food markets, butchers' shops—which always had dead, naked ducks hanging on hooks in their windows—clothing shops, trinket shops, and even a Chinese opera. I'd visited the Chinese opera with Ernie once. Let me just say the Chinese opera isn't like anything I'd seen—or heard—before. Nevertheless, Lulu and I liked to mosey through its various shops when we had a day to ourselves.

Ha! It was my lucky day! No sooner had we walked into the shop than I saw a rack of Chinese silk garments. I hurried over to it, reached for a red silk robe embroidered with butterflies, and looked around to see if there was a clerk anywhere handy.

Then, bumping into and nearly upending me, a girl tore past me to the open door of the shop, shoving Lulu out of her way in her mad dash. Trying to remain upright, I grabbed on to a pole at one end of the garment rack.

Lulu hollered, "Hey!"

Suddenly a man surged out of a back room in the shop—I guess it was the same room from whence the girl had emerged—and raced past me. He also blundered into Lulu as he ran.

"What the heck?" Lulu said, shoving her hat back into place. It had been knocked askew when she'd been bumped by two running people.

"I don't know," I said, answering Lulu's unasked question. "That man is chasing that girl."

"Yeah, I saw that much," said Lulu. "Let's go see what's up."

So we did. Leaving the rack of Chinese silks, I joined Lulu, and together we tore out of the shop. There we were just in time to see the man grab the fleeing girl in what one might call a bear hug if one were feeling charitable. It looked as if his hug wasn't one of friendly concern, but rather as if he were capturing a bank robber or an escaped slave.

Oh, dear, why did I think of slaves? I'd read about Chinese traffickers of young girls and women. This girl wasn't one of those girls, was she? I glanced around frantically, hoping to see a uniformed copper. Of course, there's never a policeman around when you need one.

Other people had gathered in the plaza to watch the scuffle. The girl, struggling violently, shrieked something in Cantonese. The man holding her, trying valiantly to keep her long fingernails from scratching his face, hollered something back at her in Cantonese.

Mumbles and mutters from the gathering throng came at us, most in Chinese and all sounding disapproving.

"Let me *go!*" the girl screamed in English.

I have no idea what the man bellowed back at her, because it was in Cantonese. But he somehow managed to subdue the wriggling girl—now that I could see more of her, I'd estimate her to be fifteen or sixteen years old—and, still holding her tightly, march her back to the shop from whence they'd come. I got a good look at both of them as they neared Lulu and me.

As a chorus of two, Lulu and I, shocked, said loudly, *"Charley!"*

Charley Wu, owner of Ernie's favorite Chinese dive, paused on his way to the shop toward which he strode, frowned at Lulu and me, and resumed his encumbered journey back to the shop.

Having heard Lulu's and my duet, the maiden in Charley's arms looked frantically at us and hollered, "Help me! *Please!*"

Oh, dear. Whatever did this mean?

I didn't get to find out, because as soon as Charley Wu and his captive entered the shop where hung the Chinese silk garments I'd been fingering moments before, he slammed the door, and I heard the lock click.

TWO

L ulu and I stared at each other in consternation.

"That was Charley Wu," said Lulu.

"I know," I said.

"Who was the girl?" said Lulu.

"I don't have a clue," I said.

"Should we do something?" asked Lulu.

Should we? Glancing around, I saw pedestrian traffic on this side of Hill in Chinatown had resumed its normal flow. No one except Lulu and I seemed ruffled by the recently enacted scene. I did notice a couple of Chinese women huddled together, shooting glances at the shop and muttering to each other, but that was it as far as any sort of commotion went.

"I...I don't know," I said at last.

"Um..." Lulu said no more but, much braver than I, she walked to the closed shop door and turned the knob. Just as the earlier click had foretold, the door, being locked, didn't open. She rapped on the glass a couple of times.

Getting a trifle nervous, I tippy-toed up to Lulu, tapped her on the shoulder, and said, "I don't think Charley is going to let us in, Lulu. He looked pretty angry."

"I know he did, but I'm worried about that kid! She was only maybe fifteen, Mercy!"

"You're right. Maybe she's his sister?"

"So what? Would you let *your* brother treat you like that?" Lulu sounded fierce.

Her attitude shamed me. "No," I said. I said it firmly, too. "I would not. I wouldn't let George within fifty feet of me if I could help it."

Nodding with vigor, Lulu clenched her hand into a fist and pounded on the wooden part of the door. "Ow!" she shook her hand. "Hard door."

Deciding on a bit of boldness myself, I went to the door and yelled, "Charley Wu! What's going on?"

Silence greeted my indignant bellow. People on the plaza turned to stare at us. Naturally, their interest embarrassed me, the well-brought-up young lady from Boston. And that made me mad. Resurrected remnants of my former life always peeved me.

Therefore, I rapped on the glass with my knuckles and hollered, "Miss! Miss? Are you all right?"

"Do you need help?" Lulu asked for good measure.

"*Yes!*" came a feminine screech from within the shop.

"*No!*" a masculine voice proclaimed just as loudly.

"Want us to call the police?"

Suddenly the door opened, startling Lulu and me into a couple of gazelle-like leaps backward. Charley Wu, his face absolutely *savage*, snapped, "We don't need your help! Go away, or I'll call the cops."

Lulu's mouth was open. She snapped it shut, opened it again, and said, "*I* was about to call the cops. On *you*! What have you done with that poor girl?"

"That *poor girl* is my sister," Charlie growled. "And she's a damn brat. Now go away! Mind your own business."

And darned if he didn't slam the door again, right in our faces. Sure enough, the lock clicked.

Well.

Lulu and I gaped at each other for a couple of seconds. I wasn't

21

sure about Lulu, but I didn't have a single idea about what to do now.

"Do you think he was telling the truth?" I finally asked. "Do you think she's really his sister?"

With a shrug, Lulu said, "Darned if I know. They look kind of alike, but they all look alike to me."

"All who? Oh, you mean Chinese people?"

"Yeah."

"Anna May Wong doesn't look like everybody else," I said, feeling a trifle unnerved by the basic truth of Lulu's statement. "And we both knew Charley Wu when we saw him."

"Well, yeah, but we know Charley. And *everybody* knows who Anna May Wong is."

"She's gorgeous," I said.

"Yeah. She is." Lulu spoke wistfully. "Betcha if I looked like *her*, I could get into the flickers."

Lulu's primary ambition in life was to become a star of the silver screen. As she spent pretty much all day, every day, filing her nails behind the reception desk at the Figueroa Building where we both worked, I didn't know how soon her aspirations would be achieved. She didn't seem to be making much of an active effort to bust down the doors of Hollywood, if you know what I mean.

"Maybe," I said. "But should we do anything about Charley Wu and that girl?"

We both stood mute for a moment or two. Then Lulu said, "I wish Ernie was here. We could ask him."

After staring at each other for another second or three, Lulu and I began frantically hurrying up the Chinatown plaza in search of a row of telephone booths. Given how little attention white people paid to people of other colors—my mother accuses me of being a Socialist when I say things like that, but I'm not—I wasn't optimistic that the telephone company would have given China-town a telephone booth. But by golly, we found one! At the very end of the plaza stood three wooden telephone boxes, all filled with people.

"You take this one, and I'll stand by this one," Lulu said,

pointing to a booth at the eastern end of the queue and then at the one in the middle. "If the other one frees up first, grab it. Or I will."

"You have Ernie's number?" I asked.

"Got it." She dug in her handbag and withdrew her little pocket address book. I'd already fetched mine.

"Good. Aha! This one's free!"

As soon as a well-dressed Chinese lady left the booth, I shocked her by dashing past her and into the space she'd vacated, Lulu hot on my heels. I swear, you'd have thought we were a couple of generals planning a battle campaign or something.

Because I'd done my research—I wanted to fit into the working classes, darn it!—I knew I'd have to have a nickel to make my telephone call. I was about to withdraw my coin purse and dig in it for change when Lulu handed me a nickel.

"Thanks, Lulu." I lifted the receiver from the hook and stuck it to my ear.

An officious voice said, "Drop in a nickel, please."

Rather than take the voice to task for being officious, I dropped my nickel into the slot provided for same. The voice then said, "Number, please."

Because I was prepared, I rattled off Ernie's telephone number. Some telephone booths were self-dialers, but I suspected the Los Angeles city fathers paid more attention to upper-crust shopping centers, and that Chinatown would be among the last places to get self-dialing telephones.

Anyhow, the operator placed the call, and the 'phone on the other end of the wire began to ring.

"Is he there?" Lulu whispered, glancing around nervously, as if she expected a gang of Chinese hatchet men to attack us as we used the telephone booth.

"Don't know yet."

"Yeah?" I'd only just answered Lulu's question when darned if Ernie didn't answer my ring!

"'Yeah?' Is that how you always answer your telephone?" I said, irked for probably no reason.

"Aw, hell. Is that you, Mercy?"

"Yes. It's I," I said. Then, deciding to forget about his terrible manners, I went on, "Ernie! I'm so glad you're there."

"Where the devil else would I be on a Saturday morning?"

"I don't know," I said.

"And more importantly, why are you happy I'm home? Mercy, if you've seen another murder or found another body, I don't want to know about it."

Crumb. You'd think all I did was stumble over bodies or witness murders if you were to judge by the tone of his voice. Again I decided not to take him to task.

"No, no, no. It's nothing like that."

"Thank god for small favors," he muttered.

"But listen, Ernie, Lulu and I are in Chinatown, and something really strange just happened. We wanted to consult you about it."

"Great."

"Honestly, Ernie! You can be such a grouch sometimes."

"What time is it anyway?" he asked.

"What difference does that make?" I demanded, becoming more annoyed as the seconds ticked past and Ernie didn't seem to want to listen to anything I said.

"I'm hungry, is what difference it makes," he said. "Exactly where are you? I'll meet you there in fifteen minutes, and we can discuss whatever this important matter is over lunch. Or luncheon, if you're you, which you are."

"But *Ernie*! *Listen* to me! This is about Charley Wu!"

"What's about Charley Wu?"

"What I need to tell you."

"Are you at Charley's noodle shop now?"

"*No!*" I pretty much shrieked. "That's what I'm trying to *tell* you! Charley Wu just kidnapped a girl off the east plaza in Chinatown!"

Silence greeted my declaration.

I said, "Ernie?" in a tentative kind of voice.

"You at the 'phone booths at the far end of the east plaza?"

"How did you know that?"

"Cripes, Mercy, will you just say yes or no?"

"Very well. Yes. That's where we are."

Before I finished my sentence, Ernie replaced the receiver on his end of the wire. He did it with force and fury, too, if I were to guess. Flustered and still more than a little irked, I replaced the receiver gently and looked at Lulu, who'd been standing there holding the door of the telephone booth open so she could hear.

"What's going on?" she asked.

"Ernie will meet us here as soon as he can."

"I heard you tell him that Charley Wu had kidnapped a girl. That might not be true, you know."

"I know," I said, feeling guilty. "But he kept interrupting me, and I just decided to blurt out the gist of the matter in order to shut him up and get him to give us some assistance. I…Well, I didn't expect he'd rush over here."

"He's probably hungry," said Lulu, who had known Ernie a lot longer than I had.

With a sigh, I said, "Yes. He said he's hungry. I think that's the real reason he's coming here. He's not precisely acting like a *preux chevalier.*"

"A what?" Lulu asked. "What the heck is a…whatever it was you said?"

"A knight in shining armor," I told her.

Lulu laughed. "Ernie? No, he sure isn't. Couldn't be if he tried." She wrapped her coated arms around herself and said, "I hope he gets here quick. I'm cold."

"It is pretty cold for Los Angeles," I agreed. "In Boston it's probably snowing." I grinned, ecstatic not to be in Boston.

"Yeah, it's probably snowing in Oklahoma, too," said Lulu. "Glad we're both here."

"Precisely what I was thinking."

"Well, as long as we have to wait for Ernie, let's see what the other shops have that we can buy for Christmas presents."

"Very well, but don't forget to keep a look-out. We don't want to miss Ernie."

"Right," said Lulu.

We did miss Ernie, but it didn't matter. Lulu and I had been fingering some cunning embroidered silk pajamas, pretty much like the one in the shop where Charley Wu had hauled his…sister? Well, whoever she was. I'd just picked up an absolutely adorable baby-sized red pair when Lulu and I heard, "*Mercy Allcutt! Lulu LaBelle! Where the devil are you?*" boom from not far outside the shop's door.

I dropped the darling pajama set and jumped a yard and a half in the air.

Lulu said, "Cripes!"

Barely keeping my wits about me, I told the hovering shop-keeper, "Please hold these for me. I'll buy them in a few minutes."

I think he nodded, but I'm not sure, because Lulu and I ran like a couple of rabbits out of the shop.

"There you are," Ernie said mildly when we screeched to a halt in front of him. "I figured you'd lose track of time and start shopping or something."

"You didn't have to yell," I told him.

"Yes I did," he told me back.

"He's right, Mercy," said Lulu. To Ernie she said, "We got cold and just stepped into that shop to warm up. I guess we got distracted."

"You're right," I admitted.

"Well, forget about that."

Ernie, I noticed, wore a fashionable, newish tan overcoat with wide lapels over his brown tweed suit. He looked quite dapper, which was a novelty. Generally, my casual boss looked vaguely like an unmade bed. He wore the tan fedora hat Phil Bigelow had stepped on, and which Mr. Buck and I had taken to be repaired. The hat maker had replaced the old worn band with a new one, and it looked quite nice. In fact, Ernie appeared as near to spiffy as made no matter that late Saturday morning.

"What was this about Charley Wu kidnapping a woman?" he went on, interrupting my musings about his attire.

"Well," Lulu temporized, "he might not have *kidnapped* her, exactly, but she sure didn't want to go with him."

"She sure didn't," I agreed. "He picked her right up off the pavement and carried her away."

Ernie heaved a king-sized sigh. "Will one of you tell me precisely what happened, please?"

Lulu and I exchanged a couple of glances, and Lulu nudged me. "You tell him," she said.

So I told him. As I did so, his face kind of screwed up into an incredulous expression, complete with a wrinkled brow and curled lip. When I finished, he stood there, gazing at Lulu and me for a few seconds. He didn't look pleased.

Lulu seemed to become nervous as he remained silent. "It's the truth, Ernie. Mercy told you exactly what happened."

"I'm not fibbing!" I cried indignantly.

"Didn't think you were," muttered Ernie. "Just wondering what it's about, is all."

"We don't know. We knocked on the shop door, but Charley told us to go away, that the girl was his sister, and if we kept bothering him he'd call the police," I said. "And here *we* were about to call the police on *him*!"

"Oh, boy. This sounds like fun," said Ernie.

And he walked up to the shop door and rapped sharply on the glass.

THREE

Lulu and I trailed behind Ernie. I don't know about Lulu, but I was kind of scared Charley Wu would get mad and yell at us again.

"Hey, Charley, it's Ernie. Open up. I want to see you for a minute," Ernie called when several fraught seconds passed after his knock.

The door suddenly swung open, and Charley Wu stood here, a frown on his face. It deepened when he noticed Lulu and me standing in a huddle behind Ernie. "What you want, Ernie? Those two"—he stabbed a finger at Lulu and me—"don't have nothing to do with me!"

Ernie grinned at Charley, at ease as ever. Nothing ever seemed to ruffle Ernie. "They were concerned because they thought they saw you kidnap a girl," he said as if this were the most humorous report he'd ever heard in his life.

"He *did*!" a voice trilled from the back of the shop.

Charley turned and shouted something in Cantonese at the voice. Facing Ernie again, he said, "They got it wrong. My sister is giving me hell. She don't want to marry the man she's gonna marry."

"I *won't!*" came the voice from the back.

Turning again Charley hollered furiously, "You *will!*"

"I don't want to butt into your family situation, Charley, but is that really your sister back there?"

"Yes!"

"Why do you want her to marry somebody she doesn't want to marry?"

Charley let out a hiss, sounding much as I imagine an irritated cobra might sound. Then he grabbed Ernie by the arm and yanked him inside the shop.

Lulu yelled, "*Hey!*"

I just stood there, not sure what to do. Then I decided I should doubtless do nothing, and Lulu doubtless should, too. Apparently, Ernie and Charley were going to hash out any prevailing misunderstandings. Turning to Lulu, who looked as if she aimed to charge up to the door and batter it again, I held up a hand. "Let's wait a little bit, Lulu. I think Ernie will…" Because I didn't have a notion in the world what Ernie might do, my sentence pretty much straggled off.

"Darn Ernie!" said Lulu.

I didn't disagree with her. "Well, I don't know what we can do now. Maybe if we visit another shop and look around, we can keep an eye on this one and see when Ernie leaves. Then maybe he'll report on what's going on."

"Maybe? Ernie? Huh," said Lulu.

It annoyed me that I agreed with her. "Well, let's not allow those two men to spoil our day. I asked that fellow in the other shop to hold those baby pajamas for me, so I'm going back there to buy them. You can wait for Ernie here if you want to."

"Naw," said Lulu. "It's too darned cold."

So we both walked back to the shop we'd been in when Ernie roared for us. Sure enough, the shopkeeper—who, I believe, eyed me mistrustfully—had kept the pretty silk baby pajamas for me, and I bought them.

"Come over here, Mercy," Lulu said when I'd completed my purchase. "Look at these soaps. They smell swell."

So I joined Lulu at another counter, and she was right. The

soaps smelled wonderful. I bought several bars each of sandal-wood, jasmine and rose-petal-scented soaps. Lulu bought some too. We were rummaging through the rest of the shop—I was particularly scrutinizing some pretty Chinese tea sets—when Ernie joined us.

"Come on, girls," he said, making me jump and almost drop a teapot. "Let's grab some lunch."

"Ernie! You scared me!" I cried, carefully setting the teapot back on its tray.

"Why? I figured you'd be waiting for me, panting to know what's none of your business."

I felt my lips pinch, then relaxed them. "Well, we thought we saw somebody being kidnapped, for pity's sake!"

"Yeah," said Lulu. "Let's grab some lunch, and you can tell us all about that girl and Charley and what's going on."

"Even though it really *is* none of your business?"

"It might not be our business, but that girl wasn't happy, Ernie, and if Charley is making her marry somebody she doesn't want to marry, there's something wrong," I said, indignant on the girl's behalf.

"The world is full of cultural differences, Mercy. You should already know that, being a member of Boston royalty and all."

"Bother you, Ernest Templeton." I hated that he'd pegged me as a rich girl the moment he set eyes on me. He was right, but I still resented it.

He laughed. *Naturally*, he laughed. He was always laughing at what he considered my naivety. I also hated that he was right about my naivety. Curse it.

Because Charley Wu was certainly not going to be at his noodle shop on the west side of Hill Street, Ernie led Lulu and me to Hop Luey's, a brightly painted pagoda-shaped building on the east plaza. He'd taken me to eat here before, and it was kind of fun because you had to walk upstairs to the dining room. Fantasies about gambling and opium dens crowded my brain as we silently trod up the carpeted steps. I suspect the opium dens were a mere figment, but I could *hear* the click-click-click of mah-jongg tiles, so there might be some substance to the gambling notion. Not that it matters.

A formally suited Chinese gent led us to a table near a window and told us our waiter would appear shortly.

"This is real nice of you, Ernie," said Lulu, looking around her as if she were in the Ambassador Hotel rather than a cunning little restaurant in Chinatown.

"Me?" Ernie said, opening his eyes wide and pointing to his chest. "I thought *you* guys were paying. You called me, remember?"

"But——" Lulu began, looking a trifle panicky.

I interrupted her. How rude, huh? "I'll pay," I said. "I just want to know why Charley Wu grabbed that girl who was trying to run away from him and took her back to that shop."

Ernie frowned at me. "You're no fun. You're supposed to make a fuss about how I invited you to lunch."

"Bother. I don't care who pays," I said, knowing Ernie'd tricked me again. "Tell us about Charley and that girl."

He didn't get a chance to honor my demand instantly because a waiter approached with a pot of tea on a tray, along with three small teacups and three menus. Therefore, I had to possess my soul in patience for another few minutes. My rebellious soul didn't *want* to be patient. Needs must, however, so I looked at the menu.

"This all sounds good," said Lulu in a voice bespeaking awe.

I squinted at her. "It is good," I told her. "At least everything I've eaten here has been good."

"Me, too," said Ernie.

It occurred to me to rejoice because Ernie and I had agreed on something for once, but I told myself not to be stupid.

"I think I'll have the number-two lunch," said Ernie after perusing the menu for a bit. "Have whatever you want, Lulu. Mercy's paying."

Not rising to his bait, I said, "That sounds good. I love the spare ribs they serve. And the fried shrimp."

"Yes, that does sound good. I've never eaten Chinese spare ribs." Squinting at me, Lulu asked, "You really like them?"

"Very much," I said.

"Okay. I'll have that, too," said Lulu.

"Excellent," said Ernie, laying aside his menu and propping his elbows on the table, probably because he knew I'd disapprove. "Okay, lunch is settled. So, what have you girls been up to? Christmas shopping?"

"Yes, but you can't evade the question any longer, Ernest Templeton," I told him severely. "What's going on with Charley Wu and that poor girl?"

Again Ernie couldn't answer because the waiter came up to our table, pencil poised above a pad in his hand.

"We'll have number two for three people," Ernie said to him.

The waiter nodded, smiled at Ernie, picked up our menus, ignored Lulu and me, and walked off.

Lulu whispered, "What does that mean? 'Number two for three people'? What's that mean?"

"It means," said Ernie, "that they'll bring enough of everything included in the number-two option for three people. I suspect they'll double the amount of food for one and bring us three plates."

"Oh," said Lulu.

"I think you're right," I said to Ernie. "But stop delaying and tell us about Charley and that girl."

With a roll of his eyes, Ernie finally gave up avoiding the question. "Very well. The girl, whose name is Wu Lian Jun, is Charley's sister. Even she confirmed their relationship."

"Her first name is Wu and her last name is Wu?" asked Lulu, clearly confused.

I decided to enlighten her, even though the following was about all I'd ever learned about Chinese names. "The Chinese use the patronymic name first. So Charley Wu could correctly be Wu Charley,"

"No, it wouldn't," said Ernie, always delighted to puncture any bubble of pride I might display. "It would be Wu Chung. He just calls himself Charley for us benighted white people."

"Oh," I said, too interested to be irked. "That makes sense. I mean, it makes sense that he'd give himself a name white people can pronounce."

"What?" asked Ernie. "You can't pronounce Wu Chung?"

"Bother! You know what I mean. It makes sense that he'd tell white people his name is Charley."

"Wait," said Lulu, stuck on a prior sentence. "What's a...what'd you call it? A patron-something?"

"Patronymic," I said. "It means your last name."

"Technically," said Ernie, again sounding pleased with himself, "It's your father's last name, and it gets passed along down for generations."

"Yes," I said, wanting to stick my tongue out at him. "If the mother's name were passed along, it would be your...matronymic? Is that even a word?"

"Dunno," said Ernie.

Thinking dark thoughts, I said, "It probably isn't. I'll bet there *isn't* a word for a mother's last name because nobody ever credits women with anything. We can't even keep our names when we get married, for Pete's sake!"

"You don't like being Mercy?" asked Ernie, all fake innocence.

"You know what I mean, Ernest Templeton," I growled at him.

Ernie's eyebrows lifted. "I guess," he said.

"Wait a minute. Let's get back to Charley," said Lulu. "So his last name is Wu and his first name is Chung, but in China he'd call himself Wu Chung instead of Chung Wu?"

"Right."

"And he calls himself Charley for us white people?"

"Right," Ernie said again.

"I guess that makes sense," said Lulu. "Who'd want to call him Chung?"

I blinked at her. "I wouldn't mind calling him Chung if that were his name, which I guess it is."

"Yeah, but it sounds so foreign," said Lulu.

"I suppose Mercedes Louise sounds foreign to a Chinese person," I said, trying to keep any note of censure from my voice. I had absolutely *no* reason to feel superior to Lulu. She was already an expert in a world I was only barely beginning to fathom.

"Yeah, I guess," said Lulu. "But Lulu Wu sounds kind of keen. Or even Wu Lulu."

"Okay, you just marry Charley, and you can be Wu Lulu," said Ernie, laughing.

"I don't want to *marry* him! But I can change my name!"

"Why would you change your name to something Chinese?" I asked, curious. "You don't look Chinese."

With a sigh, Lulu said, "Yeah, you're right." After thinking about it for a second or two, she added, "Besides I like being Lulu LaBelle. It'll look swell on a marquee one of these days."

Ernie and I exchanged a surreptitious glance as Lulu shut her eyes to bask in imaginary glory and glamour. Ernie and I both believed Lulu would have better luck achieving her ambition to be a star if she actually did something active about it. Still, everyone deserves his or her dreams, I reckon.

"Anyhow, why does Charley want Lian Jun to marry someone she doesn't want to marry?"

For the first time, Ernie's expression sobered. "He wouldn't give me a straight answer, but I have a feeling it has to do with someone attempting to blackmail him. Might be a tong problem, but I didn't think the tongs were bad here in Los Angeles. I know there have been brutal tong wars in San Francisco and New York."

I felt my eyes widen. "Good Lord. I've read about tong wars."

"What's a tong war? What's a tong? I thought tongs were something you picked up stuff with."

"Those are English tongs," I said. "Chinese tongs are supposed to be social clubs for members of the same family." I glanced at Ernie. "That's right, isn't it, Ernie?"

"Yeah. That's right. But in some Chinese populations, the tongs have taken on a brutal life of their own. Kind of like the big Italian, Irish and Jewish gangs back in Chicago and New York. If you're a merchant, you have to pay them protection money."

"I still don't understand," said Lulu. "Protection from what?"

"From them," I said.

"Huh?" said Lulu.

"Mercy's right," said Ernie. It sounded to me as if he wanted to add a "for once" to his sentence but caught himself in time to stifle it. Perhaps it was my imagination. "If you don't pay money to the gang—or, in the case of Chinese communities, the tong—they're liable to burn down your business."

"Or shoot it up," I said with a shudder, recalling a newspaper article I'd read recently about a gangster called George "Bugs" Malone and his gang attempting to murder another gang leader, Al "Scarface" Capone, in Chicago.

"Right," Ernie said. "Or maybe bomb it."

"Banana oil!" said Lulu. "Really?"

"Exactly," said Ernie. "No banana oil. Truth."

"Why do you think Charley is under pressure from a tong?" I asked, feeling worried and scared for poor Charley Wu and his sister.

"Not sure he is, but I can't think of another logical reason he'd force his sister to marry a man three times her age she doesn't want to marry," Ernie said.

"He's three times her age?" I said, thinking she'd be marrying someone as old as my father, the notion of which horrified me.

"At least," said Ernie.

"Well, why doesn't she just refuse to marry him?" asked Lulu. "Nobody in the good old U.S.A. should have to marry anybody she doesn't want to marry."

"Did you forget the part about the fires, bombs and bullets?" Ernie asked politely.

Aghast, Lulu said, "You mean somebody really *might* shoot Charley? Just because his sister doesn't want to marry an old man?"

The waiter again approached our table, this time with a tray laden with fragrant Chinese foodstuffs, so Ernie had to possess *his* soul in patience for once.

Unfortunately, so did I.

FOUR

Wow, I hadn't realized how hungry I was until the waiter set all that food on a lazy Susan at our table. He then set a plate in front of each of us and gave us each a set of chopsticks. Both Ernie and I were fairly adept at using chopsticks by this time in our lives, but Lulu looked at her set askance.

"Please bring the lady some silverware," Ernie said to the waiter, who smiled and reached into his pristine white apron's pocket. He plucked two sets of knives and forks wrapped in white napkins and set one in front of Lulu and one in front of me.

His assumption that I needed a knife and fork irked me, but I didn't let on. Maybe he thought Ernie had said "ladies" instead of "lady." Or maybe he just figured white people were too stupid to use chopsticks. He was correct about that, but it's only because most of us had been using forks and knives since infancy.

After serving ourselves from the many dishes on the lazy Susan and taking several bites each, Lulu said, "So how come you think these Chinese gangsters are going to hurt Charley if his sister doesn't marry that old man?"

After putting aside his gnawed sparerib—Ernie wasn't being impolite; there was no other way to eat them—he said, "I don't know it for sure, but Charley seemed really worried, and his sister wouldn't stop crying. They talked to each other in Cantonese, and I don't know much of that, but I think the girl kept saying, 'I know, but I don't want to', and Charley said, 'I know, but if you don't…' And I don't know what he said would happen if she didn't marry the grandpa, but I don't think it was anything good. Or even something a little bit bad, but something *really* bad."

"My goodness," I said, chewing, which was impolite, but Ernie's words alarmed me. I swallowed my bite. "So you believe there actually *will* be unfortunate consequences if Lian Jun doesn't marry the old man?"

With one of his characteristic shrugs, Ernie said, "Dunno. Just got that impression. Charley and I aren't bosom buddies, you know. He's Chinese and I'm white, so neither of us fits snugly into each other's lives, you know?"

There's no good reason for his words to have shocked me, but they did. "I thought you were pals!" I said, a shrimp halfway to my mouth.

"Well, we are. Kind of. But face it, the Chinese don't care for whites for the most part. And whites, for the most part, don't like Chinese. We co-exist with each other and make money from each other. I've tried to bust into their world a little bit, but all I've managed to do is talk to Charley about baseball games and participate in a few when one of his teammates is sick or something." He ended his statement with another shrug and a bite of chow mein.

"How depressing," I said, feeling forlorn for a second. "Why can't we human beings just get along with each other?"

"I don't know if I'd want to be close pals with a Chink," said Lulu musingly. She saw my eyes open wide and amended her statement. "I mean a Chinese person!"

Deciding to give the "Chink" lapse a miss, I asked, "Why not?"

It was Lulu's turn to shrug. "I dunno. We just seem to be so…*different* from each other. I mean, look at us." She gave a small wave of her hand, intending to point out the lavish Chinese decorations and us, three white folks, sitting in the middle of it all.

"A bunch of whites and Mexicans murdered a bunch of Chinese

folks here in Los Angeles in around 1880. It's not as if races not liking each other were a new problem, you know."

Recalling what I could of the history of the United States, I had to agree. "You're right, of course. I think it's sad, though."

Ernie lifted his eyebrows and stuffed more food into his mouth.

After a few seconds of us all chewing and swallowing and dishing more food onto our plates, Lulu said, "I guess it is kind of sad. Heck, look at the Bucks. They had to send their daughter to a college in Louisiana or somewhere because no college in California would take a Negro girl."

She was right. "You're right," I said after swallowing another bite. "Sometimes I hate people."

Both Ernie and Lulu looked at me oddly. I guess they were right to do so. What I'd said wasn't very nice. But still…"Why can't we all just get along?" I added because I thought I should say something besides what I'd just said.

"Dunno," said Ernie. "I don't have a problem with anyone unless he or she is a twerp."

"I guess," said Lulu. "I'd feel funny walking in Chinatown by myself."

After thinking about it, I admitted, "I might feel funny about it, too."

"It's different for women," Ernie said, sounding almost serious for once. "A woman probably shouldn't walk alone anywhere at any time. There are too many cranks out there who're liable to prey on a woman alone."

"That's a frightening thought," I told my boss, faintly shocked.

"It's a frightening world," he told me back.

"You're right," said Lulu with a sigh. "I think women ought to be allowed to carry weapons in their purses so we can shoot bozos who come up and try to bother us on the streets."

"You can," said Ernie. "Who's stopping you?"

"We can?" asked Lulu, visibly shocked. "Honest Injun?"

And there was another unfortunate expression. I didn't say so. "Really."

Lulu looked at me. "Say, Mercy, wanna learn how to shoot a gun?"

"I already know how to shoot a gun. I don't want to carry one. At least not the kind I know how to shoot."

Both Lulu and Ernie gaped at me.

"What?" I said. "Chloe and I had to learn how to shoot birds. I don't like shooting birds. In fact, I'd rather shoot a person than a bird." My last words were said with a good deal of grump to them. "Birds never hurt each other like people do."

"Yes, they do," said Ernie and Lulu together.

"Applesauce!"

Lulu enlarged upon the theme. "Not applesauce. You just haven't lived out in the country. Birds are always fighting with each other and robbing each other's nests and stuff. And hawks and eagles eat smaller birds, not to mention rabbits and puppies and kittens."

"And wild turkeys are mean as snakes," added Ernie. "You've lived the high life, Mercy. You just haven't seen life in the wild."

Irked, I said, "I've seen life in Los Angeles and Boston and New York, and I prefer the animals I've met to most of the people I know." Because I didn't want to be left alone at the table and it was also the truth, I added, "Present company excepted."

"We like you too, kiddo," Ernie said, laughing, curse him.

"Yeah," said Lulu. "You're real nice."

"Thanks." I actually stabbed a shrimp with one of my chopsticks. Human beings were *such* a miserable species sometimes. Often. Not always, although just then I doubt I'd have admitted as much.

We didn't talk for a while. I might possibly have rendered my dining companions unwilling to speak to me for fear I'd lash out, but I don't know for sure about that. Good thing the food was so tasty, so we could focus on it.

Eventually, however, we got full and Ernie dared to ask, "What do you gals plan to do this afternoon?"

After sharing a glance with Lulu, I ventured, "Shop some more?"

"Sounds good to me," said Lulu.

"Excellent," said Ernie. He lifted a hand to summon our waiter, who glided over and handed Ernie the bill.

I guess I was in a crabby mood that day—after having been given to understand the waiter and probably all the other people in the restaurant who weren't us only tolerated our presence because they could make money from us—because it riled me that the waiter assumed Ernie was paying. Silly, I know. Most of the time when men and women dined together, the man paid.

"Here," I said, holding my hand out to Ernie. "I said I'd pay for lunch, and I'll pay for lunch."

Ernie gave me a look I didn't deserve. "Nuts to that. I'll pay," he said.

"But—"

"When guys and gals go out to eat, the guys pay," Ernie said as if I were an infant.

Rather than argue, which would have been undignified and inevitably useless, I said, "Thank you," in a tight voice.

Bother societal norms, was my frame of mind that day. It wasn't when the day started, but the drama between Charley Wu and his sister and Ernie's subsequent explanation had spoiled my mood.

Lulu and I parted with Ernie outside Hop Luey's. I pasted on a smile and said, "Thanks for lunch, Ernie, and thanks for trying to figure out what was going on with Charley Wu and his sister."

"Happy to oblige," said my nonchalant boss. "But please don't take my interpretation as gospel, because I really don't speak Chinese well enough to understand exactly what Charley and his sister yelled at each other."

"I'll try not to," I said, knowing I'd just lied.

"Not a problem for me," said Lulu, whose sunny disposition had reasserted itself.

Thanks to Lulu and the sights and merchandise to be found in Chinatown—Lulu wrinkled her nose at the ducks and buckets of chicken feet hanging in the butcher's shop, but I thought they were interesting—my mood improved. It was a cheerful, if bogged-down-by packages, Mercy Allcutt who rode Angels Flight with her equally encumbered pal to the station up the hill. We kind of staggered home, but we pretty much laughed all the way.

Buttercup, my darling and brilliant toy poodle, met us at the door after I'd managed to get my key out of my handbag. She didn't even reproach me for having been gone most of the day.

Before picking up the packages I'd set on the porch so as to enable me to unlock the door, I knelt and petted her, apologizing for abandoning her. "Oh, you're such a good girl, Buttercup! And just wait until you see what I got you for Christmas!"

"Don't tell her!" warned Lulu squirming past Buttercup and me and staggering into the beautifully tiled entryway of my home. Our home, rather. Yes, I owned it, but I considered my tenants, and especially Lulu, my friends. "You'll spoil the surprise!"

Squinting up at Lulu while continuing to lavish love upon my precious poodle, I reminded Lulu, "She's a dog, Lulu. I don't think she understands a whole lot of English."

"Huh. Well, don't tell her anyway, just in case."

"Very well, I won't." Turning my attention back to Buttercup, I said, "You need to stop jumping on me so I can carry this stuff into the house."

Being the superbly trained poodle she was, Buttercup obeyed my suggestion eagerly. And I don't think that's merely because enticing aromas seeped from the box I'd carried home from the bakery in Chinatown. To be on the safe side, I snatched that package first and set it on a shelf in the entryway where guests parked their hats when I had guests, which wasn't very often.

Sue had come home some time earlier, and she helped Lulu and me carry our parcels into the living room. We set everything on a couple of sofas and a chair or two, then all stood back to view our bounty.

"Boy, you two did a lot of shopping," said Sue, sounding a trifle awed.

"Chinatown is a fun place to shop," said Lulu.

"It is," I concurred, although Lulu's words had reminded me about Charley Wu and his sister's problem. If it was a problem, which I didn't know. Lulu, Ernie and I only knew Charley's sister was unhappy, but I decided not to dwell on the problem. This was only partially because I honestly didn't yet know what it was.

"We popped by the Broadway Department Store, too," Lulu told Sue. "But Chinatown was more fun."

"True. By the time we hit the Broadway, we pretty much had more stuff than we could carry home with us."

"I can see that," said Sue. "You walked with that pile all the way from Angels Flight?"

"Yup. We're strong," said Lulu. She'd shed her coat and flexed an arm muscle or two. As she wore a long-sleeved sweater that day, we couldn't appreciate any musculature she'd managed to build up, if any.

"And I'm tired," I said, flopping down next to a couple of boxes on a handy chair. The house was large, the furnishings abundant and soft, and I loved everything about my home and its furniture. "Anybody else want to join me in a cup of tea?"

"No, but I'll be glad to drink one," said Lulu.

We both laughed like a couple of hyenas. Sue stared at us, although she finally grinned. "Let me make it. I've been loafing all afternoon."

"Thanks, Sue," I said, appreciating her offer. My feet ached like the dickens from having been tromping around on them for so many hours.

"Yeah, thanks," said Lulu. Eyeing the brown paper parcels lying hither and yon on the furniture, she said, "Get up, Mercy. We've got to take this upstairs."

With a sigh, I said, "You're right," and heaved myself to my feet. "First I'm going to take the bakery box into the kitchen, just in case Buttercup gets any bright ideas." Lulu and I both knew Buttercup wasn't above jumping on the sofa and opening a box of cookies.

So I took the bakery box to the kitchen and set it on the counter next to Sue, who was spooning tea into a perfectly glorious teapot I'd been given by Chloe on my recent birthday. I noticed she'd rinsed it out first with boiling water, just as she should have.

"We can have these with our tea," I suggested.

"Ooh, from that bakery in Chinatown?" Sue said, her eyebrows lifting in anticipation.

"Yup. Almond cookies and a few other kinds of baked goods I've never eaten before. But I figured we could experiment."

"Sounds like a good idea to me," Sue said happily.

Buttercup helped me carry the rest of my purchases upstairs to my sitting room. I was pleased with my haul. I'd decided to buy Chinese silk robes for Sue, Caroline and especially Lulu, who loved the ones we saw but couldn't afford one for herself. As I had no paucity of funds, I figured what the heck. I bought a blue one for Sue, a green one for Caroline and a red one for Lulu. I'd bought some Chinese silk pajamas for myself, along with a short bed jacket in the same pattern. That way I could wear red too, but we wouldn't look alike, which was a stupid thing to think in the first place. For one thing, I had brown hair and Lulu was a bottle blonde.

But it didn't matter. We'd all love our new duds.

Buttercup and I met Lulu at the top of the stairs after I'd stored my parcels. "Ready for some tea and cookies?" I asked her.

"You betcha," said Lulu, who'd changed from her heavy outdoor wear into a simple—for her—day dress. To keep it from being dull, something Lulu never was, the fabric was brilliant orange with flowers so white, they made me blink. She saw my reaction. "It's the berries, huh?" she said, twirling for Buttercup and me when we'd reached the foot of the staircase.

"Bright," I said, nodding.

"I love it. Found it today. I think you were looking at those silk pajamas. The shopkeeper told me to wash it in gentle soap. Whatever gentle soap is."

"I don't know," I said wondering myself what might constitute a gentle soap. "Maybe one of those sweet-smelling Chinese soaps?"

With a shrug, Lulu said, "Don't know, but I'll try to be careful. Don't want the white to get dull."

"You're never dull," I told Lulu with perfect honesty.

Eyeing my own costume, which was the one I'd worn on our trek today, sans the sweater and coat I'd worn over it, Lulu sighed. "I try not to be," she said.

And I tried not to be peeved with her unspoken assessment of my own duds.

In spite of Lulu's comment, she, Sue and I had fun taking tea at the kitchen table. We already knew what to expect from the almond cookies—delight—but also sampled the other sweets I'd bought.

Holding up half of an interesting concoction that looked like noodles squashed together, Lulu said, "I don't know what this is, but I'm going to take a bite." She did. Her nose wrinkled. She swallowed. "It's noodles."

"Is it sweet?" asked Sue.

"Yeah, but it's noodles."

"I guess it's a Chinese delicacy," I said doubtfully, picking up the half Lulu had left in the box. I bit into it and didn't wrinkle my nose. "Guess it's made with noodles, all right, but they must soak them in some kind of sweet syrup. It's...not bad."

"I'll stick to almond cookies," said Sue.

All in all, I think she made a wise decision.

FIVE

The next morning, Sunday, Caroline remained at her parents' home in Alhambra. Sue went to services at a nearby Presbyterian Church. Lulu and I probably should have joined her. However, except for a brief stint when we attended the Angelica Gospel Hall, presided over by Sister Adelaide Burkhard Emmanuel, Lulu and I were heathens.

Not really. But we didn't attend church regularly. Rather, we did other things with our Sundays. Today, for instance, I aimed to begin decorating my beautiful home on Bunker Hill for Christmas. In Boston, my mother had her home decorated by servants. Well, she probably had her Pasadena winter home decorated by servants, too, but I'd decided to spare Mr. and Mrs. Buck and decorate the place myself.

My decorations didn't amount to a whole lot yet, but I loved what I'd managed to scavenge so far, including a little music box. Well, it wasn't really a box. It consisted of a little boy and a little girl and a Christmas tree on a tiny stand. The tree and the kids had white stuff, meant to be snow, on them and when I turned the key on the back of the stand, it played "Silent Night." The whole scene turned a full circle. It kept turning until the key wound down, by gum. I set it on a small table in a corner next to the staircase. Anyhow, I aimed to keep adding to my Christmas decorations in the two or so weeks left until Christmas.

"Do you think I should run holly branches up the banister, Lulu?" I asked as we lolled in the living room. Lulu had been occupied in reading the latest edition of *Photoplay*, with a picture of Aileen Pringle on the cover. Lulu loved movie magazines. I think she bought every one that showed up in newspaper kiosks the second they landed. She knew more about the people who inhabited the silver screen than I did, and my brother-in-law owned a motion-picture studio!

"Huh?" Lulu looked up from her magazine. "Beg pardon? D'you ask me something?"

"Should I loop holly branches on the banister?" I said, standing back, a finger to my chin, contemplating how pretty the staircase might be if decorated properly.

"Golly, no!" Lulu said, as if the notion appalled her. "Do you know how prickly holly bushes are? We'd all stab ourselves climbing the stairs." She grinned. "That pretty stair runner wouldn't be so pretty covered in blood."

"Oh, yeah. That's right," I said, recalling the prickly nature of holly leaves. "Maybe some garlands of tinsel or something?"

After gazing judicially at the staircase for a few seconds Lulu said, "Naw. Anything you drape over the banister will get squashed."

"Hmm. You're right," I said, feeling slightly daunted.

"Hey, don't despair, Mercy. The house looks beautiful even when it's not decorated. I've never been in such a grand place before, much less lived in one."

"Thanks, Lulu," I said, my heart melting.

In her way, Lulu did more to make me recall my privileged childhood than Ernie, with all his teasing, ever did. Lulu was a young woman who'd grown up in a small Oklahoma town in what she called "the middle of nowhere." Heck, according to her, she'd never seen indoor plumbing until moving to Los Angeles. I had no reason to doubt her. It made me glad to know she was happy in my home.

"Okay, so I won't drape anything on the banister, but I can stick garlands of tinsel or swags of fake poinsettias on the outside of its whatchamacallits."

"The stair railings?"

"Is that what they're called?"

Lulu wrinkled her nose. "I think so. Ask Ernie next time you see him."

"You think he'd know?" I asked doubtfully.

Lulu, appearing slightly dubious, said, "I expect so. Ernie knows lots of stuff. I like the idea of the garlands or the swags. What's a swag when it's at home?"

"It's kind of like a bunch of fake flowers. I could stick swags on the individual railings. Or maybe hang a garland along them— below the banister itself so it wouldn't get squished and nobody would be impaled by anything."

"Sounds good to me," said Lulu. She lifted her magazine and once more became lost in the glories of Hollywood—Hollywood itself being a couple of miles up the street from us, but that wasn't the Hollywood of Lulu's fond fantasies.

Just as I was jotting a note about finding fake flowers with which to make swags or a tinsel garland to decorate the stairway, the tele-phone rang. I turned and frowned in the direction of the room I called my office. Lulu dipped her magazine and said, "Want me to get it?"

"No. I'm already up. I'll get it." And, tucking my notebook and pencil in a pocket of the apron I'd donned for decorating—I think these aprons are called "shopkeepers' aprons," although I'm not positive—I headed to my office. There, I plucked the receiver from the cradle and bent over to speak into the mouthpiece. "Mercy's Manor," I said snap-pily, deciding Lulu had chosen an apt appellation for my abode.

"Hey, Mercy, can I come over there for a few minutes? I have to talk to you."

So startled was I to receive a telephone call from my insouciant employer on a Sunday morning, I sat with a thump on my chair and said, "Ernie? What's up? You sound upset."

"May I visit you and Lulu for a few minutes?" he said, more or less repeating himself, albeit more grammatically, without answering my questions.

Figuring Ernie was Ernie and there was nothing I could do about him, I gave up asking for explanations and said, "Sure. Come on over. I can make some tea and—"

Before I finished telling him about the cookies we had leftover from yesterday's shopping extravaganza in Chinatown, Ernie said, "Thanks," and hung up on me.

"Well," I said, staring at the empty cradle. I gently replaced the receiver and toddled back out to the living room. Lulu was still engrossed in her magazine.

"Ernie's coming over," I told her.

Slapping the magazine onto her lap, Lulu glanced up at me, surprised. As well she might be. "Ernie? Now?"

"Yes."

"Why?"

"I don't know. He didn't say. He sounded a little...rattled. Or something. Kind of upset."

"Upset? *Ernie?*" said Lulu with well-deserved shock. Ernie wasn't one to become excited easily.

With a shrug, I said, "Well...Yes. He sounded...I don't know. Like he was worried about something."

"That's strange."

"Very strange. I'm going to make some tea, and we can have tea with the rest of those cookies we picked up yesterday."

"Sounds good to me. I'll help." She rose from her chair, set her magazine on the table beside it, and followed me into the kitchen.

As I boiled water and plucked a tin of Darjeeling—I loved Chinatown, but I prefer Indian tea to Chinese tea—from the cupboard, Lulu fetched a tray from another cupboard. When I'd first moved to Los Angeles, I didn't know my way around a kitchen. I still had a lot to learn about same, but at least I knew where to find all the things required to prepare tea. And the cookies resided inside the box in which they'd come, but carefully wrapped in waxed paper to keep them fresh. Sue's the one who recommended the waxed paper. Smart girl, Sue.

I had been going to write that Sue was a smart cookie, but I stopped myself in time. Wait. I guess I didn't. Well, never mind, and I apologize.

I'd just poured the boiling water into the heated teapot—a cunningly decorated one with matching cups I'd bought on one of my excursions to Chinatown—when the doorbell rang. Buttercup, better than a doorbell, had taken off at a run toward the front door a second before it pealed.

"Probably Ernie," said Lulu.

"Probably," I agreed.

We both followed Buttercup's trail to the front door. When I opened it, sure enough, there was Ernie, bundled up against the cold weather.

"Come in," I said graciously.

"Hey, Ern," said Lulu, perhaps not as gracious but quite friendly.

"Thanks," said Ernie. He entered my lovely home and bent to pet Buttercup, who was gyrating with happiness at his feet. When he stood again, he said, "It's cold out there," and unwrapped the scarf from around his neck. He stuck the scarf and a pair of gloves he shucked into his overcoat pocket and then hung the coat on the coat tree. His hat he placed on the shelf next to the coat tree in the black-and-white tiled entryway.

"Lulu and I have some tea and cookies for us," I told him once he had shed his outerwear. His innerwear was casual, leading me to believe yesterday's ensemble had been a one-time effort on his behalf. Or perhaps a fluke of nature.

"Thanks," he said. "Listen, I need to talk to you two. Is there anybody else here?"

"Not at the moment," I told him. "I'm pretty sure the Bucks are at the First AME Church they attend, and Sue's gone to the Presbyterian Church on Hill."

"Good."

By that time, we were on our way to the kitchen.

Starting to feel the least bit alarmed, I said, "Why is that good?"

"I'll tell you over tea and cookies." He gave me one of his patented grins. He'd call me *kiddo* next. I braced myself for bad news to come.

I was right to do so.

"They *arrested* him?" I cried, appalled when Ernie spilled the reason for his visit. Or part of the reason.

"Yeah." Ernie stuffed a noodle cookie into his mouth and chewed. I'd unwrapped the cookies and arranged them on a pretty plate, in case you wondered.

"Why?"

After he swallowed, Ernie shrugged. "They think he killed the guy."

I gasped.

"Golly," said Lulu, as shocked as I.

"Let me get this straight," I said, narrowing my eyes and glaring at my boss, who didn't deserve it. After all, *he* hadn't arrested anyone. "An old man was murdered in Chinatown, and the police arrested Charley Wu for murdering him? What's their evidence?"

"They don't have any," said Ernie. "They only know the old man was engaged to Charley's sister, and Charley's sister didn't want to marry him. They think Charley murdered him for his sister's sake."

"That's stupid," said Lulu, who, as already mentioned, didn't have much use for the police.

"Yes, it is stupid," I said. "Charley *wanted* his poor sister to marry the old coot, so why do the police think Charley murdered him?"

"Yeah," said Lulu. "That's really dumb."

"Who was the murdered man? I mean, what was his name? Was he a leader of a gang? I mean a tong?"

"Chan Sien Lo and yes. He came here from San Francisco, where he'd been trying to force Chinese shopkeepers to pay him protection money. I don't think he got far in San Francisco, so he decided to move to Los Angeles and try to pull his tricks here."

"Do the police *know* he was putting pressure on Charley to pay him protection money?"

"They think they do. They think the pressure was that of making Charley's sister marry him—the Chan character—so as not to get in bad with Chan, but I don't know why. As far as I know, there aren't any tong troubles here in Los Angeles, and I think their reasoning is bullsh…Uh, faulty."

"Where was he killed? *How* was he killed?" I asked.

"Close to a grocery store on the west side of Hill. Shot."

"Near Charley's noodle shop?"

Ernie tilted his head and wrinkled his nose. "No, which is another reason I think the cops are wrong. You know where Charley's noodle shop is, right?"

"Right," Lulu and I both said.

"Well, you know the street off the plaza west of Charley's shop? The body was found near the grocery store at the far south side of that street."

"That's not close to Charley's noodle shop," I said. "And it's not close to the shop where we saw Charley and his sister yesterday. Heck, that shop is on the east side of Hill."

"I know. When I talked to Charley, he said the shop where you saw him is owned by one of his uncles," said Ernie. He picked up an almond cookie and took a bite. After he swallowed, he said, "I like these better than the noodle cookies."

"So do we," I told him. "Lulu, Sue and me, I mean." Something occurred to me. "Where's Charley's sister, and what does she think about all this?"

"Nobody knows, and that's another reason I'm here."

"You mean, nobody can find her?" I asked, worried about whatever her name was. Lien? Couldn't remember. I mean, Chinese ladies don't have names with which I'm familiar like Mary or Edith or whatever.

"Not precisely," said Ernie.

"What does that mean?" I asked, a niggling sense of trepidation beginning to creep over me.

Ernie took a sip of tea and looked me square in the eye. "That means the police don't know where she is. I, however, do."

"I thought as much," I muttered darkly.

"Huh?" said Lulu.

"She showed up at my door at five a.m., crying and telling me Charley had been arrested, and asking me for help. She also asked if I could hide her from the Chan tong, or whomever it was that killed the Chan character." Ernie's attempted grin slid sideways before it could affix itself firmly on his face.

A stab of jealousy jolted me. Stupid, stupid, stupid. "How'd she know where you live?" I asked, my voice a teensy bit sharp.

"She said Charley told her to come to me and ask for help. He told her where I live."

"How'd he know?" Lulu asked.

"We go to ballgames together sometimes, and every now and then I'll play ball with his Chinese team. I have a car. He doesn't. My apartment is right there on Yale, so he'd just walk on over, and I'd drive us to the ballpark."

"I didn't know that," I said, unsure as yet if I should feel better about the sister situation or not.

"You and I don't chat about baseball or go to ballgames together," Ernie said.

"True."

"Well?" said Ernie, looking at me darned near beseechingly.

"Well, what?" I asked, confused.

"Well, can you hide Charley's sister for us?" he said as if I should have known what he meant even though he hadn't told me. "*I* can't hide her. I have a tiny apartment. No way I can keep a girl in there."

I felt better suddenly. Not sure why. "Me? Hide a Chinese girl?"

"You have more room than I have," said Ernie.

Lulu and I stared at each other for a second or three.

"Well, I know I have more room, but—"

"Listen, Mercy. The police don't even know what Lian Wu looks like. There are hundreds of Chinese girls walking around L.A. these days. Well, maybe dozens. Anyway, if you took her in as, say, a maid or something, nobody'd think anything about it. All you need to do is keep her for a while so I can investigate the murder of that Chan mug, and it'll all be jake!"

"It will, will it?" I muttered, pondering. "How'd I get a reputation as a goody-two-shoes, anyway?"

Ernie and Lulu just gazed upon me, incredulity writ large on their features.

I gave in. "Oh, very well."

Ernie let out a sigh that nearly lifted the tablecloth.

SIX

Lian Jun Wu—or Wu Lian Jun, if you're Chinese—was at that moment hiding under a blanket on the floor of Ernie's disreputable Studebaker's back seat. She had a sneezing fit when Lulu, Ernie and I all went out to rescue her from her predicament.

The poor girl looked as if she'd been through the wringer, which I guess she had. It must be unpleasant first to be coerced into marrying a man one didn't want to marry, and then to have one's brother arrested for murdering the man. Not to mention having been wrapped in an old blanket and stuffed into the back seat of an ugly old car.

"Miss Wu?" I said, aiming for a friendly, helpful tone of voice.

She sneezed again and pulled a hankie from the pocket of her skirt. "Sorry. Yeah. Call me Lily. Are you Miss Allcutt?" After wiping her nose, she sneezed a third time and said, "Sorry," again.

"Yes, I'm Mercy Allcutt, and this is Lulu LaBelle." I nodded to Lulu.

"H'lo," said Lulu.

Lian nodded at Lulu and sneezed *again*. Poor thing. Ernie's car undoubtedly needed to be washed out with soap and water. Probably bleach.

"Let's not stand here gabbing," Ernie said, grabbing Lian—or Lily—by the shoulder and shoving her at my front porch.

"Stop manhandling the girl, Ernie!" I snapped. "She's been through enough already."

"Cripes," grumbled Ernie. "I don't want any passing cop to look into your yard and see a Chinese girl and me in the same place. The cops might not know Lian on sight, but they know Charley and I are friends."

Working as a team—you'd have thought we'd been practicing for weeks—Lulu and I formed a two-woman fence around Lily while Ernie hustled her onto my front porch. Lily gazed around as if she'd never seen such a place, which might well have been true.

As soon as we all got inside, Ernie, Lulu and I let out a trio of relieved sighs. Lily stood still and gazed in awe around her.

Then she sneezed again and said, "Beg pardon."

"Bless you," I said back.

"You own this joint?" she asked of me.

Joint? This Chinese girl—who looked every inch Chinese—talked like one of your everyday flappers. I was surprised, and that's putting it mildly.

"Yes. This is my home," I said, not mentioning the "joint" angle.

"Wow. This place is the cat's meow!" said Lily, sounding like a flapper again.

"Um...Thank you."

"Can we come in and sit for a while, and maybe we can figure out something to do with Lily while she stays here," said Ernie.

After yet one more sneeze, this one not quite as violent as her first few, Lily passed her hankie under her nose and turned her attention to me. "Yeah. This is so nice of you, Miss Allcutt. I'll do anything. Ernie says you have a cook. I can wait tables or help cook or anything. I was training to be an operator at the telephone exchange until that chump came along, and Charley said I had to marry him. I couldn't believe it."

"Difficult to fathom," I said faintly.

"Come on, Lily," said Ernie, taking her arm and aiming her toward the living room and on to the kitchen.

Lulu and I hung back a pace or two and stared at each other. Not sure about Lulu, but I was quite surprised by the pert and pretty Lian "Lily" Wu. She not only talked like a flapper, but she had her sleek black hair styled into a smooth bob that might have rivaled the one sported by Louise Brooks, and her skirt and blouse were in the very height of style if not awfully warm, considering the weather.

Lulu whispered, "Golly, Mercy, I don't think I ever met a Chinese flapper before."

I whispered back, "I know I haven't."

"This should be interesting," said Lulu, and we followed Lily and Ernie to the kitchen. Ernie was just pulling out a chair for Lily to sit in. He let Lulu and me fetch our own chairs. Lily gazed with interest at the tea things and leftover cookies sitting on the table.

"I see you went to the Phoenix Bakery," she said. "Their stuff isn't awfully good."

"Really?" I said, surprised. "Is there another bakery in Chinatown that sells better pastries?"

With a shrug, Lily said, "Not really. We Chinese don't go in for desserts as much as you whites do. I'd rather have chocolate cake than anything at the Phoenix."

"Can't blame you," said Lulu with studied nonchalance. "I would, too." In fact, she seemed to be observing Lily intently.

"So, Lily," said Ernie, taking charge, which was okay by me. "Tell Mercy and Lulu—as long as we're already on first-name terms—what happened yesterday."

"May I please have some tea and maybe one of those almond cookies first? I'm starving," Lily said.

I jumped up from the table. "Oh, Lily! Of course, you may! I'll make some more tea. It's Darjeeling, if you don't mind, not Chinese."

"I don't care what kind of tea it is. Tea is tea," said Lily, making me think she actually made a better flapper than Lulu, if you went merely by vocabulary.

"Would you like something for breakfast? Toast? Eggs? Bacon?

56

Anything?" I reached into the cupboard and withdrew another teacup. Lifting the pot, which felt mighty light, I poured what was left of the tea into the cup and set it before Lily.

"Thanks. Tea and a couple of these things"—she gestured at the dwindling number of cookies on the plate—"and I'll be fine. We don't have the same kinds of things for breakfast as you white folks do. As a rule," she added in case we took her words amiss. I didn't, but it made me wildly curious.

Her comment had the same effect on Lulu. "What do you eat for breakfast?" she asked, visibly fascinated.

"Can that wait until Lian tells us what happened?" asked Ernie, sounding frustrated.

"Well, all right," said Lulu, definitely miffed. "I was only curious, was all."

"So am I," I said.

"Cripes," said Ernie.

Smiling at Lulu and me, Lily said, "We usually have dumplings for breakfast. Sometimes they'll have something in them, and sometimes they won't."

"Dumplings?" Lulu and I chorused.

The dumplings with which I was familiar were basically globs of dough cooked with and sitting on chicken or beef stew. I couldn't quite imagine eating dumplings for breakfast, although I'd never tried them and I had nothing against dumplings as a food.

"You can discuss dumplings later!" Ernie all but shouted.

"Jeeze, Ernie," said Lulu after she'd landed from her startled seated high jump onto her chair again. "We were just asking."

Lily's pretty eyes had nearly rounded as she gaped at Ernie. "Sorry, Ernie. I know you're doing me a big favor." She graced Lulu and me with a glance. "You're *all* doing me a huge favor. What do you need to know?"

"Thank you," Ernie said with a relieved sigh. "Just tell us what happened. Why were you trying to run away from Charley yesterday? You *were* trying to run away from Charley, weren't you, when Mercy and Lulu saw you?"

"Yes," said Lily in a voice bespeaking anger.

Now standing at the stove after having filled the kettle with water from the tap, I turned and watched the goings-on at my kitchen table as the water came to a boil over a burner. I watched Lily as she spoke, marveling at how pretty and flapperish she appeared. It was true that Anna May Wong, a Chinese woman from California, was a big star in the motion pictures, but you didn't see too many Chinese women out and about on Los Angeles streets. Maybe there was a cult of Chinese flappers hiding out in Chinatown.

Which sounds absolutely silly. Please forget I wrote it.

"Well, okay," Lily said, beginning her story. "Charley and I live with our mother and her brother, Uncle Yu, behind the shop in Chinatown."

"Which shop?" Ernie asked. "The noodle shop or the other shop?"

"The clothing and trinket shop," Lily said promptly. "I usually work in the clothing shop, and Charley and Mother work in the noodle shop. Mother cooks, but she doesn't like to serve customers. She's old-fashioned and doesn't like to be seen in public. I'm not," she said unnecessarily, but faintly defiantly.

"Right," said Ernie. "So you're the one who runs the shop on the east side of Hill."

"Yes. Our father died about four years ago, so Charley, our uncles and I have pretty much carried on and kept the family fed. Well, and our mother cooks for the noodle shop."

"Your mother's a really good cook," I told Lily.

Ernie shot me a scowl, but Lily said, "Thank you. I think she is, too."

"Where's your mother now?" I asked, suddenly feeling terrible for Charley and Lily's mother.

"She's staying with Uncle Wu Shen. My uncles Shen and Yu and Mother thought it better that I stay out of sight. They were afraid I'd be arrested, too. Idiot policemen!"

"You said it," said Lulu.

"So?" asked Ernie, after shooting Lulu a "be quiet" look. Lulu sniffed. "Your mother and uncle aren't living behind the trinket shop at the moment?"

"No. They thought they'd better move for a while."

"Where are they staying?"

"Behind Uncle Hop's restaurant."

"Hop Luey's?" I asked, incredulous.

Ernie shot *me* a "be quiet" look, too. But I was enthralled.

With a smile, Lily said, "Yes. Wu Hop owns Hop Luey's."

"I'll be darned," murmured Lulu.

The kettle boiled, so I had to get back to my job. I plucked the empty teapot off the kitchen table, dumped the used tealeaves into the sink garbage-strainer thing—I'm sure those things have a name, but I don't know what it is—rinsed it with boiling water, spooned in more tealeaves and filled the teapot with more hot water. Then I took the teapot back to the table, put it next to Lily, and resumed my seat.

Before anyone could say anything else, Ernie said, "All right, so your mother's staying with your uncle, and your Uncle Shen and your Uncle Hop live together behind Hop Luey's restaurant. Before this nonsense happened, you and your other uncle lived behind the trinket shop. Do I have that right?"

Nodding, Lily said, "Yes. Uncle Shen and Uncle Hop are both widowers. Uncle Shen's son Joe and his wife Mary live with them. They have two kids, Julie and Nancy. Big house, big family."

"They have American names?" I said, surprised. Then I glanced at Ernie and hoped he wouldn't yell at me. He rolled his eyes, but didn't otherwise express his displeasure. I'd have bet that's only because he was interested in Lily's answer, too.

"They have Chinese names, too, but we're American now, for Pete's sake! We were born here. We might as well have American names. Look at Anna May Wong."

I'd just been thinking about her, although I felt it prudent not to say so.

"All right. So you all live pretty much in or near Chinatown," said Ernie, getting back to the point.

"Yes. And we get along just fine. I don't know why Chung all of a sudden got into such a fuss about that nasty old man." Lily's cheeks got pink, and I could tell she was angry and upset.

"Who's Chung?" asked Lulu.

"Oh, I'm sorry," said Lily. "That's Charley's Chinese name. He was born here, too, so he's Charley to white people. And me, most of the time."

"Yeah! That's right. I'm sorry. I forgot," muttered Lulu.

"Why did Charley want you to marry this character"—Ernie pulled out his notebook, which resided in his shirt pocket—"Chan Sien Lo?"

"He thought the guy would burn us out if I refused to marry him. But I don't believe in that stupid nonsense!" Lily cried with what I considered well-deserved and righteous indignation. "There might have been tong wars forty years ago, and maybe there's trouble in San Francisco, but we don't have trouble in Los Angeles, and I wasn't about to marry the old coot! Charley got really mad at me when I told him so."

"We saw," I muttered, not looking at Ernie in case he decided to gift me with another nasty look.

"I know you did, and I'm glad," said Lily, smiling at Lulu and then me. "If you hadn't tried to stop Charley, he'd probably have made me marry that awful Chan Sien Lo, and he was *horrible*! He's older than my uncles!"

"How was he horrible?" asked Ernie. "Did he threaten your brother or your family or anything?"

"You'll have to ask Charley about that," said Lily disgustedly. "Even though I was the pawn in the chess match, I wasn't allowed to know the details. But Charley was afraid of Chan Sien Lo so he must have threatened Charley, don't you think? But I don't know how. I mean, policemen are always wandering around our shops. They can't all be crooked, can they? I mean, if Chan Sien Lo bribed all the policemen in Los Angeles, I could understand Charley's worry, but that couldn't happen, could it, especially since most of the shop owners bribe the police to watch out for us?"

I gaped, speechless, at Lily.

Silence filled the kitchen. Ernie, Lulu and I swapped glances.

The truth was that Ernie had been a Los Angeles policeman once, but he'd quit because he couldn't stand the corruption in the department. Which, all things considered, might spell either bad or good luck for Charley and Lily.

"Phil Bigelow is an honest copper," Ernie said at last. "I'll talk to him about this mess."

"And the rest of them aren't honest?" asked Lily, sounding worried, which made sense to me.

"Not all of them are crooks," Ernie said without conviction. "I think I can find some good ones to work on Charley's case."

"And you'll look into it, too, won't you?" I asked Ernie pointedly.

"Of course, I will," he grumbled, eyeing me none too kindly.

Impulsively, Lily reached across the table and took Ernie's hand. "Oh, *thank* you, Ernie!"

Startled, Ernie said, "Not a problem. Charley and I are pals." I got the feeling he wanted to yank his hand out of Lily's grip but didn't want to hurt her feelings. His wanting to do so made my feelings perk up and take notice, however.

If, of course, my feelings were correct. They weren't always. Unfortunate, that.

"Mercy and I can help, too," said Lulu enthusiastically.

"No, you can not!" snapped Ernie. "What *you* two can do is figure out what Lily can do around the place to earn her room and board while *I* figure out who really killed that Chan character."

"Might be someone from San Francisco," Lily suggested, taking possession of her hand again mainly because Ernie had removed his to snatch a pencil out of another pocket.

"You can help me decorate for Christmas," I said, thinking it a bright idea.

"That's not going to take two or three weeks," said Ernie. "Find her a job or something, can't you? Do you have a spare bedroom in this mansion?"

"It's not a mansion, and yes, there are two spare rooms downstairs off the sun porch, and there's another upstairs. Well, there are a couple of rooms up there. It's kind of an attic, but they're set up as bedrooms."

Rising from his chair, Ernie said, "You'll figure it out. In the meantime, I'm going to the jail to talk to Charley." He turned to Lily and spoke firmly. "Miss Allcutt is kind enough to put you up here. In fact, she'll probably love having you here. But don't go outside and wander around, all right? I doubt the police know what you look like, but I don't want to take any chances. No going to the Grand Central Market or back to Chinatown or anything. Or even wandering out in front of this place. The coppers know Mercy and Lulu, too." He spoke the last sentence in a grumpy voice. "They'd get mighty suspicious if a Chinese girl suddenly appeared out of nowhere the day after Charley Wu was arrested for shooting a man who was engaged to his sister, who has since disappeared."

"I *wasn't* engaged—"

Very slowly, and very loudly, Ernie said, "*The police think you were.* So *you* need to stay out of sight. Got it?"

Lily said, "Got it," in a small voice and nodded.

"And if either of these two"—he gestured first at me and then at Lulu—"get any bright ideas about investigating on their own, *don't let them!*"

"Ernie!" I cried, stung.

"And if you can't stop them," he went on relentlessly, "telephone me and don't go with them! Is that clear?"

Lily, cowed, only nodded some more.

"And you two," Ernie snarled, stabbing Lulu and me both with piercing glances, "don't try to investigate on your own! This is going to be hard enough without having you two mixed up in it."

"We've helped in the past," I pointed out mildly, although I wanted to snarl at him.

"Yeah? Well, the only way you're going to help this time is to keep Lily here. Get her one of those black maids' uniforms with the white aprons or something, so she looks like she works here if anybody sees her by accident. Is that clear enough for you?"

I heaved a sigh. "Yes, Ernie."

He turned to Lulu, who gulped and said, "Yes, Ernie."

"Good."

He marched out of the kitchen and made his way to the front

door without us at his side. Don't know about Lulu and Lily, but I was kind of afraid to follow him. Buttercup, who wasn't afraid of anything, went with Ernie to the front door. Ernie slammed the door on his way out, but Buttercup probably wouldn't hold the unkind gesture against him. She was an easy-going poodle.

SEVEN

I tiptoed to the front door and peered outside, just to see if Ernie was actually leaving my property. I didn't quite trust him not to lurk nearby in an attempt to catch Lulu, Lily or me bursting outside to do something, although I'm not sure what. Dance on the lawn? Get in my Moon Roadster and parade ourselves in front of various police stations?

But no. Ernie had driven down the long drive and I watched him turn left. Therefore, I marched back to the kitchen and said, "So, Lily, are there any domestic chores you enjoy doing?"

"Huh?" Lily peered at me, observably baffled.

"She means," interpreted Lulu, "Do you like washing clothes? Ironing clothes? Mopping floors? Dusting? Any of those icky things? Mrs. Buck is a great cook, so she probably doesn't need your help in the kitchen."

"Oh," said Lily. "Um…not really, but I'll do anything. You're helping me so much, I honestly don't mind what you set me to doing. I can wash windows! Everybody hates to wash windows, but I don't mind."

"Mr. Buck just washed the windows," I said musingly.

"I'm good at ironing. I can do the washing and ironing."

"That's a good idea," I said. "Mrs. Buck has enough to do, what with keeping the house clean and doing all the cooking. But what the heck, let's think about that later. Right now why don't you and I go up to the third floor? We can find all the Christmas decorations I have. I'll need to get some more. But we can place the decorations I have around the house." I thought of something else and frowned slightly. "You probably won't be able to go with us to buy a Christmas tree, because Ernie would kill us all if you went out of the house on an excursion."

Still at the kitchen table and washing a bite of cookie down with a sip of tea, Lily swallowed and said, "Yeah, I'd better not go with you, but my cousin Fung just set up a Christmas tree lot on College and Spring. I can write him a note and tell him to let you have a nice tree. Some of them are old and losing their needles, but our other cousin, Yu, goes up into the foothills and brings back good trees every day."

"Thanks, Lily!" I said. Then I thought of something probably more pertinent than Christmas decorations. "Er…Do you celebrate Christmas? I mean, you're Chinese, and probably have other traditions. Do you mind helping me decorate for Christmas?"

With a shrug, Lily said, "We do anything we can to make money. As for religious beliefs, we pretty much follow the teachings of Confucius, but it's not precisely what you'd call a religion. It's more of a philosophy. Kind of like Buddhism."

Lily's explanation left me more confused than I was before she tried to enlighten me. "Ah…"

With a sprightly wave of one of her pretty hands, Lily said, "Don't fret. We honor all religions." With a frown, she added, "Except those that want all of us Chinese to die."

After a pause during which I felt appalled and slightly ashamed, although I'm not sure why, Lulu broke the silence with, "Makes sense to me."

"Good. Then we'll all be fine," said Lily, still sprightly.

I decided to give the religious question a rest. It seemed her— philosophy? Well, whatever it was, it didn't seem to prohibit her from living in a home decorated for Christmas.

"Thanks, Lily," I said with more pep and considerably less befuddlement than I felt. "I'd love to get a tree from your cousin's Christmas tree lot." Then I thought of something else. "Um…Do you think Ernie will get mad if you write a note to your cousin? He doesn't want anyone to know where you are."

With a shrug, Lily said, "Fung—you can call him John—won't know where I am, and he wouldn't tell the cops or anyone connected with Chan Sien Lo even if he did. I don't think anyone in my family will cause trouble, but somebody murdered Sien Lo, so who knows what's going on?" She shook her sleek head. "Anyway, nobody I know will give me away. Or you or Ernie or Lulu."

"Good," I said. "You have no idea why that guy demanded to marry you?"

"Not a clue," said Lily, downing more tea. "But let me wash up these dishes and start earning my keep."

"I'll help," said Lulu. "We can wash up while Mercy figures out where to stick you." She wrinkled her brow. "I didn't mean that exactly."

Lily burst out laughing, so she plainly didn't take Lulu's words amiss. I don't believe I'd ever met another person as lively as Lily Wu seemed to be.

"Would you prefer downstairs or upstairs?" I asked.

"I don't care. Whatever you think Ernie will think is safest."

"Smart answer," said Lulu.

"Yes, it was," I agreed. "Okay, I'll fix the first third-floor room for you."

"Thanks." Lily said and began clearing the table as if she were an accomplished waitress.

Leaving the two "L" ladies to their task, I trotted upstairs with Buttercup, turned right instead of going straight ahead into my own suite of rooms, and marched to a little-used door at the other end of the corridor. The door opened to reveal a staircase—the so-called "servants'" staircase—which the Bucks kept swept and dusted, even though I only went up them to look for things I'd stored in the attic rooms.

Perhaps "attic" isn't the right word for the third floor of my house. The space contained a washroom without a tub, but with hot and cold running water, another small suite of rooms consisting of a sitting room and two bedrooms, and a separate, larger, room where I stored items I didn't use regularly. Like, for example, Christmas ornaments. I'd managed to acquire quite a few Christmas things during my few months in Los Angeles. That's mainly because Chloe and Harvey left behind almost all of their furnishings and unnecessary decorative items when they sold me the house and moved into their new quarters in Beverly Hills.

But this morning's trek wasn't merely to haul out Christmas ornaments. Instead, I opened the first bedroom door and stepped inside. It was dusted and tidy, but the bed wasn't made up. So I walked to the linen cupboard on the second floor, grabbed sheets, etc., and tramped back to the bedroom. To my surprise, Lulu and Lily were there, waiting for me.

"I'll make up the bed," said Lily, coming over and relieving me of the plain white sheets I held.

"Which bathroom will Lily use?" asked Lulu, sounding efficient. "I'll get her a towel and washcloth."

"Actually, there's a bathroom on this floor," I told them both. "It doesn't have a tub, but——"

"That's all right with me," said Lily, interrupting. I didn't scold. "I'm used to using a washcloth and basin, if that's what's there."

"That's what's there, all right," I told her. "But if you ever want to take a bath or something, you may use one of the bathrooms on the second floor. Or the one off the sun porch downstairs."

"Wow, how many bathrooms do you have in this place?" asked a wide-eyed Lily.

"Um…the Bucks', mine, Lulu's, Caroline and Sue's, the one up here, and there's a guest restroom off the sun room downstairs."

"Golly," Lily whispered. "You have *five* bathrooms? We only just got indoor plumbing a couple of years ago, and the whole family uses it."

"My folks in Oklahoma don't have indoor plumbing today," said Lulu.

I blinked at the both of them. Very well, I knew I'd "grown up rich," as Ernie was fond of putting it, but golly. I didn't know people still lived without indoor plumbing. The depths of my ignorance, which I occasionally thought were filling in, sometimes collapsed and made the hole even larger than I'd supposed it to be. I said, "Oh," and left it at that.

"Interesting," said Lily, moving and startling Lulu and me out of what had become postures of stunned amazement. She went to the bed and got busy.

"I'll get the towels," said Lulu. She loped off to do so.

"Um, Lily, may I help you?" I asked, suddenly feeling shy for no real reason, unless being totally useless makes people feel shy.

"Naw, that's Jake. I'm used to making beds. Sometimes I work at my uncle Mo's hotel on Broadway. It's a small place, and I help out every now and then."

"You have a lot of family here in Los Angeles," I observed.

"Oh, yeah, we've been here for decades. I think the first Wus came over when they were building the railroads. Then they passed that law, so no Chinese can get in any longer."

"What law?" I asked, feeling faintly faint.

"The Chinese Exclusion Act."

"The...I've never heard of it," I admitted, feeling fainter.

"It was passed in 'eighty-two," said Lily matter-of-factly. "Actually, they passed another law earlier, in 1875, I think, which banned Chinese women from coming to the U.S.A. Too late for us." She giggled. "We were already here."

Her giggle astonished me. "Why did they ban Chinese people from coming here?" I asked, not feeling at all giggly.

Tucking a sheet in at the foot of her bed in the approved Red-Cross manner, Lily said, "Didn't want us heathen Chinese taking white men's jobs, I suppose. A bunch of Chinese here in Los Angeles were massacred by a bunch of whites and Mexicans in the late 1870s. Not sure why, but stuff like that usually happens because people fear for their money and their jobs. That's according to my uncle Hop. He's kind of cynical sometimes."

"I don't blame him. Good Lord," I whispered, horrified.

"I doubt the good Lord had anything to do with it," said Lily tackling another sheet corner. "People hate each other for the heck of it, as nearly as I've been able to tell in my nineteen years on this earth."

"You're nineteen?" I asked, recalling another almost-nineteen-year-old who'd lived in my home briefly. Lily was nothing like her. At least I hoped to heck she wasn't.

"Yup. Turned nineteen last week."

"You…look younger."

Squinching up her nose, Lily said, "I know. That's why I wear makeup and short skirts."

"You and Lulu will get along well, I think," I told her.

Giving me a dazzling smile, Lily said, "Good." Then she suddenly stood up straight and whirled around to face me. "I know!"

"You know what?"

"I already have a couple of maid uniforms! I wear them when I work at Uncle Mo's hotel!"

Astounded, I said, "Great! That's great. I hate to say it, but it will look more normal for a Chinese girl to be dressed as a maid in my house all of a sudden than if you just walked around in regular clothes."

"Yeah," said Lily, back to sounding cynical. "You're right."

By the time the Bucks came home from their extended church services—Mrs. Buck told me the service lasted a couple of hours, and then the whole congregation got together and ate a meal in the church hall afterwards—Lily, Lulu and I were fast friends.

What's more, Lily wrote a note to her cousin Fung (or John if you were me), and Lulu and I set out to get a Christmas tree.

We got a dandy one, too. John made sure of it, passing over three or four I thought would serve. But he said he'd find us the best one, and I think he did. Six feet tall and well-shaped, John had to tie it to the top of my automobile, and Lulu and I worried about it falling off all the way back home.

But John must have been as skilled as the rest of the members of his family, because Mr. Buck had to get out a big knife in order to cut the ropes. Then he wrestled the tree into the house, and Mrs.

Buck, Lulu, Lily and I fussed about where to put it. We finally decided to put it in a corner of the living room where it could be seen from the entryway, the staircase, my office and the kitchen. And it wasn't anywhere near the fireplace, which was a condition the Bucks insisted upon, and which I heartily endorsed.

While at the Christmas tree lot, I'd also purchased a stand for the tree. It was metal and had a tub in which to stick the tree and little screws on the sides that you screwed into the trunk of the tree so it wouldn't fall over. It was a heavy sucker, too, but John assured us that, as long as we kept putting water in the metal tub daily, the tree would stay fresh until at least the new year. I thought it was a keen invention.

For the record, the Bucks accepted Lily with a mere modicum of consternation. Their consternation fled after I explained why Lily was in my home and why her presence had to remain a deep, dark secret.

"Don't you worry about a thing, girl," Mrs. Buck said after enfolding Lily in a massive hug. "Mr. Ernie will find out who killed that terrible man."

The Bucks had infinite faith in Ernie ever since he—and Lulu and I—had discovered who had really murdered the man for whose killing the Bucks' son Calvin had been arrested. They'd arrested Calvin because he'd worked for the man, according to them. According to me, they arrested Calvin because he was a Negro man.

My mother calls me a Socialist because I want everyone to be treated the same, no matter their religion, ethnicity or skin color. My mother is not only overbearing and rude, but she's blind to social inequities. I, her rebellious daughter, am not, darn it.

Ahem. I beg your pardon and shall step off my soapbox now.

Sue Krekeler and Caroline Terry, who each returned later on that fateful Sunday, accepted Lily as a new member of the household staff, even though she didn't have her maid's uniform on yet. I didn't tell them why Lily had come to stay with us, and they didn't ask. They both just smiled and greeted her, and Lily, bless her, curtseyed to them as if she were an actual servant.

"I'm having Ernie pick up Lily's maid uniforms at her Uncle

Mo's hotel tomorrow," I told Lulu as we sat in my upstairs sitting room after supper that evening. "As long as Sue and Caroline don't know any different, Lily can dress like a maid and just *be* a maid. She'll be doing a maid's work anyway."

"Sounds all right by me. I have a feeling Lily wouldn't mind if you wanted her to wear burlap. She's about the sweetest kid I've ever met. Nothing much seems to bother her, except getting her brother out of the clink."

"I think you're right."

"But Ernie will find out who really did it."

"Right," I said, but I frowned. Shoot, you'd think even *Lulu* believed me to be useless when it came to a criminal investigation.

I hoped to heck she wasn't correct.

EIGHT

On Monday morning, Lulu, Caroline, Sue and I walked to Angels Flight, paid the conductor our respective nickels, and whizzed down to Hill Street. From there we walked to our places of work, first leaving Caroline at the corner of Hill and Broadway because she worked at the Broadway Department Store. Then Lulu, Sue and I walked to the Figueroa Building. There, Sue left us to continue to her dentist's office. Well, I don't suppose he was *her* dentist, precisely, but you know what I mean.

"Be sure to ask Ernie about Charley and the case," Lulu said to me as we entered through the polished glass doors of the Figueroa Building. When I first entered this building the preceding June, the glass had been dirty and the brass plaque announcing its name had been dull and ugly. Now the whole place shone. That's because Mr. Buck was the custodian there now, just as he was at my house.

"Of course I will!" I said, surprised she'd even suggest I do something I was sure to do without any prompting from anyone.

"I know you will, but I want to know what's up, too, so tell me, okay? You can fill me in over lunch or something."

"Sounds good to me," I said, and I meant it. I'd developed an almost insatiable longing for corned beef sandwiches since I'd moved to Los Angeles, and not merely because I knew the notion of her daughter dining on corned beef sandwiches enraged my mother. I loved 'em!

Because I'd had an unhappy experience regarding the elevator in the Figueroa Building during my first month of secretarial duties to Ernie, I generally took the stairs up to the third floor where Ernie's office was located. I did so that day.

To my surprise, when I got to the office, Ernie was already there. My perpetually casual employer generally slouched into the office at nine or nine-thirty of a morning, although I always got to work promptly at eight, or even earlier. I was earlier on Monday, by about five minutes.

"Ernie! What are you doing here?" I asked as I hung my coat on the rack near the door. For the record, my voice was sunshine itself.

"I work here," he called back, sounding grouchy. And on the first day of the workweek, for pity's sake!

I'd headed toward the door to his room, which was off the one in which I worked, when the telephone rang. Disgruntled, I detoured to answer it. "Mr. Templeton's office. Miss Allcutt speaking," I said as I always did when answering the telephone at work. I tried at all times to behave like a professional secretary.

"Mercy? Gimme Ernie, okay?"

I recognized Phil Bigelow's voice, only it sounded a trifle testy. And his greeting was positively *rude*. I'd come to expect better of Detective Philip Bigelow. However, I said as icily as possible, "Hold the wire for a moment please, Detective Bigelow."

Finishing my trek to Ernie's room, I paused in the doorway and said, "Phil Bigelow."

Neither of those men deserved courtesy from me, curse them.

Without acknowledging my presence, Ernie plucked the earpiece off the cradle and spoke into it. "Phil? So what's the verdict?"

Verdict? What was the man talking about? I decided to find out for myself, so I went to my desk, sat in my chair—trying to be silent as I moved—and picked up the receiver I'd laid on my desk blotter. Holding it to my ear, I heard Phil say, "...find a gun. But the guy was shot with a revolver with dumdums. Shot in the back."

"And what makes you think Charley Wu used it? You already told me you can't find the gun, and you searched Wu's place and didn't find any weapons at all."

"We found a baseball bat," said Phil grudgingly.

"Right. It would take some incredible ingenuity to get a baseball bat to shoot dumdums. I know the Chinese are supposed to be smart, but I'd really like to see this miracle of a baseball bat revolver that shoots dumdum bullets. Any idea where the trigger is on this wonder baseball gun?"

"Cripes, Ernie, just because we couldn't find the gun doesn't mean he didn't use the thing. He was seen and heard arguing with Chan not very long before Chan was shot. Everybody in Chinatown knew he had it in for that Chan character."

"You've got it backwards, Phil," said Ernie. "Everybody *I* talked to in Chinatown knows Chan had it in for Charley."

"Dammit, Ernie, the guy's right for the crime!"

"The hell he is. I know Charley Wu! He'd no more shoot anybody than he'd fly to the moon!"

"But he's the only suspect we have!" Phil's voice had taken on a plaintive note.

"He's the only suspect you have because you haven't looked for another one, and you know it! You're a detective, Phil. Go out there and *detect*, for Christ's sake!"

"Nobody can get those Chinks to talk, Ernie. You know that!"

"Baloney. They'll talk to me. If you won't do your job, I'll do it for you. Cripes, you know damned well the Chinese in Los Angeles don't commit crimes like that. They have the occasional numbers-running racket or gamble on Mah Jongg, but they don't kill each other."

"Not necessarily true, Ernie. There were those tong wars, you know," said Phil, attempting to redeem himself.

"Bushwa! Those were more than twenty years ago. Besides, they used hatchets, not revolvers with dumdum bullets. Anyhow, there were no tong wars in Los Angeles. San Francisco and New York, maybe, but not L.A. You know that as well as I do."

"Ernie, I don't know what you expect me to do!" cried Phil, sounding as if he were out on a rickety limb and someone was sawing at it from the tree-side.

"I expect you to do your *job*, dammit! Listen, Phil. You say they won't talk to you in Chinatown. Well, take me with you. They'll talk to me. Well, as long as you stay in the background and they don't see you."

"Cripes, Ernie, you know I can't do that."

"Maybe not officially, but you can take me unofficially, and don't pretend you can't. We've been through this before several times, remember?"

"Aw, shi——" Suddenly, Phil stopped talking. "Ernie?"

"Yeah?"

"Is Mercy listening to this call? The line sounds funny."

Curses! Found out. Well, too bad. "Yes! Yes, I'm listening to this call, blast you, Phil Bigelow, and Ernie's right! Charley Wu would no more shoot somebody than *I* would."

A short silence ensued. Ernie broke it.

"Yeah," said Ernie. "She doesn't shoot people. She shoves them down elevator shafts."

"I do not! Well, only that once. And he was trying to kill me, so my action was more than justified."

"Aw, crud," said Phil.

"Come to the office, Phil. We'll hash this out. You and I both know Charley isn't your killer."

"I don't either," said Phil grumpily. "Do you know where his sister is? The girl the Chan guy wanted to marry? We can't find her, and nobody in Chinatown claims to know where she is."

My heart stopped for a second.

"His sister? Hell, no, I don't know where she is. Didn't know he *had* a sister. She's with her family, I suppose."

The old ticker recommenced ticking.

"No, she's not. We can't find her and they won't say where she is."

"Why doesn't that surprise me?" asked an extremely sarcastic Ernie Templeton. "I mean, they all look alike, don't they? Besides, they probably think you'll arrest her next."

I heard Phil huff out an aggrieved breath. "I'll be there in a little while," he said. Then he hung up his receiver. I did the same to mine. I heard Ernie's receiver click into the cradle.

"Mercy," said Ernie.

"Yes?" I said, not feeling as brave as I had a few seconds prior. But I had a girl to protect, and I wasn't going to allow Ernie's bad mood to stop me. Besides, I wanted to know what a dumdum bullet was. Therefore, I stood, picked up my pad and a couple of pencils, clutched them tightly to my chest, and marched into Ernie's office, back straight, prepared for any barbs he might fling at me.

I forestalled him by asking, "What is a dumdum bullet?"

After blinking a couple of times, Ernie said, "A dumdum is a lead bullet with an X carved into its nose."

"Golly, isn't that dangerous? Carving bullets?"

"Why would it be dangerous?"

"I don't know. The notion of doing anything at all with a bullet sounds dangerous to me."

"They're only dangerous if you shoot them from a gun. Maybe if you ate enough of them, you'd get lead poisoning, but it would probably take a while."

"Oh. Yes, I guess that makes sense," I said, still a trifle doubtful, not to mention attempting to keep Ernie's attention from my perceived misbehavior. "Why do they carve an X into the bullet? Does that do something special to the bullet?"

"Yeah. The crossed lines make the bullets expand when they hit a target. A dumdum makes a hell of a hole in a body."

"They expand when they penetrate?"

"Yeah."

"Oh. Ew."

"Yeah. It's no fun being shot with a dumdum. But how's Lily doing?" he asked mildly, surprising me. I'd prepared for a battle over me listening in on his conversation with Phil.

Slumping a bit in relief, I sat in one of the chairs facing his desk and said, "Okay so far. Sue and Caroline think I hired her as a maid. The Bucks know her story, but they're not going to tell a soul."

"Good," said Ernie. "Thanks for taking her in, Mercy."

"I don't mind at all. She's a nice girl. Oh, and you need to go to her Uncle Mo's hotel on Spring Street today and pick up two maids' uniforms. She says she wears them when she works at the hotel."

Shaking his head, Ernie said, "I swear to god, those people own or operate nearly all the businesses in this part of Los Angeles."

"Yes. They're quite energetic and enterprising. Lulu and I got a Christmas tree from Lily's cousin Fung's Christmas tree lot yesterday afternoon."

Ernie's face crunched into a ferocious frown, but before he could yell at me for exposing Lily to Los Angeles, I said, "Lily didn't go with us! She wrote a note to her cousin and asked him to get us a good Christmas tree."

"What did you do with the note?"

"Gave it to Fung. What else was I supposed to do with it?"

"Great. And if some smarter-than-average policeman finds the note and figures out Fung and Lily are related, what do you think's going to happen then?"

"Lily wrote it in Chinese characters, Ernest Templeton, and I crumpled it up and stuck it in my coat pocket as soon as Fung read it. Then when I got home, I tossed it in the fireplace! Do you really think I'm *that* much of an idiot?" When he opened his mouth to say something, I forestalled him. "Don't answer that. But honestly, Ernie, Lulu, Lily and I *all* know she has to remain hidden. For pity's sake, why do you think I want you to get her maid uniforms?"

After heaving a gust of air that ruffled the *Los Angeles Times* on his desk, Ernie said, "Sorry. This situation has me worried."

"Understood. But *you* need to understand that *I* understand. Lily can wear her maid's uniform all day, every day, and nobody will think anything about it if they happen to see her at my house."

"Yeah? What's she going to be doing at your place? Doesn't Mrs. Buck do most of the cleaning and so forth?"

"Yes. Lily will do the laundry, including the ironing. She says she doesn't mind washing and ironing."

"Better her than me," said Ernie.

"Me too."

We both heard the door to the outer office open, so I sprang nimbly from my chair and hastened into my room, still carrying my notebook and pencils. Sure enough, Phil Bigelow was just shutting the door behind himself.

"Good morning, Phil," I said, trying not to sound as irate as I felt about a police department that arrested people without investigating all aspects of a crime first. Because I couldn't seem to help myself, I said, "Why'd you arrest Charley Wu? Do you have any evidence at all that he killed that awful man?"

"Mercy!" came Ernie's voice from his office. "Shut up."

"Bother!" I said. "Go on in, Phil. Ernie's there."

Hanging his coat and hat on the rack beside the door, Phil said, "Yeah. I heard." When he turned around and started on his way to Ernie's office, he apparently noticed my grim expression because he lifted his arms in a helpless gesture and said, "It's not my fault, Mercy! He's the only suspect we have. And he's a good one."

"That's only because you haven't looked for another one," I said in a snippy voice.

"Phil!" Ernie called from his office. "Get in here and stop harassing my secretary."

"Nuts. It's the other way around," said a visibly distressed Phil Bigelow. "She's the one harassing me."

"As is only fitting," I said as I sat behind my desk and straightened my desk blotter.

"She's right, you know, Phil," said Ernie.

"Aw, cripes," said Phil. Then he gave up attempting to justify the L.A.P.D.'s arrest of an innocent man, clumped into Ernie's office, and shut the door, blast him.

The telephone rang, so I stopped fuming in anger long enough to answer it. "Mr. Templeton's office. Miss Allcutt speaking."

"Mercy," whispered Lulu into the receiver. "Are you alone in your room?"

Surprised, I said, "Yes, I'm alone. Ernie and Phil are in Ernie's office and they shut the door, the rats."

"I'm glad they did, because I need to tell you something."

"Oh? About…Well, you know. About that?"

"Yes. Actually, it's Junior. He's the one who has the skinny."

The skinny? I wasn't sure, but presumed the word meant information. Oh, and Junior was a youngish lad, I suspect about twelve or thirteen, who worked in the Figueroa Building as a runner for various attorneys in the building. He occasionally ran other errands, too, like fetching meals from the diner across the street. People tipped him to do the chores they asked him to do.

"Is Junior there with you now?" I asked.

"Yeah, but you need to hear what he has to say because I'll probably get it wrong if I try to repeat it."

"Can he come up here?" Recalling who now sat in Ernie's office, I said, "No, that won't work. Phil Bigelow is here. When can Junior and I talk?"

I guess Lulu covered the mouthpiece on her telephone, because I heard muttering sounds on my end of the wire.

Then Lulu said to Junior, after having removed her hand from the mouthpiece, "If this is just an excuse—"

"No!" I heard Junior say. "I don't need no excuses. But I could use some lunch, and we can talk there."

Hmm. Apparently, the enterprising youngster was bartering information for food. Well, why not?

"He says if we take him to lunch, he'll spill everything he knows about the murder in Chinatown."

"He does, does he? Where does he expect us to take him to lunch? The Ambassador?"

Lulu laughed. "No. He said we should go to the diner around the corner. In fact, he says if we give him money, he'll go out and pick up lunch for the both of us, and we can eat in seclusion downstairs in the janitor's closet."

"That's kind of a small space, isn't it?"

"Yes, it is," said Lulu. "But we can probably find an empty room

79

somewhere in the building where we can be alone—well, the three of us, I mean—and he can spill the beans."

I heaved a sigh. "Very well. Send him up here, and I'll give him money for three…Well, whatever the diner offers."

"What's for lunch, Junior?" Lulu asked.

I heard, faintly, "Chinese."

"Chinese," said Lulu.

"Oh! Wow, maybe he *does* know something."

"He probably does. The kid gets around."

"Okay. Send him up. Thanks, Lulu."

"You paying for all of us?" Lulu asked, sounding surprised for no good reason. I was the only one of the three of us who had spare money.

"Yes. Don't worry about it."

"I'm not worrying. Just asking," said Lulu.

She replaced her telephone on its cradle. I did likewise and opened my desk drawer, where I always stored my handbag and other miscellaneous things—primarily the manuscript I was at present working on. Have I mentioned that my ultimate goal, even more ultimate than becoming Ernie's assistant private investigator, is to become a writer of mystery novels? Well, it is.

I probably jumped a foot when Ernie's door opened suddenly and Phil stepped out, looking as if he wanted to punch something. Turning his head in Ernie's direction, he barked, "We *are* looking, curse it! I don't want to convict an innocent man any more than you do, but Charley Wu looks good for it! He was seen and heard arguing with the man shortly before he was shot."

"When was he shot? Was it still daylight?"

"Well, no. The coroner thinks he was shot at around ten or eleven p.m."

"In that case, nobody could have seen him. The city fathers haven't been generous with the electrical lighting in Chinatown, as you well know, Phil."

"Nut to that. Wu was heard, if not seen, arguing with the Chan mug, and he looks good for the crime!"

"He does not," came Ernie's sarcastic reply. "You just don't know what to do when it comes to policing Chinatown."

"And you do, I suppose," snapped Phil, still standing in Ernie's doorway.

"Better than you and the entire L.A.P.D., yes, I do."

"Well, if you can help us, please do," Phil said. Snidely, I probably don't need to mention.

"I'll be damned if I'll do your job for you, Phil. I'll go along with you and talk to folks in Chinatown, but they won't talk if they see you there. You know Charley Wu didn't kill that man. It's *your* job to find out who did. Unless you want to fry an innocent man just because he's Chinese."

"I *don't*—" Phil stopped yelling, took a deep breath, and said, "I don't want to fry anyone just because he's not white. You know me better than that, Ernie."

"Huh," said Ernie.

I could hear Phil grind his teeth as he stomped from Ernie's office doorway to the front office door. I didn't feel sorry for him.

NINE

E rnie, grinning, strolled out of his room after Phil left the office. "Phil's not happy with me."

"I noticed." I grinned too. Then, on a more sober note, I asked, "Why do the police suspect Charley of killing the man? They haven't even found the weapon used to kill him, have they?"

"No. They found a baseball bat in Charley's house. Well, you heard, because you were spying on our conversation—"

"I wasn't spying!"

"Give it up, Mercy. When you listen in on another person's telephone call, it's spying."

"Huh."

"Anyhow, the only possible weapon they could find at Charley's place was a baseball bat."

"But the man was shot, not battered to death," I said, faintly bewildered.

"Yeah. Phil knows that. You and I know it."

"If they didn't find a gun, did they find any…What did you call them? Dumdum bullets? Any ammunition at all?"

"No. No gun and no ammo. They had better grounds for

arresting me for killing that crazy woman a few months back than they have for arresting Charley."

I don't think I mentioned that Ernie had been suspected of murdering one of his clients, did I? Well, he had been, but he didn't do it. In fact, it had been *I* who had discovered the guilty party back then. I did it by accident and nearly died for my efforts, but I did it, by golly!

"I agree," I said. "How are you going to make them change their minds?"

With a shrug, Ernie said, "Beats me. Hurts, too." He flopped onto the chair beside my desk.

"Do you know many other merchants in Chinatown? Can you talk to them?"

Shaking his head, Ernie said, "I know several of them, and they all smile and say they're glad to see me but face it, I'm white, Mercy. I doubt they'd want to talk to me about anything important, and the murder is important. Charley's the only Chinese man I consider an actual friend. They stick pretty much together. Well, so do we all. You don't hang out with the Bucks, do you?"

"Well…We don't precisely hang out together," I said, beginning to feel uncomfortable.

"Yeah, and you don't know any of their friends either, do you?"

I sighed heavily. "No."

"There you go then. The races don't regularly mingle."

"That makes me sad."

"It's the way the world works, Mercy. You wanted to learn the wicked ways of the world. Well, that's one of 'em."

"I guess. I don't like it though." I thought of something. "But I'll bet Lily will become a friend to Lulu and me!"

"Could be."

The door to the corridor opened, and Junior swaggered in. As soon as he saw Ernie, he stopped swaggering. In fact, he stopped walking entirely. Unfortunately, he also began looking guilty.

"Hey, Junior," said Ernie, smiling at the lad.

"Morning, Mr. Ernie," said Junior. He shot a quick look at me as if begging me to intervene and somehow tell him what to do.

Ernie, no slouch at detecting things, instantly realized something of a secret nature was unfolding before him. He stood, braced his right arm on my chair, and squinted at Junior. "Okay, kid, you look like you're up to something. What's going on here?"

"Nothin'," said Junior.

"He came up here to get some money from me because he's going to a diner around the corner to fetch Lulu and me some lunch. That way, she and I can look at the flyer from the Broadway Department Store we picked up this morning. I want to get some of those cunning Christmas ornaments they're advertising."

Physically relaxing, Junior said, "Yeah. That's all. You want me to get you something, too, Mr. Ernie?"

"Both of you need to take acting lessons," said Ernie grimly. He turned to me. "What's up, Mercy? If you're recruiting this kid to go snooping for information about a murder, I'm going to have to take steps."

"I'd never do such a thing!" I lied passionately. "Whatever gave you that idea?"

"Because the diner around the corner is a Chinese place, is why," said Ernie.

Whoops. I guess Ernie knew his way around this neighborhood better than I did. Because I felt caught out, I said, "So what? I like Chinese food." Then, thinking quickly and—I believe—brilliantly, I said, "Charley Wu's place must be closed today, so we can't eat there. Anyhow, the place around the corner is nearer to us than Chinatown."

Quirking a finger at Junior, Ernie said, "Come over here, Junior. Take a seat. I want to talk to both of you."

Oh, dear.

"Yeah?" said Junior, looking scared. "What about?" He backed up a step, preparing to bolt if I were to judge.

"Lunch," said Ernie.

"Come on over, Junior," I said, giving up the pretense. "You might as well tell Ernie your information, too. He's better at detecting than Lulu and I are."

"Uh..."

"It's okay, Junior," said Ernie. "If you know something that'll help Charley, tell me about it. Charley's a pal of mine, and I know damned well he didn't kill that man."

"Oh," said Junior. With relief, he whipped off his flat cap and resumed sauntering, this time to one of the chairs in front of my desk.

"So," said Ernie once Junior was comfortably seated, "do you know anything about the murder of the Changuy in Chinatown? The one they arrested Charley Wu for killing?"

"Well," said Junior, casually lifting his dirty, holey shoes and propping them on my desk, "I have a pal in the Chinese place around the corner, and he told me there's a whole 'nother story behind that guy getting bumped off."

"Get your shoes off my desk instantly, young man," I said, frowning at Junior. He might be young and he might be useful, but he needed to learn manners. "Your shoes are filthy."

After a brief eye-roll, Junior removed his shoes from my desk. I got out my dust rag and flapped off the dirt he'd left behind.

"You ought to know better, Junior," Ernie said with a twinkle in his eye, but with reproof in his voice. There might have been a twinkle in his voice, too.

"Sorry, Miss Mercy." Junior turned back to Ernie. "So anyway, my pal, Fong, he told me the guy who was killed was blackmailing Charley Wu because of a debt his father owed him."

"A debt Charley's father owed the dead man?" I asked because Junior's explanation hadn't been clear to me. "What kind of debt? Why didn't Charley's father pay it?"

"How should I know? Fong doesn't know either," said Junior in disgust at my ignorance. "But them Chinks think a lot of what they call family honor, according to Fong. Anyway, somehow or other, the dead bozo aimed to tear up the debt if he could marry Charley's sister."

"Oh," I said, appalled, which seemed to be my default position of late.

"Ah. Does your friend Fong know what kind of debt it was?" asked Ernie.

"Dunno. I know the dead guy was coming to Fong's family for an old debt, too, but I don't know for what. They're real secretive about family stuff."

"Okay. Got it," said Ernie. He appeared troubled, which troubled me. My boss wasn't easily troubled. "So Fong thinks the Chan chump pressured Charley to get his sister to marry him, and he'd forgive Charley's father's debt to the dead guy?" His lips twisted a bit. "If that makes sense."

"You mean, Chan would forget about the debt if Charley's sister married him?" asked a slightly confused Junior.

"Couldn't have said it better myself," said Ernie, telling the truth.

"Yeah. I think so. But on Saturday, there was a big scene in Chinatown when the girl tried to run away, and that guy Charley ran after her, and a couple of white women got involved, and Fong thinks that might have triggered somebody into offing the dead guy. 'Cause it wasn't just Charley Wu the guy was trying to get money out of."

Ernie presented me with a non-too-jolly look. I remained appalled, the notion of anything I'd done having contributed to a murder being quite unpleasant. Even if the murdered man was an evil blackmailer. Or is it blackmail if you request payment of a parent's debt from a child? Did that sentence even make sense?

"Do you know the names of any of the other people Chan was going after, Junior? Does Fong?"

"Dunno. I can ask him, but he probably won't tell me even if he knows."

"Don't do it," I said suddenly. "You might get hurt, and then I'd be responsible for two murders!"

"Who'd you kill?" asked Junior, looking avidly interested.

"Well, nobody. I was thinking about you, if you ask questions."

"Me?" Junior stabbed his chest with a forefinger. "Why me?"

"I don't know, but I was one of the white ladies in Chinatown on Saturday who contributed to the scene you spoke of. If the bad men connect you with me and the both of us with Charley Wu, there might be trouble."

"Holy moly! No kidding? That's the *cat's*!" Junior looked as if he'd won a jackpot.

"Calm down, you two," said Ernie. To me, he said, "Mercy, you weren't responsible for the murder. You witnessed something that worried you and, being you, you took steps. The guy getting killed had nothing to do with you. The whole thing stinks like rotten fish though." He held up a hand. "Lemme think for a minute. Don't either of you talk."

Junior clamped his lips together. So did I, in spite of being annoyed. But the thought of Charley Wu being electrocuted for a murder he didn't commit made me hold my sometimes—oh very well, often—too-ready tongue.

I don't have any idea how long Ernie sat and thought, but it seemed like an hour and a half. However, just as I was about to burst and Junior blew his third or fourth bubble, Ernie lifted his chin from his hand and said, "Okay. Junior, how about you and me go to the Chinese place around the corner and bring back food for the ladies and ourselves?"

Junior leaped from his chair, popping yet another bubble and sucking it into his mouth. "Swell! Yeah. That's the berries, Mr. Ernie!"

Feeling left out, I said, "May I come, too?"

"*No.*" Ernie stood from the chair he'd occupied next to my desk and loomed over me. "If the Chan guy wasn't working alone, the people who work with him might recognize you from that mess on Saturday. Nobody knows Junior or me or that we have anything to do with you and Lulu."

"But you came to lunch with Lulu and me on Saturday!"

"That doesn't matter. Everybody in Chinatown knows I'm a pal of Charley's. Nobody's going to connect you with me or with Junior."

"But—"

Ernie pointed a forefinger at me. His finger got so close to the bridge of my nose that my eyes crossed. "*No!* For once in your life, you're going to do as I say and stay out of this. There may be a point when you can get involved. Well hell, Mercy, you're already involved! For God's sake, you took in Lily! Junior and I will gather any information we can gather, and you can take it back to Lily and see if she can make anything out of it. Got it?"

"Oh," I said, subdued. "Yes. I see. That makes sense."

I resented Ernie's eye-roll, but I didn't say so. I did say, "And you'll pick up those uniforms, right?"

"After lunch," said Ernie. "Come on, Junior. Let's go get Chinese for lunch."

"Swell, Mr. Ernie!" He looked back at me. "Hope you like chop suey, Miss Mercy! And Chinese spareribs!"

"Love them," I said, feeling a bit downhearted. On the other hand, Ernie was correct in that I was helping out in the case. And I could write down information gathered by Ernie and Junior from Junior's friend Fong and ask Lily about it. Maybe she knew something about her father's debt and why it was so important for Charley to pay it. With her entire self as payment.

Nuts.

At about noon, Lulu came upstairs and walked into my office. She said, "Ernie said he and Junior are going to the Chinese place and will bring back lunch for us. He wouldn't let you go with them, huh?"

"Right," I said. "Mr. Chan might have been murdered because of that scene we participated in on Saturday, and Ernie doesn't want us anywhere near Chinatown or anyone who knows anything about the murder. Oh, but Lulu, let me tell you what Junior said!" I patted the arm of the chair next to my desk.

"Y'mean about the Chan guy claiming Charley's father owed him money?"

Well, darn. "Junior told you about the debt thing?"

"Yeah. He said the old man would forgive the debt if he could marry Charley's sister."

"That's positively medieval! Using a human being as a pawn to settle a debt. Have you ever heard of such a thing?"

"Nope. I never have. It is kind of icky. I'd hate to have to marry an old guy because my father owed him money."

"And why would the old man be murdered because Lily tried to run away from Charley because she didn't want to marry the old man? Could there be more people involved than just the dead man?"

"Who knows? It's Chinatown," said Lulu as if that explained everything. Maybe it did.

"I suppose so. Ernie said he's only nominally a friend—"

"What's that mean? Nomina— Whatever. What's that mean?"

"He meant he can never be bosom buddies with Charley because the races don't mix. If they were both Chinese, they could be close pals. Same thing if they were both white."

"Oh, yeah. That makes sense."

"It doesn't make any sense to me," I said, getting riled. "Why do people dislike each other because of the color of their skin? That's just silly, Lulu!"

"Well," said Lulu judiciously. "I think there's more to it than that. I mean, we don't have ceremonies and big parades with dragons and firecrackers and stuff like that. The Chinese do. And we don't eat dumplings for breakfast or noodles for dessert, either."

"I guess." I put my elbows on my desk and lowered my chin to my hands. "What do we white people do that other races don't do? I guess donuts for breakfast are kind of like dumplings. What else?"

With a shrug, Lulu said, "Beats me. Eat with knives and forks? Oh, wait a minute. Doesn't Pasadena put on a big parade on the first of the year with flowers and stuff? Pasadena's full of white people, isn't it? Well, except for servants and maids and cooks and people like that."

Servants and maids and cooks and people like that. Right. "I don't know why people of color have to be servants. Why can't they be just like us?"

"Because, from everything I've heard, we'll kill them if they tried," said Lulu, being so cynical, she made me want to cry. "You heard about that colored section of Tulsa in my home state of Oklahoma, didn't you? There was a really prosperous Negro community there, and the white people in Tulsa actually burned it out and bombed it. Couldn't stand for Negros to have brains and money, I guess. Made me sick when I heard about it."

"It makes me sick, too."

"But the Bucks are Negros, and they're your servants. And Lily is playing the part of a maid. Right?"

"Right," I said dismally.

"But I'll bet Lily can be our friend, Mercy. Buck up…So to speak." She giggled.

"I hope so," I said, still feeling dismal.

Lulu and I sat in my room, she finding fault with her nails and filing the occasional rough edge and I deploring humanity, for I don't know how long before Ernie and Junior returned bearing a big cardboard box. From the box came enticing smells that reminded me of Chinatown.

"All right, girls, we come bearing food," said Ernie, sounding pleased with himself.

"Yeah," said Junior. "We got lots of stuff."

"Did you learn anything from your friend Fong?" I asked, hoping.

"We'll tell you all about it during lunch," said Ernie. "Clean off your desk, Mercy. Please." He probably added the "please" because I'm a prig. Sometimes I feel totally hopeless.

However, in spite of my personality faults, Ernie plopped the cardboard box on a chair in front of my desk as I quickly cleaned everything off the top of it. The blotter I slid into my middle drawer, and I stuffed everything else into the bottom right file drawer, which had plenty of room because we had so few files. That's because we had so few clients.

As soon as everything except the telephone was gone from the desk, Ernie and Junior began placing white paper containers on the desk. It looked to me as if they were full of food.

"My goodness, what clever containers!" I said.

"You never get Chinese takeout?" Ernie asked. "They always use these white pails. Don't know what they're made of. Looks like paper, and they have these little wire holders." He demonstrated by hauling out a deep container from the box. I noticed the white boxes were stamped with Chinese characters, and I wondered what they meant.

"I never get Chinese anything unless I go to Chinatown. What do you call it? Take out?"

"Sure. I live right near Chinatown, so I eat a lot of Chinese food," said Ernie, hauling out more white boxes.

They were cunning things, and I admired the ingenuity of whoever invented them, but I foresaw a problem. "Um…Do you have any plates, or do we just all eat out of the boxes?" The notion sounded unsanitary to me, but I'd already behaved like a prig once, so I decided not to say so. However, if Junior stuck a fork— Oh. I foresaw another potential problem. "Um…Did they provide forks or anything?"

Ernie reached into the cardboard box again and withdrew a bundle of chopsticks tied with a string. "We have these."

"Oh. That's fine by me. I'm pretty good with chopsticks thanks to you," I said, brightening minimally. "But…" I didn't ask about plates again. If worse came to worst, I could use the water glass in my drawer. The resulting food therein might be kind of a lumpy mess, but it would probably taste pretty good even if everything was mixed up.

"Stop worrying, Mercy," said Ernie. "Everything's jake."

"I wasn't worrying," I lied.

"Yes, you were."

I decided not to lie again. But boy, those boxes were taking up a lot of space on my desk. "How much food did you get?" I asked, my voice a trifle weak.

"Enough for four lunches and two dinners," said Ernie.

"Yeah," said Junior happily. "Mr. Ernie said I can take some leftovers home for my dinner."

"How nice," I said.

"And here!" Ernie said, triumphantly removing four forks from the cardboard box. "Fong didn't believe me when I said we could use the chopsticks, so he lent us these."

"Thank God," muttered Lulu. "I can't use chopsticks. Did they send any plates?"

I was *so* glad it was Lulu who asked about plates! Nobody'd think *she* was a prig for doing so. The word "prig" and Lulu would never be used together in the same sentence in a million years, especially if you saw the outfit she wore that day, which was bright red with a green bow. "For Christmas," according to her.

"Yup. They even sent plates," said Ernie. Again, he reached into the cardboard box, this time hauling out four more little white boxes, holding them by their metal handles.

"Those are boxes," said Lulu. "We could use a few plates."

"Ah, but you don't understand the miracle of these containers," said Ernie in what was probably supposed to be a mysterious voice.

But darned if he didn't perform an arcane act right in front of our very eyes. Pulling the metal wire out of the holes in a container, he unfolded it until it flattened out into a by-golly plate!

"Wow," I said. "Those Chinese people are so inventive."

"An American guy invented these," said Ernie, popping my happy assumption like a soap bubble. "But the Chinese grabbed onto them and have used them ever since."

"Well, I'm glad somebody invented them," said Lulu, taking the "plate" Ernie handed her. I did likewise with my flattened box, and we all dug into the foodstuffs in the various containers. Boy, was it good!

TEN

As we ate, Ernie gave us a synopsis of what he'd learned from Junior's friend Fong. And *there* was a friendship between a white boy and a Chinese boy, so I still maintain it's possible for races to get along with each other if they want to.

After consuming several bites of different Chinese delicacies, including a sparerib, Ernie swallowed, wiped his fingers on a napkin provided by the restaurant—I assumed Junior would take the napkins back to the restaurant along with the dirty forks—and said, "Very well, so we know the murdered man, Chan Sien Lo, came from San Francisco."

"I didn't know we knew that," I said. I neglected to swallow my noodles first, moreover, thereby making a disgusting pig of myself.

"Yeah, we knew that," said Ernie, spearing a fried shrimp and dunking it into the amazing sauce provided for same. "He arrived about a month and a half ago, and it's become evident that he's caused trouble for more people than just Charley."

"How so?" I asked.

After devouring his shrimp, Ernie continued. "Chan's game, if it *is* a game, is to approach people in Chinatown and show them papers claiming to be debts owed by parents or other dead relations."

"Why would that be a problem? Why would a kid be responsible for his or her parents' debts? Especially if they must be pretty old debts, if the guy had to come from San Francisco to collect on them and nobody knew about them until he showed up," said Lulu, ever practical even if she didn't look it.

"The Chinese as a culture," said Ernie in a lecturing tone, "put a good deal of emphasis on family honor. 'Saving face' is a term they use. Well, they say it in Chinese, but it means the same thing."

"'Saving face'? I'm not sure what that means," I told him.

"It means not embarrassing yourself or your extended family. Say you lived in Scotland, and you were a Macdonald and Lulu was a Campbell. You'd hate each other just because of that, and you'd never allow one of your kids to marry one of Lulu's kids."

I only had to ponder this statement for about three seconds. "That's not the same thing at all, Ernie. That's a feud. Like the Hatfields and McCoys. This Chan-Wu thing isn't a feud."

Ernie lifted his head, looked at the ceiling, and chewed for a second as he pondered my comment. Then he swallowed and said, "Yeah. You're right. Okay, so let's say it would be a disgrace to the Wu family if it became known Charley's father owed Chan a debt and the debt was never paid."

"Has Chan ever lived in Los Angeles?" I asked. "For that matter, did Charley's father ever live in San Francisco?"

"Don't know. I'll have to ask Charley when I visit him in jail."

"And the Chan guy had better have provided legitimate papers detailing this so-called debt," Lulu said. "Otherwise, the guy's all wet and lying."

"That's right," I agreed. "Depending on the type of debt, you might be able to check with a bank or a government agency or something for legal documentation."

"Good points, girls," said Ernie.

"Huh?" said Junior.

Ernie enlightened him. "Depending on the type of debt, there might be documentation about it at, say, the Los Angeles County

Department of Records. If it's a gambling debt or something like that, there won't be."

"If it's a gambling debt, how the heck can Chan claim anything at all about Charley's father owing him money?" I asked indignantly. "Not only is gambling illegal, there can't be any documentation for something like that!"

"You don't know how the Chinese keep tabs on these things," said a grim Ernie. "They keep their own documentation."

"Do they?" I asked skeptically.

"Kind of. Depending on the debt, its origin, its date or whatever, and if this Chan guy was part of a bigger gang, he might have threatened Charley's businesses. You know, like the protection rackets the Italian, Irish and Jewish gangs have going in New York and Chicago. And the Chinese like to gamble. Hell, walk anywhere in Chinatown and you can hear the mah-jongg tiles clicking away."

"Yes, I recall hearing mah-jongg tiles clicking when we went to lunch."

"But Los Angeles's Chinatown isn't like San Francisco's Chinatown or New York's Chinatown. Our Chinatown has a strong self-regulating system, and it pretty much keeps interfering people from other cities or states out of its affairs."

"How does it do that?" I asked.

"They pay the L.A.P.D. for protection, and the L.A.P.D. doesn't allow others to interfere with their own protection racket," said Ernie in a casual voice.

"I think it's terrible that citizens have to bribe the police to do the jobs city taxpayers already pay for," I said with a sniff.

"Come on, Mercy," said Ernie in a pitying voice. "You know what the L.A.P.D. is like. I quit the force because I couldn't stand the corruption. It hasn't changed in the four years since I left. It's about as corrupt a force as you can find in the entire country." He added judicially, "Maybe New York is worse. Chicago. Detroit. I dunno."

I set my chopsticks down on my paper plate and stared at Ernie for a few seconds. "Yes," I said, "I guess I did know that. I tend to forget unpleasant facts when they rear their ugly heads."

"Like your mother," said Lulu, grinning at me whilst holding a forkful of fried rice with vegetables mixed into it.

With a deep and heartfelt sigh, I said, "Yes. Like my mother."

"But wait a minute," said Junior, who'd been stuffing food into his mouth as if he hadn't eaten for several days. Actually, that might have been the case. The kid was only about twelve and if he had a family, I didn't know where it was. Guess he wanted to get in on the action, because he swallowed and said, "Fong heard his father and grandfather talking, and he heard the names of a couple of other families who were approached by the Chan character. I think Chan had another goon working with him."

"The names might be helpful," I said, pleased with Junior's pal Fong.

"They might be helpful if we can get any of the other families—or the Fong family—to talk to me."

"Well, maybe they'll talk to you, because you sometimes play baseball with them." I swallowed my shrimp before speaking that time.

"Possibly. Still and all, I'm white and don't really fit in except when it comes to baseball."

"Well, how discouraging," I said.

"No. Not as helpful as it might be, is it?"

"No."

Squinting into a white carton containing chicken with almonds, Ernie said, "But I guess I can try. I might have a chat with your maid, too. She seems to be pretty Americanized. She might not have the same prejudices as her elders." He grinned.

"That's a good idea," I said, although I wasn't sure I wanted Ernie to be cozy with Lily for any length of time. Then something occurred to me. "I can take notes."

"Great idea. If Charley or your maid—"

"What maid?" interrupted Junior.

Lulu, Ernie and I swapped glances. Then Ernie said, "Mercy just hired a Chinese maid. She might know what's going on in Chinatown. Mercy lives on Bunker Hill and not in Chinatown.

Therefore, Mercy's maid's family won't find out about it if she can be persuaded to spill what she knows."

"If she knows anything," I added.

"Right," said Ernie. "If she knows anything."

"Oh," said Junior. He gazed at me in something resembling awe. "Do you really live on Bunker Hill, Miss Mercy?"

"Yes, I do," I said.

"Wow. I didn't know you were an egg, Miss Mercy."

An egg? I looked to Lulu for an explanation.

"She's not an egg," Lulu said. "She's got money, but she takes in lodgers. She's not a rich snob. She's just rich."

I wasn't sure that was much of an endorsement, but I let it go.

"Yeah," said Ernie. "Mercy's all right. She's not a Mrs. Grundy."

"That's for sure," Lulu said, wiping her vividly red lips with a napkin and leaving what looked like a crime scene behind on the napkin. "Mercy's a sweetie, and she likes helping people."

Junior didn't bother to swallow before he said, "Oh. Well, that's jake, I guess." He eyed me speculatively as he chewed. "Didn't know you had money, Miss Mercy."

"I've been fortunate," I said in a repressive voice. "And let's not talk about it any longer. It has no relevance to the Chan situation."

"True," said Ernie. "But Junior, you might see if Fong knows the names of any of the other families who have been approached by Chan. And if he knows the names of any of Chan's goons, if he had any."

"Please don't ask him to snoop," I told Junior. "We don't want those horrid men to do something awful to Fong."

Opening his eyes wide and staring at me with an open mouth full of Chinese food—it didn't make for an enticing sight—Junior said, "Golly. You're right."

"Darned right she's right," said Ernie, sounding stern for the second time in one day. "I don't know how many people worked with Chan, but they might be killers. I personally don't much care if they knock off people like Chan, but I sure don't want them to go after the local kids. And we don't know why Chan was killed. If he had goons, maybe they killed him and plan to take over his extortion racket."

"Do you think they had goons?" asked Junior after he'd—thank god—swallowed.

"I don't have any idea," said Ernie. "At the moment, we know nothing except that Chan is dead and Charley's been arrested for killing him. For all I know, Chan had buddies who plan to set up a protection racket and blow up businesses if the owners don't pay."

"Golly," said Lulu. "For real?"

Shooting her a "Just go along with what I say" look, Ernie said, "Yes. Don't you read the newspapers? Happens all the time in Chicago and New York. Rum-running gangsters blow up restaurants and stores all the time. And, of course, they shoot each other wholesale."

"I only read movie magazines," said Lulu in a small voice. "Think I'll keep it that way."

"I don't blame you," I told Lulu. "The real world is full of evil people and woe."

"Woe?" Ernie grinned at me.

"I'd call it woe if my family was blown up as it was dining in a restaurant," I said. Then I reconsidered my words. "Well, I'd consider it woe if Chloe and Harvey were blown up, anyway."

Everybody laughed. I hadn't meant my comment to be funny. Ah well.

After they all stopped laughing, we ate in silence for another minute or two. Don't know about anyone else, but I was getting full. The food was *good*. What's more, it didn't look as if the four of us had made much of a dent in those white pails. Ernie and Junior would probably have dinners for a couple of evenings if either of them had an ice box in his home. If Junior had a home. Oh, he must, mustn't he? I hated to think about all the poor children in the world. At least Junior earned money, even if he had to skip getting an education to do it. My thoughts were cut short when someone spoke. Good thing. I'd begun to wallow again.

"Hmm. Wonder if Charley kept any of the papers Chan

showed him," mused Ernie, wiping his own mouth. As he didn't use bright red lipstick, his napkin only looked dirty when he finished.

"Are you going to visit him in jail?" I asked.

"Yes. Right after I visit your maid's uncle's hotel."

"Thank you, Ernie," I said. "Do you think Charley can get out on bail?"

"They don't generally post bail for suspected murderers, but I'll find out. They're holding Charley on the flimsiest of flimsy evidence."

By then, we were all slowing down in the dining department. I looked at my paper plate, contemplated placing one more sparerib on it, and decided not to. Let Ernie and Junior feast on the leftovers. Lulu and I would have a lovely dinner prepared for us by Mrs. Buck.

"I don't think I can eat any more. It was really good," I said.

"Me, either," said Lulu. "I'm stuffed. And it was really good. What's the name of that place anyway?"

"The Canton Palace," said Ernie.

"Oh. Well, I guess they think highly of themselves, too," I said. "Can't say as I blame them."

"Yes. Their food's tasty. Glad it's close to work. But I'm full, too," said Ernie. "What about you, Junior?"

Junior scooped one more lavish portion of lo mein noodles onto his paper plate and said, "Right after I finish this."

We all had a laugh. Junior was a skinny kid, but he could sure pack it away. I guess growing boys need their nourishment.

When he finally finished off his last gigantic helping of noodles, Lulu and I began packing everything away again. We tossed the paper boxes we'd used as plates in the wastepaper basket and then began tucking the leftovers away. All of the little paper pails folded at the top so the food wouldn't fall out, and we just lifted them by their metal handles and packed them back into the cardboard carton.

"Want me to wrap the forks in the napkins for you to take back to the Canton Palace, Junior?" I asked politely.

"Aw, nertz, I guess so."

"Nertz nothing," Ernie told him in yet another stern voice. "You told Fong you'd return the utensils, and you'll return the utensils. And the dirty napkins." Squinting at a sulking Junior, he added, "What's more, you'll do it now."

"Aw, do I gotta?" Junior.

"Yes. You gotta." Ernie.

"Do they have paper menus to give away to customers?" asked Lulu.

I stared at her, puzzled, wondering what she was talking about.

"Yeah," said Junior.

"Come back with a paper menu, and I'll give you a nickel," said Lulu.

Brightening, Junior said, "Thanks, Miss Lulu! I'll do it."

"You'd do it anyway," said Ernie.

"Yeah, I would. But I like to make money," said Junior. He picked up the bundle of napkin-wrapped forks and bounced out of the office. I heard him whistling "Yes, Sir, That's My Baby," as soon as he hit the hallway.

"Energetic kid," said Lulu. Neither Ernie nor I contradicted her.

"What do you want to do with the cardboard carton?" I asked Ernie.

"Keep it here. I'll put it on the desk in my office. Just give it to Junior at the end of the day if I haven't come back yet."

"You aren't going to keep any for yourself?" I asked, surprised.

"Naw. The kid needs it more than I do. Besides," he said, smirking at me, "I have to bring Lily's uniforms to your house and have a chat with her about Charley, so I figured you'd invite me to dinner at your place."

Lulu and I both burst out laughing.

"Consider yourself invited," I said.

ELEVEN

The rest of the day was nominally boring. Or normally boring, I guess. Perhaps because it was the Christmas season and people had begun behaving themselves better than usual, business had been slow at Ernest Templeton, P.I.'s, office for a week or so. I answered the telephone twice and made one appointment for the following day, but that was it.

Ernie left the office right after Lulu and I had packed away all the uneaten food and he'd carried the carton into his office and set it on his desk. I figured he'd pick up Lily's uniforms and then visit Charley Wu in jail. I didn't envy him. Visiting people in jail sounds so sordid.

Or is that Boston talking?

No. Visiting people in jail is sordid. Being in jail had to be considerably worse, and I hoped bail would be set for Charley Wu. Ernie would probably let me know that evening.

At any rate, I hauled out the mystery novel I was writing and stuck a piece of paper in the typewriter. I'd already murdered an unpleasant person—I didn't like killing off good guys—but I didn't know who did it yet. Do all authors have these problems? I can't imagine Agatha Christie not knowing beforehand what she aims to write and who did what when and where, but I haven't reached that stage yet. And that's putting it mildly.

I was sitting at the typewriter, glumly looking at a page with two typewritten lines on it, brain empty and fingers poised over the keys with nothing to do, when the front office door opened. Looking up, I beheld Junior waving a paper in his hand.

"Good afternoon, Junior," I said politely.

"Hey, Miss Mercy," he said back. "I picked up two paper menus in case you wanted one, too." He trotted to my desk and placed the sheet of paper thereon. By golly, it was a printed menu of Chinese delights from the Canton Palace.

"Thank you, Junior," I said, picking up the paper and gazing at it in wonder. Modern technology has sure come a long way, hasn't it? The Canton Palace offered about thirty-thousand different items on their menu. I wondered how big the place was. Probably not very, to judge by other businesses in this neighborhood. Maybe Chinese cooks were merely efficient and didn't need a whole lot of space in which to work.

"You're welcome," he said, and continued standing in front of my desk.

"Did you need something, Junior?" I asked.

"Naw."

"Are you leaving for the day? Ernie said you may take the box of Chinese food home because he won't be eating at his place tonight."

"Gee, really? That's swell!"

"So be sure to pick up that cardboard box—it's on the desk in Ernie's office—before five o'clock, because that's when I leave work."

"Will do. Thanks, Miss Mercy."

"Do you have people to share it with?" I asked. "There's still a whole lot of food left."

"Oh, sure. I'll take it home. My ma will be glad she don't have to cook."

His mention of a mother made me feel better. I'd entertained visions of Junior sleeping in doorways and so forth.

Still he stood. I furrowed my brow, wondering what the kid

wanted. Then it was I remembered Lulu's nickel. With a sigh, I opened my desk's bottom right drawer in which resided my hand-bag. I reached into it, fished around for my coin purse, and found several pennies and a dime. Oh, what the heck, I gave the kid the dime.

"Gee, thanks, Miss Mercy!" said Junior, whirling around and heading for the door.

Before he reached it, I said, "Did Fong tell you anything more about the criminal activity going on in Chinatown?"

Turning at the door to look at me, Junior said, "Naw. He was busy so we didn't get to talk much. He washes dishes after the lunch crowd."

"His hands must get chapped," I said, thinking about poor Fong with his hands in dishwater for hours at a time.

"Naw. His grandma rubs lanolin on his hands before bed."

"Oh." Quite effective and enterprising. Wonder how he managed to keep the grease off the sheets on his bed. I didn't ask.

When it was time to leave in the evening, Ernie hadn't returned to the office, Junior had hauled off the cardboard carton stuffed with paper pails filled with Chinese food, and I'd managed to type two more sentences of my novel. I still didn't know who murdered the fellow. Not, in fact, unlike the Los Angeles Police Department regarding Mr. Chan Sien Lo. Unlike them, however, I wasn't going to arrest an innocent person for doing the deed. Although…

Hmm. That might be a good plot point. I'd have to think it over.

After picking up my handbag from my desk drawer, I went to the coat tree beside the front door, retrieved my nice warm coat and cloche hat, and donned them. Then I left the office, locked the door, and headed for the staircase. I think I've mentioned that I don't care to take the elevator. At least not when I'm alone.

When I arrived at the lobby, I saw Caroline had already joined Lulu at the reception desk. Both women waved at me. It looked as though they'd been palavering with Junior, who'd set the cardboard box full of Chinese food on the reception desk.

"Good evening, Caroline. Did you have a good day at work?" I don't know why I asked that. She worked in the hosiery department at the Broadway Department Store. How good a day *could* she have? Not that I'm maligning the Broadway, but selling hosiery doesn't sound awfully thrilling to me.

"It was all right. Same as usual," said Caroline. "My job isn't terribly exciting at the best of times."

See? Sometimes I'm right about things.

Lulu glanced at the front of the building and said, "Here's Sue."

We all turned to see Sue Krekeler, her white uniform and cap covered by her own warm coat and hat, pushing open the glass door of the Figueroa Building.

"Evening, Sue," I said. "Ready to go home?"

"I sure am," she said as she shut the door. "We had a really busy day today and my dogs are barking." I knew she meant her feet hurt and felt proud of myself. Very well, so sometimes little things make a person happy.

Checking her footwear, I was pleased to note she wore sensible shoes. If a woman had to be on her feet a lot, she ought to be prudent and not torture herself with pointy toes and high heels. Lulu would probably disagree with me, but that's only because she could sit behind the reception desk at the Figueroa Building and didn't have to be a receptionist in a busy dentist's office and see people from the reception area into the dentist's torture chamber all day long.

As she approached the desk, Sue said, "What's going on here? Looks like a meeting of business associates or something." She grinned at us, and most of us grinned back. Not sure about Junior.

"Mercy's boss is trying to find a murderer," Lulu said in a thrilling voice.

"A *murderer?*" said Sue. "Good heavens, I thought that's what the police were for. Finding criminals and so forth."

"Not if the murderee is Chinese or a person of another color. Other than white, I mean," I said, indignant again. Doesn't take much for me to become indignant.

"Oh," said Sue. "I didn't know that."

"Yeah," said Lulu. "Why, just a couple of months ago…" She stopped speaking, and I was glad. I didn't want Lulu to tell anyone who didn't already know that the Bucks' son had been arrested for a murder he didn't commit. Anyone who wasn't as involved in the case as Lulu and I had been might make false assumptions. Well, Caroline had been a tenant then, too, and had even participated in some of the action, but still….

"Just a couple of months ago what?" asked Sue.

I decided to butt in and save the day. "A friend's son was arrested for a murder he didn't commit, and the police only arrested him because he was a colored fellow. The murdered man's housekeeper saw another colored fellow walking on the street on the day of the murder, and she just assumed it was Calvin, but it wasn't."

Was that saving the day? Not sure.

"Yeah. That housekeeper woman was really dumb," said Lulu.

"How terrible," said Sue. "I didn't know you had colored friends, Mercy and Lulu. That's quite…intrepid of you."

"Why's it intrepid?" I asked, indignant again. "Friends are friends."

"Well, I know, but you don't often see the mixing of races," said Sue as if she found nothing to quarrel with about in the status quo.

I was about to enlighten her when Lulu piped up, which was probably for the best. "But I fingered the real killer because I identified the car he drove by the hood ornament." She looked proud of herself, as well she might.

"And Caroline saved the day when the killer was holding us all at gunpoint," I said, nodding to Caroline, who blushed.

"Golly, really?" said Junior, avidly interested. "That's the berries, Miss Caroline!"

"I had no idea," said Sue, looking somewhat shocked.

"I didn't really do much to save us," said Caroline, forever modest.

"Well, let's get going," said Lulu. "I ate so much lunch, I hope I can do justice to Mrs. Buck's dinner."

"Me, too," I said, because it was true.

"Guess I'll head out, too," said Junior, hefting the cardboard box in both hands.

A little worried about his load, I said, "Where do you live, Junior? Do you need help carrying that home?"

"Naw. I live just a block and a half away, and it's not very heavy. It'll sure be nice to feed the family tonight." He grinned a wide grin, scattering his rainbow of freckles all the way to his ears.

Curious—or perhaps merely nosy—I asked, "How many people are in your family, Junior?"

"My ma, my two sisters, and me. My dad died a couple of years ago, so Ma has to work, and so does my older sister. My younger sister still goes to school."

"I see. You have quite a burden to bear, young man," I said, feeling sorry for the kid.

"It really ain't heavy, Miss Mercy," Junior assured me, lifting the carton and misunderstanding my statement. It was probably just as well. Most people—and I believe this is particularly true of young men—don't want people feeling sorry for them.

"Have a good evening with your family," I said to him as he toted the box to the front of the building, turned around, and used his skinny backside to shove the door open.

"Imagine having to support a family when you're only...How old is Junior?" I asked Lulu.

She shrugged. "I dunno. About thirteen, I think. And kids supporting families has been going on forever, Mercy. There aren't any guarantees in this life. If a father dies or abandons his family, lots of kids have to work."

"You're right, of course," I said, wishing she wasn't.

"We're all lucky to have good families," said Caroline, who was quite prim and proper.

Mind you, those are good qualities. I'd met my fair share of "flappers" and other loose women who had moved to Los Angeles to get into the flickers. Heck, one of my former tenants had turned out to be a murderess. I didn't like to think about her, mainly because I had been at fault for allowing her into my house.

Lulu, too, had bundled her red-and-green self up in her warm coat and hat, so the four of us left the building and walked to Angels

Flight. We chatted about this and that as we walked. When we boarded the car, Sue primarily mentioned how glad she was to get off her feet and sit for a minute in the train car. A minute was all it took to get from one end of Angels Flight to the other. After the train stopped, of course, she had to walk the two blocks to my house, but then she could go to her room, take off her shoes, and lounge around in carpet slippers for the rest of the evening if she wanted to.

Lulu, Sue, Caroline, and I had barely walked through my front door and been greeted by a deliriously happy Buttercup when I heard the rattle of Ernie's decrepit Studebaker pull into the driveway. I was about to go outside and welcome him when I was distracted.

"May I take your hats and coats, ladies?"

And darned if Lily didn't show up on the heels of Buttercup, looking as much like a maid as she could without a maid's uniform on.

"Thanks, Lily," said Lulu, shrugging out of her coat and revealing her bright red dress and green bow.

"That's all right, Lily," said Sue. "I'm going to my room. I'll take my coat off there. *And* my shoes."

"You don't need to take our hats and coats, Lily," I told her. "We're able-bodied young women." I smiled gratefully at her, though.

"I know," she said, "but I was helping Mrs. Buck in the kitchen and when she heard you guys at the door, she suggested I help relieve you of your outer garments."

"She did, did she?" I said, hoping Mrs. Buck wasn't being hard on Lily. Or that Lily wasn't annoying Mrs. Buck. "But Ernie just showed up, so why don't you and I go out and greet him?" Then I remembered Ernie's edict about not allowing Lily out of the house. "Well, you wait here, and *I'll* greet him."

"Okay," said a cheerful-sounding Lily.

So I slipped my coat on again, opened the door, and stepped onto the front porch as Ernie brought his machine to a shuddering stop in my driveway next to the paved path to the front porch. I watched as he twisted in the driver's seat to reach into the backseat and withdrew a paper parcel. Maids' uniforms? We'd see.

"Good evening, Ernie," I called.

"C'n I use your telephone?" he said by way of a reply. "And can you help me with this stuff?"

With a sigh, I walked down the porch steps and to Ernie, where he seemed to be struggling with two paper parcels. He shoved one at me. "Here. You take the shoes. I've got the dresses, aprons and caps in this sack. Damn, how many clothes do maids have to wear, anyway?"

"Lily doesn't have to wear any clothes at all to be a maid in my house," I told him before thinking through my sentence properly.

Ernie burst out laughing.

Grumpy, I said, "You know what I meant. She doesn't have to wear a uniform if she works for me. The uniforms you brought are merely costuming in case the police pry."

"Yeah, yeah, yeah," said Ernie. "C'n I use your telephone? I want to call Charley's uncle Hop."

"Yes, you may use my telephone, Mr. Templeton. As you're doing that, I'll tell Mrs. Buck we have an extra person for dinner."

"Crumb, you haven't told her yet?" Ernie sounded worried.

"I just got home from work myself," I snapped.

"Well, hell, I figured you'd call from the office."

That probably would have been a good idea. I didn't say so. "No, I didn't call from the office."

"Well, I hope there's enough food. Junior took all the Chinese grub home with him, didn't he?"

"Right."

"I hope Mrs. Buck doesn't mind."

"She probably won't," I said. Ungraciously, I fear. But really. Ernie could be so exasperating.

When I opened the front door a second time that evening, it was to find all of my tenants—including Sue, who hadn't taken off her shoes yet—and Lily all gathered in the beautifully tiled entryway. Ernie took a startled step backwards. I grabbed his arm.

"No need to be scared, Ernie. You know everyone."

"I know," he said, snarling slightly. "I didn't expect them all to gang up on me the second I walked into the house."

"Good grief," I muttered. To the gathered throng, I said, "Why don't you ladies go on up to your rooms and get comfortable? Sue, take off your shoes and put on some slippers."

"Good idea," said Sue with a sigh as she limped through the archway to the living room. Caroline and Lulu left, too.

As soon as the three of us were alone in the entryway, I said, "Lily, Ernie brought some things for you."

"Oh, you went to my uncle Mo's hotel?" she asked, sounding excited.

"Yes. I picked up the uniforms he said were yours along with some shoes and some little white caps." Frowning slightly, Ernie added, "I don't know if Mercy'll make you wear the caps. They look kinda stupid to me."

"You needn't wear a cap, Lily. In fact, the uniforms are only a disguise if anyone pries around the house. They'll just think you're a maid I've hired. Mrs. Buck doesn't wear a uniform, and if you were a real maid and not in hiding, you wouldn't have to either."

That didn't make any sense.

"Right," said Lily with a shrug. "I don't mind wearing the entire uniform. I do it when I work at Uncle Mo's place. Why not here?"

"Why not indeed," said Ernie. "Here. Take these, will you?"

He gave me the other paper parcel, the one containing the dresses and aprons. Turning to Lily, I said, "I'll help you get this stuff upstairs, Lily. You may start wearing them tomorrow. I can't see why you need to put on a uniform for this one evening."

"Okay," she said, still cheerful.

"Thought you were going to ask Mrs. Buck if I can stay for dinner," Ernie said at my back as I turned to walk off with Lily. He sounded a little whiny.

"I shall, as soon as I assist Lily," I told him.

"Huh," he said.

Lily and I giggled as we carted her packages up the stairs.

TWELVE

Mrs. Buck didn't mind at all that Ernie had invited himself to dinner.

"Oh, laws, Miss Mercy. You know I always cook enough for an army. Tonight I've got a pot roast in the oven along with onions, potatoes, turnips and carrots; and there's two different desserts. The Grand Central Market had some good-looking pears and persimmons, so I made a pear pie and a persimmon pudding. If you like the persimmon pudding, I'll make one for Christmas. Kind of like Mrs. Cratchit's plum pudding only without the nasty candied orange peels. Can't say as I like candied peels much."

"I don't either," I told her with a shudder. My mother always had her cook prepare an enormous plum pudding stuffed with raisins, currants, chopped candied citrus peelings and dates. What's worse was that she always made us eat a helping. I could pretty much handle everything except the candied fruit peelings. Ew.

"Then that's fine. Is Lily around? Maybe she can set the table. She was in here before you and the other gals came home, but I don't really need a cook's helper. I need a table-setter and a furniture-duster more than a cook's helper."

"Absolutely. I'll have her set the table, and I can't wait to try your persimmon pudding. I've never had persimmon pudding before. Actually, I haven't eaten persimmons very often."

"I like 'em as long as they're really ripe. If you try to eat an unripe persimmon, it'll be as bitter as gall."

Whatever gall was. I'd heard the expression before, but I still didn't know what gall was. I should look it up. "Interesting. I hope one day you'll teach me to cook, Mrs. Buck."

"Any old time, Miss Mercy," said Mrs. Buck with a laugh. I wasn't sure about her laugh. Maybe she didn't think I meant my words, but I did. Cooking was what the female members of the working world had to do, and I felt it my duty to learn.

When I returned to the living room, Ernie stood in the middle of the room petting Buttercup and looking peeved. Lily was just coming down the staircase, so I spoke to her first.

"Lily, will you please set the table? There will be five at dinner tonight, because Ernie's joining us."

"Sure will," said the eager Lily, veering toward the dining room as soon as she got to the bottom of the staircase.

Ernie stopped petting Buttercup and stood abruptly, frowning at me.

"What's ailing you?" I asked my irritated employer.

"I need to use your telephone."

"I already told you that you could. Why aren't you using it?" I asked, becoming slightly irritated myself.

"Where's the telephone?"

Taking a cue from my boss, who is always rolling his eyes at me, I rolled mine at him for a change. "You know very well it's in my office. Right there." Defying my mother's teachings, I pointed to the room in question.

"Well, I wasn't sure," whined Ernie. "All the doors are closed."

"Oh, brother."

He didn't snipe back at me, but walked to the office door, opened it, and entered the room, which was quite tidy, thank you very much. As he sat in my chair, he picked the receiver up from the cradle, then used the dialing pad to dial a number, perhaps

Charley's Uncle Hop. Who owned Hop Luey's! I thought that was special.

I didn't snoop on Ernie's call, figuring once a day is enough for that sort of thing. Rather, I walked upstairs with a happy Buttercup and went to my room. There I removed my sensible work ensemble and donned a flowing silk robe with embroidered flowers I'd bought in Chinatown a few weeks earlier. The background color was forget-me-not blue, and the flowers were all different colors. I loved it, and it was the most comfortable garment I'd ever owned. I'd worn it before around the house, but never in front of a gentleman. As Ernie was about as far from being a gentleman as a fellow could get, I figured nobody would mind if I wore it that evening.

The fact that the robe complemented my eyes and looked gorgeous on me—according to Lulu—had nothing to do with my choice.

Ernie was pacing back and forth at the foot of the stairs when I descended them. He glanced up and blinked at me several times. "You look different," he said.

He would.

"Is that supposed to be a compliment?"

Tilting his head and observing me—which made my face heat up, darn it—he thought for a moment and said, "Yeah. You look great in that blue thing."

"Thank you, Ernie," I said, giving up on him. Not that I had ulterior motives, mind you, no matter what my sister and Lulu think. "Why did you have to call Charley's Uncle Hop?"

"Because the judge set bail for Charley, and Charley said Hop was the fellow to go to for the money."

"I'm so glad Charley can get out on bail!"

"Yes. I have a feeling the judge didn't think much of the evidence collected by the police department, because judges don't often set bail when it comes to suspected murderers." He grinned. "Phil was irked. But they honestly don't have *any* evidence to suggest Charley killed the guy. People heard them arguing, but you can't shoot a man with your mouth any more than you can with a base-ball bat."

"Good," I said, reaching the bottom of the stairs and heading for a nearby sofa, where I sat and pooled my silk robe round me. I patted the sofa and Buttercup joined me. Delicious aromas filled the air and even after our enormous Chinese lunch, my tummy began to tell me it wanted a refill.

The rest of the tenants of Mercy's Manor slowly gathered in the living room and sat on various chairs and sofas. I was pleased to see Sue had taken my advice and was wearing a pair of what looked like comfy slippers. They all listened as Ernie and I conversed, which was perfectly all right by me and a normal human reaction to an interesting tale.

I stroked Buttercup's fluffy fur as I asked, "How much did the judge ask for Charley's bail?"

"A thousand smackers."

Gasps went up around the room. I swallowed my own gasp, but holy Moses, that was a lot of money!

"How generous of him," sniped Lulu.

"Yeah," said Ernie sarcastically. "The judge was a very generous guy."

"Oh," I said, interested, "it's the judge who says if there will be bail and sets the amount? Did that sentence make sense?"

"Not much," said Ernie, "But yes. The police arrest the bozo, the family finds a bail bondsman, the D.A. gets involved along with the public defender, and the judge decides if there will be bail and, if so, how much."

"And Charley's Uncle Hop is going to foot the bill?" I asked.

"Yes."

"Then what happens?" I said, "I mean, Charley will get out of jail on bail. Will he just go back to work? What about hearings and a trial and all that stuff?"

"He will be required to attend all hearings and, of course, his trial. If it comes to a trial. I aim to do my best to find the actual killer before then." Ernie scowled. I didn't blame him.

"Just out of curiosity," said Sue, sticking in an oar. "If somebody gets out on bail and then doesn't go to the hearings and trials and so forth, what happens?"

Ernie answered, which was a good thing. I sure didn't know what to tell her. "If someone skips out on bail, a warrant will be issued for his arrest, and whoever bailed him out will lose all his money."

"Oh, dear," said Sue. "I hope this man you know is honest."

"He is," said Ernie rather forcefully. "I've known Charley for years."

"Of course he is," I said, frowning slightly at Sue.

"Oh, you know him too?" she asked.

"Slightly, but yes. And I trust him. He'd never run out on a family commitment, and his uncle is definitely family. Why, he owns and runs Hop Luey's restaurant in Chinatown!"

"My goodness!" Sue said. "I've dined there. It's quite elegant."

"But Hop will end up paying something, right?" said Lulu, who knew more about the mean streets of Los Angeles than anyone else in the room except Ernie. "Isn't it a percentage of the bond?"

"Ten percent," said Ernie.

"Hmph," I muttered. "When we—I mean when you find the real killer, the Los Angeles Police Department ought to refund all of Hop's money."

"Good luck with that one," said Ernie sardonically.

Then Lily appeared in the doorway leading to the dining room. "Dinner is served," she said in an exceptionally maid-like voice.

"Oh, good," said Caroline, murder seemingly wiped from her mind.

"Yes, I'm starving," said Sue, her attention likewise averted.

I heaved a big sigh.

"Smells good," said Ernie.

"Mrs. Buck's meals are always good," I told him.

I was correct. Our meal was delicious, and I decided persimmon pudding would make an admirable dessert for a Christmas dinner.

THIRTEEN

The following day, Lily dressed in her maid uniform, which was black and had a white apron pinned on it. She even wore one of her white caps and black low-heeled shoes. She looked as if she'd been a maid all her life, in fact. As we working girls straggled from our bedrooms to the living room and on into the dining room, she was filling dishes on the sideboard as if she'd been doing *that* all her life, too.

As usual, I was the first one in the dining room. I always set aside whatever I aimed to wear to work the night before so I didn't have to do any heavy thinking in the morning. I blinked when I entered the room. "You look perfectly maidly, Lily," I said to her, amazed.

With a wide grin, she said, "I've had lots of practice. Want me to serve people's plates, or do you serve yourselves?"

"We can lift the lids and scoop stuff ourselves. Thanks for offering. Does Mrs. Buck need you for anything?"

"Naw. She just asked me to fill the various serving dishes and make sure nothing runs out."

"She's too good to us," I said as I made my way to the sideboard. "So are you. I swear, when I was a kid, I had to eat oatmeal every day of my life. We never got anything interesting except on weekends." I lifted the first lid. "And here Mrs. Buck is giving us both bacon *and* sausages! The woman's a saint."

With a laugh, Lily said, "She's really nice."

The rest of our merry band showed up shortly after I did, and Lily vanished into the kitchen again, only reappearing to check the serving dishes and to ask if anybody needed anything else. Nobody did.

Before we all left for work, I visited Mrs. Buck and Lily in the kitchen to see what, if anything, Mrs. Buck thought Lily might do that day to earn her keep.

"If you'd wash the towels and hang them out in the backyard, that would be a good thing, child," Mrs. Buck told Lily with a smile.

"Sounds good to me," said Lily. I swear, the girl was always happy. Must be nice. I got down in the dumps sometimes.

"Excellent. Be sure to wear a coat or something when you hang out the laundry. It's cold today."

"Will do," said Lily, still chipper. Don't know how she did it. The notion of washing anything at all and hanging it out on a cold, windy day made me feel icky.

But I had to go to work, so I said a friendly goodbye to my staff and joined the rest of my tenants in the living room, where they'd all gathered. We walked to Angels Flight together and then, as usual, walked to the Broadway where Caroline left us, and then to the Figueroa Building where Sue left us.

"You know, Lulu," I said as the two of us pushed open the glass door and entered the lobby, "I was thinking about that man's murder last night. He couldn't have been working alone, could he? I mean, he must have had henchmen, don't you think?"

Lulu thought about my question as she went behind the reception desk, took off her coat and hat—making me blink, as she'd chosen bright green with a red bow today—and stuffed her handbag into a drawer. After pursing her lips in thought for a second she said, "I don't know. Would he need henchmen?"

"I don't know, but I can't imagine he'd try to blackmail all those

Chinese families unless he had henchmen to do some dirty work for him if they didn't pay up."

"Was he blackmailing them?" asked Lulu, sounding surprised.

"I should think it would be called blackmail if a person goes to other people and claims they owed him money because of some dead relative's debts."

Sitting and opening the drawer in which she kept her manicure supplies, Lulu said, "I don't know. If they're legitimate debts, I guess it's not blackmail."

"Hmm. But *were* they legitimate debts? And is, under law, a child responsible for his parents' debts? Wonder how to find out about that."

"Leave it to Ern. He'll figure it out."

Bother. "Well, I think I'll ask him about it." Something else occurred to me. "Say, Lulu, would you like to visit Chinatown either for lunch or after work? I want to see where that guy was killed. Maybe we can find a clue the police didn't bother to look for."

"Ernie will kill you if you snoop on your own, Mercy. You know that."

"I won't be snooping!" I said, lying through my teeth. "I want to get some of those red Chinese lanterns to hang in the entryway, and we can see where the man died while we're looking for lanterns. And I want more Christmas ornaments, too."

"Well, I sure don't mind going to Chinatown. I love browsing through all those shops. But if Ernie finds out, he'll kill us both."

"Stop saying he'll kill us," I said, perhaps too sharply. "Ernie can't stop us from going on a little shopping trip, even if it does take us to Chinatown."

"Whatever you say, Mercy. Anyhow, he'll probably only kill you if he finds out."

"How comforting," I said as I headed to the staircase.

I had to admit, if only to myself, that Lulu was right. If Ernie knew Lulu and I aimed to trek to Chinatown, no matter how legitimate our reason, he'd kill me. But I didn't have time to worry about my ultimate demise because when I got to the office, the door was unlocked! On Tuesday, meaning it was the second day in a row this phenomenon happened. I didn't trust it.

Pushing the door open with trepidation, I called out, "Ernie? Are you here already?"

"Yes!" he called back, sounding grumpy.

"Already in a bad mood, I see," I said waspishly as I entered the outer office, looked at the clock I'd bought and hung on the wall to see it was only five minutes until eight o'clock. Ha. So we were both early.

"Yes. I'm in a bad mood," growled Ernie. "This case of Charley's is driving me nuts."

Before bearding the lion in his den—and wishing I'd brought some of Mrs. Buck's oatmeal cookies to work with me to sweeten the beast—I hung up my hat and coat. After I drew off my gloves, I shoved them in the pocket of my coat. Then, prepared for the day, I went to my desk. There I wound the cunning pagoda-shaped clock I'd bought in Chinatown and which adorned my desk, placed my handbag into the bottom right desk drawer, and drew out my dust cloth with which I proceeded to dust all wooden surfaces in the room. I decided to give Ernie's office a miss that day because I had questions for him, and I didn't want to be yelled at before necessity called for same.

For the record, I no longer had to wash the windows in either Ernie's or my room, because Mr. Buck washed all the windows in the Figueroa Building. He said it was his job and not mine to do so. Fine by me.

I must have been silent as I went about my business, because I'd just dusted off the picture I'd bought and hung on the wall when a roar came from Ernie's cage. I mean his office.

"What the devil are you doing? Get in here! You've got work to do!"

After glancing at the clock once more, I said, "It's two minutes until eight, Mr. Templeton. My hours are from eight a.m. until five p.m., or have you forgotten?"

"Damn it, come here! I need to talk to you."

Well, this was interesting. As a rule, Ernie preferred not to talk to me about his cases. He'd made this stricture abundantly clear about Charley Wu's case the day prior. Therefore, curious, I picked up a secretarial pad and two sharp pencils—I kept a supply of freshly sharpened pencils in a cup on my desk—and walked to Ernie's office.

The door was slightly ajar, so I pushed it open and walked in. On a normal day, Ernie sauntered into the office with a copy of the *Los Angeles Times* tucked under his arm, went to his room, flung his hat at the hat rack, picked it up if he missed, sat at his desk, plopped his feet on his desk and proceeded to read the newspaper.

Not that day. That day, Ernie slumped at his desk, his elbows on it and his head resting in his cupped palms.

"Good heavens, Ernie, whatever is the matter?"

"I don't know where to start with this damned case is what's the matter," he snarled.

"Well, it's not my fault, so don't bark at me for it."

Lifting his head from his palms, he frowned at me. Squinting, he said, "Sorry."

I could tell he didn't mean it.

"May I ask you a question or two that have been bothering me about the case?" I asked with some trepidation.

"Aw, hell, you're going to do it, aren't you?"

"Do what?" I asked, trying to sound innocent.

"Butt in on the case."

"I only want to ask you a couple of questions, Ernie. Maybe my questions will spark an idea in your head."

"What I need is a damned firecracker," he groused.

"You'll have to wait until February for firecrackers," I told him. "That's when the Chinese New Year is."

"Huh. Well, sit down and ask your questions."

So I did.

FOURTEEN

I n fact, I'd thought of another question to ask before I asked about possible henchmen. "Can you tell me how the body was lying when it was found? And precisely where?"

Eyeing me with doubt writ large on his features, Ernie said, "Why do you want to know? You're not going to snoop. It's not safe."

"I'm not going to snoop," I lied. "I just want to know where the dead man lay and in what position. I mean, I heard Phil say he was shot in the back. But he also said the dead man had been arguing with Charley. Did the shooting take place the instant he and Charley stopped arguing? If it did, it's unlikely Charley could have shot the fellow in the back, isn't it?"

"Why?"

"Because *if* Charley shot him at the time of the argument—and I know he didn't—he'd have shot him in the front, wouldn't he? Unless the man had turned to go into a building or something. Did he own a building in Chinatown? Or a shop or a business? Or did he live elsewhere and just venture into Chinatown to torment shopkeepers?"

Ernie's eyes squinched up and he sat up straight in his chair, uncupping his hands but leaving his forearms draped in front of him on his desk. "I don't know. I hate to say it, but those are good questions, Mercy. I'll ask Phil."

"Will Phil know? Did the police bother finding out?"

"I'll call Phil and let you know."

"Good. Also, it seems to me that if this Chan fellow was going after people and telling them their dead relations owed him money, wouldn't he have a henchman or two to back him up? I mean, if he approached a family that knew its history to be impeccable, he might find himself in physical danger, don't you think? I know the Chinese here aren't violent as a rule, but still…"

"Family honor means pretty much everything to most of the Chinese I know," said Ernie. "That's another good question, damn it."

"There's no need to swear at me because I've asked some good questions, Ernest Templeton."

"Nuts. You know me by this time, and you know I swear."

"Yes." I sighed deeply. "I do know."

"Yeah, well, stay there. I'm going to call Phil."

Holding out a hand, I said, "Wait a minute. Before you place the call, can you tell me precisely where Mr. Chan's body was found? You said it wasn't near either of Charley's businesses." I thought for a second. "Although his family seems to own businesses all over Chinatown. Maybe they own the grocery store where he was found."

"I don't know about the grocery store, but yeah, they do own or operate several of the businesses there." Ernie squinted at me suspiciously for a second or two before he, too, sighed deeply. "I guess I can't stop you from prying, so it's probably better to tell you than to have you going around asking questions on your own."

"Yes, it is," I said firmly.

"All right. You know Charley's noodle shop is right there on the west side of Hill, almost at the corner."

"Yes, I know where it is."

"Okay, the Chan character's body was found at the end of Chinatown. Same side of Hill, but at the south end of the street that curves in front of those other businesses. You know, Fong's Toy Shop and Jewelers— Crumb."

"Another Fong," I said, recognizing Ernie's exclamation for what it was.

"Yeah. Another Fong. Or, more likely, a sprig from the same Fong tree."

"But I've been to Fong's. It's nowhere near the south end of that street, either. The grocery store is at the very end, on the other side from Fong's, kind of next to an alleyway." It also stank, but I decided not to say so.

"Yeah. The body was found across the street from the grocery store, but not near any open businesses."

"But near a building or two?" I asked.

"Yeah. Near what are supposed to be a couple of empty buildings."

"I see. I wonder if they're truly empty."

"Don't know, and I don't know if the cops bothered to check."

"I think we should check," I said decidedly.

"What's this *we* business?" snapped Ernie. "I really don't want you to get involved in this case, Mercy!"

"I'm already involved. I'm hiding Charley's sister, and I want to help. Lily's worried to death about her brother."

Very well, so Lily had been upbeat and cheerful ever since she'd come to Mercy's Manor. What was a little fib, especially since she *must* be worried about Charley?

"Cripes." Ernie lifted his elbows, cupped his hands, and proceeded to bury his face in them again.

After considering the matter for a second or two, I decided it might not hurt to take Ernie into Lulu's and my confidence. Actually, to be fair, it *might* hurt, but Ernie couldn't hold me captive. If he didn't like my plan, he could just go do something else.

"Um…Ernie?"

"Yeah?" He didn't even lift his head to speak.

"Lulu and I want to get some of those red Chinese paper lanterns to hang in the entryway of my house, and the only place to get them is in Chinatown."

"Uh," said Ernie, wise to my wily ways.

"I think Fong's would be a fine place to look for them," I went on, undeterred by Ernie's crotchety mood.

"You do, do you?"

"Yes, I do. And then we might just visit the grocery store and see if they have anything interesting to buy."

"Like chicken feet and pigs' trotters?"

My nose wrinkled of its own accord. I know people all over the world eat different things, but I had to admit those buckets of chicken feet, pigs' trotters and dead ducks held no appeal for me. "Maybe they sell…I don't know. Almond cookies."

"Right."

"Well, Lulu and I plan to visit Chinatown to get paper lanterns, and we also aim to see where Mr. Chan's body was found. I'll bet anything if you went with us, you could detect something the police missed."

I resented the eye-roll he gave me. Guess he didn't feel like being buttered up that morning.

"Just stay there in the chair," he said as he reached for his telephone.

As I hadn't planned on moving, I ignored his officious tone of voice. I remained in the chair, notebook and pencils in my lap, and gazed as Ernie picked up his receiver and dialed the number of the station where Phil Bigelow worked.

When the operator answered, Ernie said, "Phil Bigelow. It's important."

I doubt the operator cared if Ernie's call was important, but she connected him anyway because a few seconds later he said, "Why the hell are you in your office instead of beating the paths in Chinatown trying to figure out who killed the Chan character?"

Phil said something I couldn't hear. I thought about going to my desk and picking up my own receiver as I'd done before but decided doing so might be pressing my luck. Besides, Ernie took that opportunity to give me a "don't you dare move" glare, which cemented my decision.

"Bushwa," said Ernie. "If Charley was arguing face-to-face with Chan, how'd he shoot him in the back?"

Again Phil spoke.

Again Ernie said, "Bushwa." Interesting slang term. I know what it means, and I'm glad he didn't use the term it was meant to replace.

More noises from Phil's end of the wire.

"You don't have a single, solitary clue, do you, Phil? And you don't have a single solid piece of evidence against Charley. Is he out on bail yet?"

Phil said something.

"You're not telling me something, Phil. What is it? Spill, dammit. Or are you going to keep it to yourself because it might exonerate Charley?"

I heard a loud sound through the receiver, but I didn't catch the word Phil hollered. Then his voice lowered and he talked to Ernie for a minute or so. Ernie's eyes got rounder as he listened. Hmm. Ernie'd better tell me what Phil was telling *him* or I might have to take steps.

"Interesting. And you still think Charley's your man? You think he actually owns one of those?"

I guess Phil said something, although he didn't yell this time. I didn't hear it, at any rate.

"Huh. Well, maybe I'll just toddle down to Chinatown and have lunch at Charley's noodle shop. I'm sure I'll get more from him than any of your men will. I don't suppose you've checked to see if those supposedly empty buildings near where Chan's body was found are truly empty, have you?"

Phil again.

"I thought not. Well, don't bother. I'll check when I'm in Chinatown for lunch."

This time I heard Phil because he bellowed, "Dammit, Ernie!" before Ernie hung up on him.

Ernie looked at his wristwatch. "Huh. Too early for lunch. Want to go snooping with me?"

"Yes! Please!" I said, leaping from my chair. "I wish Lulu could go with us, but she has to stay at the reception desk until her lunchtime."

"I'm not sorry. Looking after you is trouble enough for any detective."

"It is not! I mean, I'm not a bother! I gave you some good ideas, didn't I?"

"Yeah," said Ernie, rising and lifting his coat from the rack beside his desk.

As he shrugged it on, I went into the outer office and put on my own hat and coat. I thought about leaving my handbag in my desk but thought better of it. After all, something we saw in Chinatown might strike my fancy. I'd leave the Chinese lanterns until I could visit the place with Lulu.

Therefore, I was ready for Ernie when he walked out of his room into mine. In fact, I opened the door and held it open for him. Only then did I recall the one appointment I'd made for him that day.

"Oh, crumb!" I cried.

"What now?" said Ernie.

"You have an appointment at eleven-thirty this morning."

Again taking a peek at his wristwatch—and what handy things they were—Ernie said, "We'll be back by then if we need to be. I just want to look around the place where the body was found and listen at the buildings. Maybe talk to a couple of the shopkeepers. Mr. Fong and I know each other."

"Oh. The man who makes the toys and jewelry?"

"Yeah. Him. He makes some pretty things out of a stone—or maybe it's some kind of mineral—called cinnabar. I got a cinnabar bracelet for my sister. Already sent it to Chicago."

"Are you in close touch with your family in Chicago, Ernie?" I asked, never having heard him speak of his family except in disparaging terms. From prior conversations, I gathered his father, at least, had shuffled off this mortal coil. Didn't know about his mother. Or any siblings.

"Gawd, no," he said with a pretty fair facsimile of a real shudder. "Can't stand any of them except Suzanna. She's my sister.

That's why I sent her a Christmas present. I wouldn't touch any of the rest of them with a barge pole."

"Families can be a lot of trouble sometimes, can't they," I said with true sympathy.

"Not if you don't let them be. Of course, none of my family has followed me to Los Angeles. You're not so lucky. But you're doing pretty well. I heard you tell your mother you wouldn't go to Pasadena for Christmas. Felt like cheering."

We'd stepped out into the hallway, and Ernie had turned his back on me so he could lock the office door. Therefore, he didn't see me shudder. Mine wasn't a facsimile, but a real live shudder. The notion of visiting my parents in Pasadena gave me a cold grue.

"Thank you." I'd managed to get my emotions under control by the time Ernie turned around again.

We walked down the hallway to the elevator. I believe I've mentioned I don't mind taking the elevator as long as someone is with me. In actual fact, the elevator saved both Ernie and me from being attacked by a monstrous dog a month or so prior. Actually, that particular dog would probably have only jumped up and licked us to death, but we didn't know that when we saw it barreling down the hall at us.

Ernie opened the elevator door. I made sure the cage was flat against the floor of the hallway and stepped inside, which is one more reason I preferred using the staircase unless someone was with me. You could take a nasty tumble if a person hadn't stopped the elevator flush with the hall floor, either by tripping over it or taking a sudden step down.

When we left the elevator in the lobby, Lulu turned to look to see who was entering her realm. "Hey, you two. Whatcha doing?"

I did mention Lulu was a vision in green that day, didn't I? Well, she was. I blinked a couple of times even though I'd seen her earlier.

"Holy cow, Lulu, you're all dressed for Christmas, aren't you?" said Ernie, blinking in his turn.

"I like to dress for the holidays," said Lulu, fluffing her red below-the-waist fabric belt that tied with a big bow on the side. I knew Lulu didn't sew, so she must have a good contact at a consignment shop, or something equivalent, because she owned more clothes than I'd ever seen any other woman wear.

"Well, you did a good job with this outfit," said Ernie, still blinking.

"But what are the two of you doing? Usually, you make Mercy stay in the office when you go out detecting," said Lulu.

"We're not precisely detecting," said Ernie. "We're just going to visit Chinatown to see where Chan's body was found."

Lulu looked at me in deep reproach. "Mercy! I thought *we* were going to do that!"

Ernie glanced down at me and said, "Ha. I knew it. You two were going to pry and snoop on your own. Never mind that there's somebody in Chinatown who shoots people for fun. No. Not you two. You'll never rest until you both get killed, will you?"

"We weren't going to pry and snoop!" I said, even though it was a fib.

"Yes, we were," said Lulu, who didn't have my scruples. Actually, I guess she had more scruples than I did because she didn't fib. What a lowering reflection. "It's because the police are idiots." This statement kind of redeemed her negation of my own personal lie.

"Well, you don't need to now," said Ernie. "Mercy and I are going to check out a few things."

"Darn!" said Lulu, unappeased.

"We'll still go there for Chinese lanterns, Lulu," I told her. "And we can look at the buildings near where the body was found to see if they're empty."

"That's what *we'll* be doing today, Mercy," said Ernie sternly. I don't know why he suddenly wanted to be stern all the time recently. He never used to have a stern bone in his body.

"I know it, but I can still show Lulu where the body was found when we go there for paper lanterns," I said lamely.

"Gawd," said Ernie. "You two are impossible."

"We are not," I said as Ernie turned and headed to the front door, where Mr. Buck kindly held the door open for him. I hurried after him.

"Tell me what you find out!" Lulu called as I scuttled away.

"Will do!" I called back.

Mr. Buck always made sure Ernie's dilapidated Studebaker had a parking spot directly in front of the Figueroa Building, so Ernie stepped up to the rusty passenger door and opened it as if the car were a Rolls Royce instead of a falling-apart Studebaker. Then he picked up the crank, but Mr. Buck walked over and offered to crank the thing for him.

"Thanks, Buck," said Ernie, rubbing his hands together. As soon as he got to the driver's side of the car, he pulled his gloves out of his coat pocket and put them on. "Cold today."

"Not as cold as Boston," I muttered.

"Nor as cold as Chicago," he said. "Which is why I don't live there any longer."

"I don't live in Boston any longer because I wanted to get away from my mother and father. Then they followed me out here," I said, my tone dismal.

Ernie turned the switch to "on" and pulled out the choke, then Mr. Buck cranked the car. Once the Studebaker shuddered to a start, Ernie took the crank from Mr. Buck and drove off down the street, laughing. And he'd met my mother and father!

FIFTEEN

As soon as Ernie began driving down the street, I said, "All right, Ernie, what was the information Phil gave you about the gun that made you think Charley wouldn't have one?"

With a grin, Ernie said, "When they did the autopsy, they found a .32 slug. They figure it was probably fired from a Colt Positive 32 with a snub-nose barrel."

"I don't know anything about guns. And you think Charley wouldn't have that kind if he owned a gun?"

"It's new, and it's mostly used by coppers. It's a lightweight point-and-shoot pistol that uses soft-nosed bullets. Soft-nosed bullets make big holes in what they hit."

"Oh. Well, they didn't find one of those at Charley's place, did they?"

"The only thing they found that might possibly be used as a weapon was a baseball bat. Baseball bats can't fire soft-nosed bullets."

I gave a tiny shiver, only partially due to the cold. The notion of people shooting each other didn't appeal, even if the man who was shot last week was a bad one. It must be said also that I was still worried about Charley. If Ernie and I—and maybe Lulu—couldn't find the real culprit, the police would still likely blame Charley for the fellow's death. And all because Charley was known to have had an argument with Chan. What a stupid world!

Ernie easily found a parking place on Hill Street near Charley's noodle shop. When we walked to the shop and Ernie tried the doorknob, it was locked.

"Hmm. Wonder if he's not open yet or if he's not going to open," muttered Ernie. He tapped on the door and called out, "Charley! It's Ernie. If you're in there, open up."

Listening hard, I heard no sounds issuing from the noodle shop. Would the shop open for the luncheon—I mean *lunch*, curse it!—crowd? Perhaps Charley's family was too disturbed and their routine too disrupted by current events to open up that day.

"Well, let's go see where the body was found," I suggested after Ernie had knocked harder and stood there, glowering at the locked door. "We can come back later and see if the shop's open."

"Yeah, I guess we might as well," said Ernie. He started walking toward the small street that bisected the plaza, I at his side. We turned left when we got to the little street and marched past Fong's shop. It, too, was closed. Most of the Chinatown businesses must open rather late and stay open rather late in the evening to be available for people getting off work. I preferred my own work schedule.

As we walked past Fong's, Ernie glanced in the window thereof and said, "Hmm. I think I see Mr. Fong in there. If he's open when we walk back, we can pop in and I'll ask him some questions. He's always struck me as a nice man who isn't as distant from white folks as a lot of the other Chinese folks hereabouts. He told me all about how he makes his cinnabar jewelry."

"I'd like to see some of it. Maybe I can get Lulu a piece of cinnabar jewelry for Christmas."

With a loud guffaw, Ernie said, "Lulu? You need to get something bright red and glowing for Lulu. Maybe your sister might like something made of cinnabar. It's red, but it's quite subdued."

"Oh. If it's subdued, you're right. Lulu wouldn't care for it."

"Chloe might," observed Ernie.

"Yes, she might. I already got her a lovely Chinese silk robe, but it won't hurt to get her something besides the robe."

"Must be nice to have money," said Ernie. He was always ribbing me about having been born to money, blast him.

"It is," I said frigidly. The frigid part wasn't due to the weather, either. I *hated* when Ernie teased me about having been born into a wealthy family. This was especially true since Ernie had met both of my parents and knew how dreadful they were. Besides, it was my great-aunt, Agatha, who'd left me an annuity, and that's mainly what I used when buying houses and so forth. Not that I'd bought more than one house, but...Oh, never mind.

"Sorry, Mercy. I shouldn't rag you about your moneybags."

"No," I said, still frigid, "you shouldn't."

"Forgot I said anything, okay?"

"Maybe," I said.

We'd made it to the end of the street, which opened out onto an alleyway. I'd been this way with Ernie before, shortly after I'd gone to work for him, when we trailed a bad guy who'd kidnapped a woman. The grocery store at the east side of the street was as smelly as ever. Well, it wasn't the grocery store itself that stank, but the trash receptacles lining the alley near the store. Ick.

Coming to a halt, Ernie took off his right glove and fished into his jacket pocket, withdrawing a paper. It looked to me as if he'd sketched something on the paper.

"What's that?" I asked.

"When Phil told me how the body was found, I made a drawing of it, so I wouldn't forget. I think this is pretty much how the guy was found." He leaned over, being considerably taller than I, and showed me the sketch. It was darned good, although I didn't say so.

"Oh," I said, squinting at the paper. "And the guy was shot in the back?"

"According to the L.A.P.D., yes."

"Well, it makes even less sense than it did before that Charley shot him after an argument," I said, peering from the paper to the grimy street. "His head was pointing to the grocery store, and his feet were heading the other way, toward the building. If he and

Charley had been fighting, how could Charley have got behind him?"

"Good question, especially since they think he fell out of the window there." Ernie pointed to a ground-floor window. "According to the accounts I've heard from Phil, Chan and Charley were arguing on the street. How could they both get into the building so that Charley could shoot him in the back and shove him out the window?"

After giving his question approximately two seconds' consideration, I said, "He couldn't."

"Right."

"Is that building empty? It must not have been empty when the guy fell out the window. Did he have a business there?"

"Not according to any of the city's records, he didn't," said Ernie.

Looking up at what appeared to be a four-story, bleak and dismal building, I gave another little shiver. "It seems kind of abandoned to me," I ventured.

"Does to me, too." Ernie walked up to the door, which had boards nailed in an "X" pattern across it, and knocked loudly.

Nobody came to the door. I walked up closer to the place, which was uninviting to say the least, and listened with all my might. "Do you hear something?" I asked Ernie.

"No," he said.

I listened harder. I'd thought I'd heard something before, but I couldn't hear it any longer. "I thought I heard some kind of squeaking. Or something."

"Probably mice or rats if you heard squeaking," said Ernie prosaically.

"Ew."

"Yeah."

I heard it again. "But listen, Ernie! It's not like the squeaking of a mouse or anything, It's more like a sort of trilling noise."

With a shrug, Ernie said, "Maybe a bird got in. Birds find their way into all sorts of small crevices in buildings. Maybe some birds built a nest in there."

"In December?"

"Well, what do I know about birds?"

"I don't know, but I think there's something or somebody in the building."

After heaving a huge sigh, Ernie said, "All right. Let's walk around it and listen. If you hear anything else, let me know."

"Very well."

So we walked around the building, which sat so close to the building next door, we had to kind of sidle between the two. I didn't hear anything else. But darn it, I *knew* I heard something inside that building. In fact, as I thought about it, I believed it might have been a girl speaking Chinese. The noise was high-pitched. Maybe a very young girl.

Nuts. Ernie was probably right and it was a bird. Still….

Well, Lulu and I could visit during lunch and take a closer look. Maybe get in somehow. I didn't tell Ernie my thoughts, because he'd have lectured me on breaking and entering. In truth, Lulu and I might actually have to break something—say, one of the grimy windows—in order to get into the place.

I decided to think about it later, especially when Ernie said, "All right. Let's check out the grocery store. Maybe somebody in there speaks English and will talk to us."

He discovered a wrinkled old man behind a cash register who spoke English, sort of, but Ernie couldn't pry any information about the murder from him. The old man just shook his head and said, "See nothing. Hear nothing."

With a sigh, Ernie said, "Thank you. I'm trying to get information to show the police that Wu Chung didn't kill Chan Sien Lo." I guess he was frustrated, because he tried his sentence again in Cantonese.

Still, the old man only shook his head and said, "See nothing. Hear nothing."

I'd been glancing here and there in the small store, trying to find something to purchase in order to soften the old fellow's heart, but my luck was out. Every label on every item was written in Chinese. That made sense, but it didn't help me much. And the unlabeled things I could see didn't appeal to me. I wasn't in the market for dried scorpions, buckets of dry seaweed, or big hunks of ginger root. It occurred to me that perhaps some of the Chinese food I'd eaten since moving to Los Angeles had been prepared with seaweed or scorpions. I'd ask Lily. The notion was kind of nauseating. Make that *extremely* nauseating.

So we left the shop. We'd taken a few steps back toward Fong's shop when a young woman hurried up behind us. She tapped me on the shoulder, and I spun around, feeling creepy after examining that filthy building and the insides of the grocery store. I think I yipped a trifle.

"So sorry to startle you," said the young woman, "but I heard what you said to my grandfather. Are you really trying to help Charley? I know he didn't kill that man."

"So do we," said Ernie.

"Come over here. Grandfather will be angry if he knows I'm talking to you," said the young woman, pulling my arm and guiding Ernie and me into a little nook between shops.

"Thank you for helping us," I said. "My name is Mercy Allcutt, and this is Ernie Templeton. Will you tell us your name?"

With a small grin, the woman said, "I recognize Mr. Templeton from baseball games."

"Yeah, I help Charley sometimes when a teammate can't make it to the game," Ernie said with a smile of his own.

"I'm Jade Chew. Well, that's the English version of my name. In Chinese I'm Chew Mingyu."

"Happy to meet you, Jade," I said and added, "I think Mingyu is a lovely name."

"Well, I'm an American, so I call myself Jade," said Jade. "And I know that evil Chan man was doing something terrible in the building you two were looking at before you came to Grandfather's grocery. This sounds terrible, but I think he…" Here she paused and looked at Ernie. To me, she said, "I don't want to say in front of him. Will you come with me a little way farther?"

Instantly I considered the idea that this pretty Chinese girl aimed to lead me into the arms of a criminal gang. Then I whacked my internal thoughts upside the head and said, "Of course."

We walked a few paces farther into the nook she'd chosen. Frowning, Ernie watched, but he didn't attempt to stop us.

"All right," Jade said in a whisper. "It's too embarrassing to talk about in front of a man, but I think that Chan devil was running a…" Her voice trailed off again, but then she seemed to give her own internal thoughts a whack upside the head because she burst out (still in a whisper), "I think he had kidnapped some Chinese girls and was making them work as…as…as prostitutes!"

Shocked but somehow not terribly surprised, I said, "Good Lord, did you ever see any girls?"

"Not very well. He sort of shuffled them in and out of that dirty old building at night. He had another fellow—just as horrible, but I don't know his name—who worked with him. They'd block our view from what they were doing, but I *know* I've heard women talking or crying over there. I *know* it."

"That's terrible. And you say Chan wasn't working alone. Do you know if he had more than one henchman?"

"More than one what?" Jade looked confused.

"More than one man working with him," I explained.

"I only ever saw the one. He was ugly and had a scarred face. He reminded me of some sailors I met once. Horrid people. Chan was fat and ugly. The other guy was skinny and ugly."

"And you haven't heard anything from that building since Chan's body was found?" I asked avidly, not sure what I hoped she'd say. If she'd heard women in the building, I hope Chan had left them supplied with food and water. "Have you seen the ugly, skinny man since Chan was killed?"

"No. He hasn't been around. He probably ran when Chan was shot. In fact, maybe *he* shot Chan!"

"Oh, I like that idea!" I said.

Jade, who had been smiling, became sober again. "I do, too, but only if somebody can find him. If nobody can find him, they'll probably convict Charley."

A curious brightness in her eyes and a twist of her mouth made me ask, "Are you fond of Charley, Jade?"

She lifted her hand and wiped it under her eyes. "Yes. We were going to marry. Then he got this crazy idea that Lily had to marry the horrid Chan man.So I got mad at him and told him I wouldn't marry him. And now I hate myself!" She turned around, and I heard a stifled sob or two.

Feeling terribly sorry for her, I turned her around, gave her a hug—she stiffened up like cement setting—and said, "Try not to worry. We're determined to clear Charley of this trumped-up charge. Charley didn't do it."

"I-I know," Jade said, sliding out of my arms. Guess she wasn't accustomed to having strange girls hugging her in sympathy. Can't say as I blamed her. "Thank you for trying." Her voice was strong again. "And you'll tell that man"—she pointed at Ernie—"what I said?"

"You bet I will," I told her stoutly. "I'll tell him right away."

"Thank you. I've got to get back to Grandfather's store now, or he'll get mad at me."

"All right. Oh! Before you go, do you cook with the dried scorpions and seaweed?"

Jade probably could have looked more shocked, but I'm not sure. "Good grief, no! Some of the old folks still use old Chinese remedies that involve those icky scorpions. And some of them eat the seaweed. I don't like either of them."

"Aha. What about those huge hunks of ginger root?"

"Oh, yes!" she said with strong conviction. "If you like Chinese food—even the food we cook for Americans—you'll always eat ginger. Ginger is great. It's good for a stomachache, too. You should try it sometime. It's also good in tea."

"I'll be darned. Thanks, Jade! I might just pick up some ginger root next time I'm in Chinatown."

"Be sure to peel it first," she advised me as she took off at a trot, past Ernie, and on to her grandfather's grocery store.

SIXTEEN

E rnie was gazing after Jade when I walked up to him again.
"What's her problem?" he asked.

"Nothing. She was embarrassed to speak of her suspicions in
front of a man, so she spoke of them to me."

"How poetic," growled Ernie, taking my arm and leading me
down the street toward Fong's. Again he shook down his coat sleeve
and looked at his wristwatch. "We don't have a lot of time left if I
have an appointment at eleven-thirty," he said. "Let me just talk to
Mr. Fong for a second, and then let's see if Charley's place is open."

"What time is it?" I asked, thinking we hadn't been in Chinatown all *that* long. Heck, we'd left the office before nine.

"Almost ten," said Ernie.

"Oh. Well then, I guess we don't have a whole lot of time."

So Ernie and I entered Mr. Fong's shop. I loved the place. Mr.
Fong not only had displays of the lovely toys he'd made, but he had
exquisite Chinese vases and jewelry and fans and…oh, just everything. But I wasn't allowed to browse. Ernie marched us both up to
Mr. Fong, who sat behind the counter working on something that
appeared rather delicate. A piece of jewelry? I squinted and saw
him twisting some kind of wire into an intricate pattern with a thin

instrument that looked kind of like a fat needle. He glanced up and smiled as we approached, shoving his work aside. He didn't mess it up, since it resided on a board. Clever man, Mr. Fong.

"Good morning," he said in a pleasant, unaccented voice. Guess his family had come over to the U.S.A. a long time ago, possibly to work on the railroads.

"Good morning, Mr. Fong," said Ernie. "I'm Ernie Templeton. I'm a private investigator and friend of Wu Chung. I'm doing my very best to discover who killed Mr. Chan Sien Lo. The police arrested Charley—I mean Chung—and I know he didn't do it."

"Yes. All of us in Chinatown know he didn't kill that man. Unfortunately, the police don't much like talking to us."

"To be fair," said Ernie, "I've tried to talk to some folks here in Chinatown, and they don't much like talking to me, either. And I'm on Charley's side and not even with the police."

With a chuckle, Mr. Fong said, "I saw you walking toward Chew's Grocery. He won't talk to anyone who isn't Chinese."

"His granddaughter spoke to me," I said, sticking my bit in.

Mr. Fong smiled at me. He had a soft, friendly smile. "Mingyu is a modern young woman. And I know she was worried about what was going on in the building across from her grandfather's store."

"Yes, she told me," I said. Then it was I discovered within myself a serious case of mortification about speaking of an alleged brothel in front of Mr. Fong. Therefore, I didn't say anything else.

"Many of us businessmen in Chinatown were attempting to discover why Mr. Chan was making allegations against some of the shopkeepers," said Mr. Fong. "He claimed deceased members of some families owed him debts. He didn't approach me, so I don't know if he had paperwork in some way proving his claims, but I did notice he seemed to select his victims in a certain way."

"What way was that?" asked Ernie.

"It came to the attention of some of us that the only families he approached were those containing young daughters. He didn't bother me. I have two sons. I believe he spoke to Chew Bao, but Chew Bao isn't a fellow to trifle with. I understand he went after Mr. Chan with a meat cleaver."

"Too bad he didn't chop off his head," I said. Both Ernie and I laughed.

We shouldn't have, though. Mr. Fong said, "Then it would have been Chew Bao who was arrested for Chan's murder instead of Wu Chung. And Chew Bao would have been guilty. I doubt the police would have taken Chan's provocation of him into account."

"Yeah, you're right. They wouldn't have," said Ernie. "I was with the L.A.P.D. for a couple of years, but I couldn't stand the corruption. That's when I set up my own business. Made more money with the police, but it would have been dirty money and I didn't want it."

"An honorable young man," said Mr. Fong with a little bow of his head.

"Don't know about the honorable part, but I couldn't take the police guff any longer. I don't suppose you know any other families who were plagued by Chan, do you? And who might be persuaded to talk to me?"

After giving the matter some thought, Mr. Fong shook his head. "I believe Wu Chung and Chew Bao were approached. He also talked to my cousin, Fong Gui, who operates the Canton Palace. We had a family conference about it, and we came to the conclusion that Chan was trying to pull a confidence trick on Gui. Gui has a daughter named Shu Fang, which means gentle and sweet in English and doesn't suit her at all because she's quite a hellion. However, we believe he might have wanted to get his hands on her. I don't know what he aimed to do with the girls, but I doubt it was anything good."

"So it wasn't just Charley whose sister was in peril from this Chan character," said Ernie.

"No indeed," said Mr. Fong. "I attempted to explain this to a policeman who came into my shop to ask questions, but he wasn't interested in anyone but Wu Chung."

"That figures," said Ernie in disgust. "Well, thank you, Mr. Fong. If you think of anything else that might give me a clue about who killed Chan, please give me a call." He handed Mr. Fong his business card.

Mr. Fong glanced at the card and said, "Ernest Templeton, P.I. That means private investigator, doesn't it? The P.I. part, I mean."

"Yes, it does."

Mr. Fong bowed his head again. "Thank you. I'll talk to some more people, and we might discover something together we couldn't figure out by ourselves. If we do, I'll be sure to telephone you."

"Thank you," said Ernie.

"Thank you, Mr. Fong," I said. Then, because I couldn't resist and it was the truth, I said, "You have *such* a beautiful shop."

"Thank you, miss," said Mr. Fong with another smile.

When Ernie opened the door to Mr. Fong's shop, the wind darned near blew my hat off. I slapped a hand on it. "Stupid wind."

"Santa Anas," said Ernie. "We get 'em this time of year."

"I know. We've had them before recently. The steeple blew off a church a few blocks away from my house during the last batch of Santa Anas in November."

"Ah. Charley's is open. Let's pop in there and see if he's available. If he'll open up for lunch, maybe we can go back to work, I'll keep my appointment, and then we can come back here and eat."

"Brilliant idea!" I said. "May we bring Lulu? I really do want to get some of those Chinese lanterns."

"Gawd," said Ernie. "Yeah, we can bring Lulu."

"Thank you, Ernie," I said sweetly.

We'd made it to Charley's noodle shop and, after a tussle with the wind for possession of the door, Ernie managed to get it open and we walked in. Sure enough, Charley stood behind the counter, chatting in Cantonese to a whole bunch of his Chinese pals. He glanced up and said, "Ernie!"

"How's it going, Charley?" asked Ernie, walking up and sticking his hand out for Charley to shake. I don't know if hand-shaking is a Chinese custom, but Charley didn't seem to mind if it wasn't. He shook Ernie's hand with vigor.

"Can't say I'm not scared, but thank you for trying to help me," said Charley with feeling.

The crowd of Chinese men that had been gathered at the counter faded away until only Ernie, Charley and I stood there.

When I glanced around the little restaurant, I noticed people sitting at the few tables against the wall, so I didn't feel too guilty. I sure didn't want Charley to lose business because we'd invaded his shop.

"Okay," said Ernie, getting down to business. "I have to get back to work because Mercy made an appointment for me at eleven-thirty, of all stupid times—"

"It's my job!" I cried, interrupting him.

Naturally, he merely rolled his eyes. "Anyway, I don't have much time, so I'll just get to it. The police say witnesses have placed you at the end of the street, across from Chew's Grocery Store arguing with Chan Sien Lo shortly before he was shot. That's the main reason they nabbed you for his murder."

"I did argue with him, but it wasn't shortly before somebody shot him. It was about seven-thirty in the evening. He wasn't shot until later that night, right?"

"Not sure. It was dark when whoever shot him shot him. It was dark when you argued with him, too, wasn't it? I mean, it's December and it gets dark early."

"Yeah, it was dark, but I didn't shoot him. I don't even own a gun!" Charley said with passion. "The cops only want to pin it on me because I'm the only one they know of who argued with the pig. But others have squabbled with him, too! Talk to Chew Bao and Fong Gui! They both fought with him. With words, I mean. Well, Bao went after him with a cleaver, but he didn't hurt him."

With a grin, Ernie said, "Yeah, Mr. Fong told us about that."

"I'm glad he didn't chop him to death," said Charley, not grinning, "because the police would have fried him for sure. Never mind that Chan wanted to take Chew Mingyu."

"I thought he only wanted to marry your sister," I said, unable to hold my unruly tongue. "But now people are saying he wanted other girls, too."

Although it didn't look as though he wanted to, Charley answered my question. Talk about a male-dominated culture! And I thought we white folk were bad. Anyway, Charley said, "He wanted to *marry* Lian Jun. He said he had jobs for the other girls." He shook his head in disgust. "I didn't know about that until after you"—he pointed at me—"and your friend chased her last Saturday. Then I talked to the other families and found out Chan wanted their daughters and sisters, too."

"Then you should be glad Lulu and I got involved," I said stiffly.

This time *Charley* rolled his eyes at *me*!

"Don't pay attention to her, Charley. She wants to be a detective. Still, she might have a point. If she and her snoopy friend got you businessmen here in Chinatown to talk to each other, they probably did you a good turn."

"Huh," said Charley. "Maybe."

"Listen," said Ernie. "We've got to get back to work now. Will you be open for lunch today? Save three stools if you are, because I'm coming back to talk to you some more."

"I'll be open. My mother's back there cooking as if there'll be no tomorrow. When she gets upset, she cooks. You'll probably have to eat something more than pork and noodles," said Charley.

He sounded glum about his mother's industry, but I was pleased. Her pork and noodles were delicious, but I wouldn't mind sampling some of her other offerings. Well, as long as they didn't involve seaweed. According to Jade, I wouldn't have to worry about dried scorpions at least.

"All right. We'll see you later, Charley."

"See you later, Ernie. And you, too," he added as a tepid after thought to me. "And thanks, Ernie."

I only smiled at him.

We got back to the Figueroa Building in plenty of time for Ernie's eleven-thirty appointment. We even had time to stop by the reception desk, where Lulu was painting her nails Christmas red, and ask her to go to lunch with us in Chinatown.

"Charley's place will be open for lunch," said Ernie.

"Oh!" cried Lulu. "He's out of the clink?"

"Yup. His Uncle Hop bailed him out, and he opened his shop."

"And," I added to Ernie's brief explanation, "he said his mother's in the kitchen cooking up a storm. She's upset, and when she gets upset she cooks, according to Charley. So we might get to eat something besides pork and noodles."

"I like pork and noodles," said Lulu.

"I do, too, but we can try something else, too," I told her.

Lulu got a faraway look in her eyes, and as she flapped her newly painted nails in the air, she said, "I have an aunt like that. Aunt Maisie. Every time one of her kids gets into trouble or Uncle Fergus does something she doesn't like, or a cow dies or whatever, she cooks up a storm. She makes really good pies, too."

"I want Mrs. Buck to teach me how to cook," I said.

"Ha!" said Ernie.

"I do!" I cried fervently.

"Get a book from the library," suggested Lulu. "Betcha they've got tons of cooking books there."

"What a brilliant idea," I said. "Thanks, Lulu."

"Sure. After Christmas, we can go to the library and look for cooking books."

"Come on, Mercy," said a bored Ernie. "Let's get upstairs and see what's up with my eleven-thirty."

"I think he saw something bad," I said. "Or thinks he did. Or maybe he's being blackmailed. Or something. He was kind of rambling when I talked to him yesterday."

As we got to the elevator, Ernie said, "Great. Just wonderful. All's I need is a rambling blackmailee when I'm trying to save a pal from the electric chair."

"Well, *I* didn't know you were going to put your business on hold while you helped Charley, did I? You didn't *tell* me you were."

As Ernie opened the elevator cage for me, he said, "Right, right, right. You're right. I'm just worried, is all."

"Well," said I as I stepped into the cage, "we know more now than we did earlier this morning. Maybe Charley can tell us more over lunch."

"Maybe," said Ernie.

It then occurred to me that Lulu and I could pop by Chinatown after work and check out the awful building where I thought I heard something. Might as well do it that day as another, although…No. I should drive Lulu and myself to work tomorrow, so we wouldn't have too far to walk in the dark. It might not be *too* dark when we got to Chinatown to snoop. Chinatown was kind of a creepy place for a couple of white girls to be in the dead of night. I couldn't recall there being many street lights around the repellant building. I could bring a flashlight, of course.

"What are you daydreaming about?" Ernie asked, jolting me out of my thoughts.

"I'm not daydreaming," I said. "I'm thinking about getting red Chinese paper lanterns. I think I saw them in a shop we passed today."

"You're not going to Chinatown alone, Mercy Allcutt," said Ernie firmly. "I know you'll pry. Red Chinese paper lanterns, my foot."

"That's not fair! I *do* want some of those lanterns. I also want to browse in Mr. Fong's store. It looked to me as if he might be working on a piece of jewelry when we walked in there today. I'd like to see more of his jewelry. And some of those ornaments were just gorgeous."

"Yes, Miss Rich. While I talk to Charley at lunch, you and Lulu can prowl the streets of Chinatown. At least it's daylight."

"Lulu and I want to eat lunch, too, darn it!"

"Yeah, yeah, yeah. Eat fast," said Ernie, uncaring, the beast.

SEVENTEEN

When our eleven-thirty client came in through the outer office door and spoke to me, I was almost sorry I'd made an appointment for him. He'd been fairly incoherent on the telephone the day before. I'd thought he was just upset then, but he was incoherent today, too.

Short and thin, he had a nervous tic in one eye and a monocle in the other. He carried a cane with a silver handle, and he wore black gloves with his black suit. He appeared quite formal, actually. When he doffed his hat, I saw he was bald, although he had a red mustache that curled up on both sides, reminding me a bit of Hercule Poirot from *The Mysterious Case at Styles* by Mrs. Agatha Christie, which I'd read recently. Only Mr. Poirot's mustaches were black. This man's bald head was dotted with freckles.

I smiled sweetly at him as I do to all our clients, and said, "Are you Mr. Brentwood?"

"Me? Brentwood? No. No." He shook his head hard. "I mean, yes, I'm Mr. Brentwood, but you're not Ernest Templeton."

"No, I'm Miss Allcutt, Mr. Templeton's confidential secretary."

"But I came here to see…to see…to see…Mr. Templeton, not you."

I maintained my serenity. For all I knew, this guy was an eccentric millionaire who wanted to shower money upon Ernie's head. "Let me take you to Mr. Templeton's office," I said, even though an idiot would know the open door to Ernie's office led to...well, Ernie's office.

"Uh. Er. No. Yes. Er, thank you," said Mr. Brentwood. He minced toward me as I stood and stepped out from behind my desk.

I took another step or two and stood at Ernie's open office door. Turning my head and talking to Ernie, I said (and with a smile, too, darn it), "Mr. Templeton, Mr. Brentwood is here to see you."

"Thank you," said Ernie without enthusiasm. "Send him on in."

So I gestured to Mr. Brentwood, who stared at my hand for a second or two, then jerked himself forward and lurched into Ernie's office. As soon as he'd cleared the doorway, I shut the door. I didn't want to be in there. Let Ernie handle the weird little man.

They didn't remain long. After maybe seven minutes, the door to Ernie's office opened again, and Ernie smiled as he held the door for Mr. Brentwood to exit. "I'm sorry I can't help you, Mr. Brentwood. I think you really need to talk to the police about this matter. Unless you have more information, I don't know of any way I can assist you."

"No. No. Um, the police? Do they know about things of this... this...this nature?"

"They're supposed to be able to help with things like that. You might want to consult a policeman."

"Oh dear. Oh dear," said Mr. Brentwood. "No. They won't let me. No, they won't let me."

"Who won't let you?" asked Ernie, his smile fading.

"Oh. Oh, no. Nobody. No one. No one won't let me," said Mr. Brentwood, making no sense at all.

"Well, if you're able to give me more information later, be sure to do so. All right?" Ernie's smile returned, and he spoke as if he were talking to a confused little child.

"No. Yes. Yes, I will do that," said Mr. Brentwood, as fuddled as ever.

"Very good," said Ernie, still gentle as a lamb.

Turning with a jerk, Mr. Brentwood squinted at me, popping his monocle out of his eye. Plainly, he was familiar enough with this type of accident that he dealt with it deftly, catching its ribbon and screwing the glass back where it belonged. I never understood the use of monocles. If you need cheaters, get cheaters why don't you? Especially if you looked like Mr. Brentwood. Eyeglasses wouldn't hurt his appearance at all. In fact, he'd appear less odd if he wore spectacles rather than that silly monocle.

I still smiled sweetly at him. "May I see you to the door, Mr. Brentwood?" He acted as if he didn't know the direction, although it was right in front of him.

He said. "No. No. No. Let me think about it. Yes. I'll think about it and let you know. Door. Oh, yes. The door. Let me out? I'll let you know."

"You do that," said Ernie. He sounded sweet, too, this time as if he were humoring a lunatic.

"Yes. No. Yes. No. Yes, I'll do that," said Mr. Brentwood.

"Thank you for coming to see me," said Ernie.

Because Mr. Brentwood seemed to have stationed himself in the middle of my office, looking from Ernie to the hallway door and not moving, Ernie decided to help him out. He strode to the door and opened it for his client. After watching Ernie's movements for a second or two, Mr. Brentwood gave one of his jerks and lurched out of the office and into the hall. Ernie shut the door behind him and turned to me.

"Why in God's name did you make an appointment for me with that idiot?"

With a shrug, I said, "I didn't know he was an idiot. He seemed a bit confused on the telephone yesterday, but I didn't realize befuddlement was his normal aspect."

"His 'normal aspect'? What the devil does that mean?"

"I didn't know he was always like that," I snapped. "Do you like that phrasing better?"

"Yeah." He snatched his coat and hat off the rack beside the door and put them on. "I do. Now let's grab Lulu and get back to Chinatown."

Glancing at my clock, I said, "It's kind of early for Lulu to take off for lunch. The building management might not like it."

"Aw, hell, I'll get someone to fill in for her."

"You will?" I asked, surprised.

"Sure. Junior can talk on the telephone as well as anybody else in the world, I should imagine."

I walked to the coat tree, retrieved my own outerwear, and donned it. "But can he transfer calls and so forth?"

"I have no idea. But he can give people the right numbers to call, tell 'em the switchboard is broken, and suggest they call whatever office they want directly."

"Oh. I guess he can, can't he? Do you know where Junior is at the moment?"

"No, but he probably won't be hard to find."

We exited the office only to find Mr. Brentwood standing, staring off into space, a few feet away from Ernie's door. I heard Ernie mutter, "Cripes."

Nevertheless, he walked up to the man and said, "Mr. Brentwood? Do you need assistance?"

Poor Mr. Brentwood jumped a foot, jerked his head toward Ernie, and said, "No! Yes! Yes. Where's the elevator?"

Good grief. He'd been standing still, staring at the elevator when Ernie and I exited the office.

"We're going to take the elevator, too," said Ernie kindly. "Why don't you come with us?"

"Oh," said Mr. Brentwood. "Yes. No. Yes. Thank you. I shall do that."

Ernie took his arm and Mr. Brentwood meekly walked with us to the elevator. Ernie opened the door and guided him in, and we descended the three floors to the lobby.

As soon as we stepped from the elevator cage, I heard a loud, "Oh, my goodness gracious! Thank *God*!"

After giving a startled leap of my own, I looked at where the commotion was coming from. Lulu stood in front of the reception desk with Mr. Buck and Junior crowding there, too. A woman in a nurse's uniform and cap broke through the knot formed by the trio and took off toward Ernie, Mr. Brentwood and me like a greyhound after a rabbit.

"Jerome!" the nurse-type person cried, reaching us and grabbing Mr. Brentwood's arm. "Oh, Jerome, you worried us so much!"

Mr. Brentwood frowned at the woman, but he didn't yank his arm away. He said, "No. No. No. I didn't worry."

"It's all right, Jerome. We'll get you right back to the home." She glanced at Ernie and me and said with true and grateful fervor, "Oh, thank you for taking care of him. We didn't know where he'd gone!"

"Uh…Sure," said Ernie.

I only smiled. Sweetly, darn it.

The nurse-ish female led Mr. Brentwood carefully to the lobby door. Mr. Buck hurried and opened it for them. *Such* a polite man, Mr. Buck.

After we watched the nurse and Mr. Brentwood leave the building and Mr. Buck walked back to us, Ernie said, "Glad you two are here, Junior and Mr. Buck. Do either of you know how to handle the reception desk when Lulu's gone?"

"What?" cried Lulu. "Where am *I* going?" She looked scared.

"To Chinatown with Mercy and me," said Ernie. He turned back to Mr. Buck and Junior. "Well? Do you know how to handle the calls and transfer them to the right places and such?"

"Sorry. Don't have a single clue," said Mr. Buck.

Junior piped up, "No, but m'sister does. She works for Doc Clutter down the hall. There's lots of people working in that office, so he can probably spare her for a while."

"Can you ask her? I'll be happy to speak to the doctor if you need me to," said Ernie.

"Well," said Junior, "he's pretty nice, but it would be better if you came with me."

"Okay. Lead me to Doc Clutter's office," said Ernie.

And Junior did. Soon he and Ernie came back to the reception desk with an almost precise double of Junior, only she was definitely female. And cute as a button, although I've never known why buttons are considered cute.

"This's m'sister," announced Junior, who'd stuck another piece of gum in his mouth. Unless he'd had it hiding behind his ear, as I've heard some children do and which sounds utterly unsanitary to me. "Her name's Glynis."

Junior's sister Glynis reached out and smacked him lightly on the head. "Don't be rude, Sylvester," she commanded.

"Aw, don't call me that!" whined Junior.

Oh, poor Junior. I couldn't fault him for rebelling. I'd never burden a child of my own with a name like Sylvester.

"All right, you two," said Ernie, gaining control of the siblings with ease. "Miss Glynis O'Fannin, please allow me to introduce you to Miss Mercy Allcutt and Miss Lulu LaBelle."

"Oh, Glennie and I already know each other," said Lulu, smiling at Glynis, who smiled back.

"And my name is Mercy. Please don't call me Miss Allcutt, Glynis," I said.

"Fine with me," said Glynis with a grin. Turning to Lulu, she said, "You gotta go somewhere, Mr. Ernie tells me. Doc said I can sit at the reception desk for as long as you need me to. It's a slow day in the office."

"Have you helped at the reception desk before?" I asked, a little surprised.

"Oh, sure," said Glynis, moseying behind the reception desk as Lulu put on her coat and hat. "Last time Lulu was sick, I was here for a week and a half."

"Goodness," I said. "That must have been before I moved to California."

"Last February, I think," said Lulu. "Had the flu something awful. Hope I don't ever get that sick again."

"We all thought you was gonna die from pneumoney," said Junior in a solemn voice.

"I wasn't *that* sick," said Lulu, snapping a little.

"Well, our pa died of pneumoney, and it was pretty bad," said Junior.

"I'm sorry," said Lulu, chastened. "But I didn't have anything close to pneumonia."

"And I brought you hot soup every day or so," said Ernie.

"You did?" I gazed at my boss, astounded.

"I'm good for one or two things besides detecting," said Ernie, perceptibly peeved at my astonishment.

"Yeah. Old Ern was real good to me. So were Junior and his ma. Mrs. O'Fannin made me gargle with some horrid-tasting stuff, and she brought me soup, too. And aspirin tablets. And cod liver oil." She shuddered as she spoke the last three words.

"How nice people are," I said, my heart feeling all soft and squishy.

"Yeah, yeah, yeah. People are saints. Now let's get back to Chinatown," said Ernie, stomping toward the door. A grinning Mr. Buck held the door for him—and for Lulu and me when we hurried after him.

"Have fun," said Junior a little wistfully.

"Be careful," said his older, wiser sister. She didn't appear much older, though. Then again, I've never been good at guessing people's ages.

As we raced after Ernie, and although I didn't say so, it made me glad to know that if Lulu did get sick again, she could be sick in her rooms at my house instead of the miserable boarding house in which she'd lived before I bought Chloe and Harvey's house on Bunker Hill. I could get her medical attention, too, which is probably more than she got the last time she caught the flu.

As ever, Mr. Buck had beat all of us to Ernie's disgraceful Studebaker. He opened the front passenger door and smiled at me, so I sat there. I'd have been glad to take the back seat, but oh well. Anyway, Lulu climbed in the buggy's back seat and said, "Gee, Ern, you've gotta get another car one of these days."

"Yeah, yeah," he said as he opened his own door and climbed in. "I'll do that with my next million bucks."

"You don't need a million bucks to buy a car, Ernie Templeton," said Lulu. "A couple hundred would get you something better than this."

"Stop talking about my car like that. Hubert doesn't like it."

"Who's Hubert?" asked Lulu.

"My car, of course!" said Ernie as if Lulu should have known that.

"Oh, brother," said Lulu.

I laughed.

Once we were safely on the street—it took some tricky maneuvering to get the machine through passing traffic without getting hit—I asked Ernie something I'd been meaning to ask ever since Mr. Brentwood's sudden departure from our presence. "What did Mr. Brentwood see you about, Ernie? Was he ever coherent enough to tell you?"

Shaking his head and squinting, Ernie said, "Not really. He said he'd lost a girl. Then he said he'd found a girl. Then he said he saw a girl in a window."

"That's it?"

"No, that wasn't quite all of it. He said he saw a girl who had black hair with her hands tied."

"Good heavens! When?" I cried, aghast.

"He didn't know."

"Oh."

"I think the fellow's brains are muddled," said Ernie. "There's a home for the mentally confused about a block and a half away from the Figueroa Building. You'd never guess what it was because it doesn't have a sign or anything. It's just a nice big house. Over on Los Angeles Street. Got a wrought-iron fence around it and a pretty gate. You'd never know it was a loony bin unless you knew it was a loony bin."

"And Mr. Brentwood came from there, did he?" I asked.

"Evidently," said Ernie. "That nurse took him away, so I guess that's where he came from.

"How strange," I murmured.

"He was strange, all right," said Ernie.

However, my mind had already begun churning, and I paid no attention to Ernie's snide comment. So Mr. Brentwood, disturbed in his mind as he was, recalled seeing a woman with her hands tied, did he? "Did he say where he saw the woman?"

"What woman?" asked Ernie distractedly. He was watching traffic, so I didn't get mad at him.

"The one Mr. Brentwood said he saw. Seeing her must have disturbed him."

"I think he was already disturbed," muttered Ernie.

"Yes, I agree, but it seems clear that he isn't supposed to leave the place where he lives by himself. Did he escape again, or was he with other people when he saw the girl?"

"How should I know?" he grumped at me.

"Well, did you ask him where he was when he saw the woman who had her hands tied up?"

We'd made it down Hill Street to Chinatown, and Ernie slid into a parking place not too far away from where Charley's shop was. He didn't answer my question until he'd turned off the engine and the Studebaker had shuddered to a stop. Then he turned to me and said, "I didn't hear your last question. Mr. Brentwood was nutty, you know."

"Yes, I know, but he might actually have seen something that disturbed him. As, for instance, if he was in a group of people from the…I don't like to call it a loony bin. If he was in a group of people from the institution in, for instance, Chinatown, he might have seen something that might help Charley."

Ernie stared at me as if I'd lost my mind for a second or two and then shook his head. "Damn," he said. "I didn't think of that. You may be right."

Hallelujah! I didn't say so. "Can we go to the home and ask someone? Perhaps they take their…what would you call them? Wards? Inmates? Perhaps they take their inmates on pleasure trips to interesting places around Los Angeles sometimes. For instance, they might like to go to Chinatown. Or one of the museums or something."

"They might. Give the loonies something to entertain them," said Ernie.

"I wish you wouldn't call them loonies," I said. "It's not their fault they're…different."

Lulu whooped from the back seat. "Different? That guy with the monocle looked like he belonged in a book!"

"Well, it's not his fault."

"I guess not," said Lulu. "Somebody ought to teach him to dress himself in something that isn't so outlandish."

Lulu, who wore the most garish clothes I'd ever seen on a female person, had said the above. One just never knows, does one?

"The loony bin might be a good start," said Ernie as he opened the front and back passenger doors for Lulu and me to get out. So we did.

EIGHTEEN

After checking his wristwatch, Ernie said, "It's a little after noon. Let's get something at Charley's. If he's not too busy, I'll question him some more."

The wind didn't fight him this time, but when Ernie opened the door, we discovered Charley's noodle shop was packed as full as it could hold with Chinese men, all talking in Cantonese.

Ernie said, "Damn." Then he lifted his voice and said something in Cantonese. I don't know what it was, but he was answered instantly.

"Ernie!" came Charley's voice, loudly and happily. "Come here! I've saved seats for you."

"Thanks, Charley," said Ernie as Chinese men stepped aside and allowed us to pass, Ernie first, then Lulu. I brought up the rear, feeling a bit awkward as I did so.

"I saved you three seats," said Charley as soon as we'd climbed up onto the tall stools set before the counter.

The first time I'd been to Charley's place (which was the day Ernie hired me), I'd had a scramble to sit on one of those tall stools, but I'd learned to climb up them, using the two rungs holding the legs together. Lulu, who was taller than I by a couple of inches, didn't suffer from my problem. She just plunked herself down.

"Thanks, Charley. Appreciate it," said Ernie.

"I appreciate you helping me," said Charley. He turned, walked a few paces, opened the door to the kitchen, and hollered something to whoever was in it. Then he came back to us, ignored Lulu and me, and spoke to Ernie. "I've been talking to other businessmen here in Chinatown. They're eager to help if they can. I've got them to write down all the things they can remember about Chan Sien Lo and his claims of debts owed."

"Thanks, Charley," said Ernie, noticeably impressed. "That should help a lot."

"Maybe. I'll have to translate them for you," said Charley, reaching under the counter and lifting out about three inches' worth of papers. They weren't all the same size, and they weren't all the same color, and almost all of them were covered with Chinese characters. I noticed a couple of papers sticking out from different places in the stack had English words on them.

"Oh, my," I murmured, amazed. Charley had spent a productive hour or so while we'd been dealing with Mr. Brentwood and the Los Angeles traffic.

Charley gave me a look. It wasn't a hostile look or anything. It was mainly indifferent. Obviously, women weren't worth much in his eyes.

Then the door of the kitchen opened and a tiny, wizened Chinese woman in a once-white apron and wielding a large wooden spoon hollered something to Charley, who jumped to attention and hurried to the kitchen door. Clearly, the woman was Charley's mother, and also clearly, he didn't disparage *her*. The fact that he jumped at her command told me as much.

The woman spotted Ernie sitting at the counter and said in a singsong voice, "*Chinese word, Chinese word*"—obviously, I don't know what the words meant—"Ernie!" She smiled hugely, so it was plain she and Ernie were well acquainted.

Ernie stood up, leaned over the counter, waved, smiled hugely back at Charley's mother, and said something in Cantonese that sent the woman into whoops of laughter. I aimed to ask Ernie about their exchange and what was so funny about it when we got back to the office.

Then Charley's mother took Charley by his own apron strap and yanked him into the kitchen. He emerged therefrom a minute or two later with a tray filled with so much food, I wasn't sure it would fit on the counter.

"Holy Moses," said Ernie. "Did your mother fix all of this, Charley?"

After shooting a glance at the kitchen door—I believe to determine if it was shut, which it was—Charley said, "Yeah. I told her you and these two"—he gestured at Lulu and me—"were coming, and she said to bring you all of this. I hope you can eat everything, because she'll be irked if I have to take much of it back."

"Oh, my," I whispered.

"Glad I'm hungry," said Lulu.

Charley put plates and chopsticks before us then set out dishes and dishes and dishes of food. The other people in the little noodle shop watched, smiling and nodding, as we filled our plates. Lulu asked for a fork, which Charley provided.

Boy, was that food good! I didn't recognize most of the dishes, because they weren't the types of Chinese foods sold to us white folks in Chinese restaurants. Much of it was quite spicy, and I appreciated Charley for keeping our water glasses filled.

"Some of this stuff is so hot, I can't eat it," whispered Lulu in my ear at one point. "It's hotter than Mexican food!"

"It's spicy, all right," I said, perspiration bedewing my brow, "but it's *so* good."

"It is good," admitted Lulu. "The parts of it I can eat, anyway."

"Eat up," ordered Ernie under his breath. "Mrs. Wu will be offended if we don't stuff ourselves."

"Oh, my," I said. I'd started the meal feeling kind of brave about it, but my courage was slipping as my stomach filled. "I wish we'd brought Junior. He could probably eat all of this and then some."

"Brilliant idea," said Ernie, surprising me. He didn't generally consider my ideas brilliant. He gestured to Charley, who came over to us. "Do you think you can pack some of this so we can take it to a poor orphan boy we're trying to help out, Charley?"

Charley squinted at Ernie and said, "You're lying, aren't you? You just can't eat it all. I told my mother nobody could eat that much food, but she insisted."

"I'm not lying," lied Ernie, sounding earnest, which was almost appropriate. "There's a kid who works at the Figueroa Building who has to help support his sisters." He didn't mention Junior's mother. "He could really use the food we can't eat. If we try to eat it all, we'll just get fat."

Charley stood at the counter thinking for a second or two, then said, "Yeah. I can do that. I'll tell my mother about your orphan." He tipped Ernie a wink. "She'll think you're even more of a hero than she already does."

"Crumb," said Ernie. "Why does she think I'm a hero?"

"She's deluded," said Charley with another big smile. Then he said, "No. Really, she appreciates it that you believe I didn't kill that pig and that you're trying to help me. So do I," he added.

"I know you didn't kill him, Charley. We just have to convince the police and maybe figure out who *did* kill him."

With a shrug and a sorrowful face, Charley said, "There's no lack of suspects. I just hope it wasn't one of the other guys trying to make a living here in Chinatown. It's hard enough without people thinking they'll get killed if they visit here."

"Yeah," said Ernie. "Well, please ask your mother if she can pack some of this away. We're going to talk to a few other shop-keepers around here and then come back and pick up the food, if it's all right with you."

"Fine with me," said Charley. I noticed, however, that he took a deep breath, adopted a stoical facial expression, and squared his shoulders before walking to the kitchen to tackle his mother.

"How long have you known Mrs. Wu?" I asked Ernie, keeping my voice soft, although there was so much chatter going on in the little restaurant, I doubt anyone else could have heard if I'd spoken in my normal voice.

"Oh, criminy," said Ernie. "I don't even know. I met Mrs. Wu when I was in the L.A.P.D. That's when I met Charley, too."

"Interesting. She seems to like you a lot."

With a grin, Ernie said, "We kid around some."

Lulu said, "She *kids* you? She looks like a tiny little dragon woman."

"Looks can be deceiving," said Ernie.

Charley exited the kitchen in a hurry, looking back over his shoulder. I hope this didn't mean we'd offended Mrs. Wu. When he reached where we three sat, he said, "Whew! She'll give food to your orphan, but you have to take some of it for yourself, too."

"Not a problem," said Ernie. "I love your mother's cooking."

"Yeah," said Charley. "So do I. She's a dragon woman, though."

Ernie, Lulu and I all burst out laughing. Charley stared at us for a second or two before he said, "She is. Trust me."

"We believe you," said Ernie.

"Speaking of dragon women," said Charley, turning to me, which startled me into stiffening on my stool, "how's your new maid coming along? Ernie told me about her. Thank you."

Aha. "She's a dragon woman?"

Charley rolled his eyes and said, "Oy," which nearly made me burst out laughing again, but I contained myself.

"She's doing quite well, thanks. She's a lovely girl and works very hard." This was pretty much only an assumption on my part, since Lily had been with me for a mere couple of days. "She's helpful around the house, and was instrumental in getting us a nice Christmas tree."

Charley nodded. "Fung?"

"Yes."

"But she didn't go with them to pick it up," Ernie assured Charley.

"Good. Yeah. Keep her indoors," said Charley. "Thanks for your help."

"Happy to do it," I said.

"Have the police been in to talk to you any more since you got out?" asked Ernie.

"Yeah. Once."

"Do you know which officers came? Did Phil Bigelow interview you?"

Charley looked blank for a moment, then said, "Don't know. You all look alike to me."

"Right," said Ernie. "Well, we're going to pry around some more, Charley. Keep safe. And thank your mother for us, will you? And the kid—we call him Junior—at the Figueroa Building will be grateful for your mother's contribution to his family's dinner."

"I'm going to tell her you ate most of it. She doesn't give a rap about a white kid going hungry. She likes you, so she wants you to eat her food."

His words shocked me, although I don't know why. I'm sure millions of white people would say the same thing about Chinese kids going hungry. And all looking alike. I swear, people were more similar than they cared to admit, weren't they? Sometimes I despaired of the world. Often, in fact.

However, that's neither here nor there. We all said thanks and good-bye to Charley, told him we'd be back to pick up the food when we were through snooping, and took our leave. Mrs. Wu didn't leave her kitchen to wave us away.

Once we were on the plaza again, Ernie said, "Whew, I'm stuffed to the gills. Don't think I've eaten so much since the last time Mrs. Wu cooked for me."

"Does she cook for you a lot?" I asked.

"Naw. Just when I pick Charley up for a ballgame or something. She's a pistol, though. Funny old lady."

If he said so.

"All right," said Ernie in a getting-down-to-business voice. "I'm going to interview shopkeepers. Can you keep these papers in your handbag or something, Mercy? I can't very well carry them around with me."

I looked from the three-inch stack of miscellaneous papers to my handbag, which wasn't awfully large. Then I glanced at Lulu's bag, which was a tiny bit bigger than mine. "Maybe Lulu and I can split the stack and each carry some of them."

"Okay by me," said Lulu.

"All right. Just don't lose any of them. I'm going to have to get most of them translated before I can use them, unless I talk to some of the people who wrote them while I'm investigating this afternoon. You two, go and shop for lanterns or something. *Don't* ask any questions about Mr. Chan or the murder."

I saluted. "Yes, sir."

"Okay, Ern. This is nice of you. I don't get to shop during the week very often because everything's closed when I get off work."

"Well, don't buy out Chinatown," said Ernie as he buttoned up his overcoat—the wind had picked up again—and strode across the plaza to the first shop on the side opposite Charley's noodle shop.

As soon as he was out of hearing distance, I said to Lulu, "Listen, I want to check out a supposedly vacant building around the corner up there." I pointed, again defying my overbearing mother's teachings. "I swear I heard something in there, but the place is supposed to be empty. It's all boarded up. Even the windows."

"Well, if you *did* hear something, why do you want to investigate it?" asked Lulu skeptically. "What if it's another bad man with a gun or something else awful?"

Hmm. I hadn't actually thought of that. "Well, let's take a look. I won't do anything drastic."

This time *Lulu* rolled her eyes at me. "Like the time you tackled the killer-woman at the Angelica Gospel Hall? That wasn't drastic at all, was it?"

"*I* didn't know she was a deranged murderess!" I cried in my own defense. "But nobody else seemed to care that everything centered around the church so I decided to check it out myself. And I found the guilty party."

"Yeah. She almost killed you too."

"I don't want to talk about it," I said in a voice sounding stuffy even to my own ears. "I just want to listen at various places around that building and find out if I can hear anything."

"All right, but I want to shop, too."

"We'll shop. I want to see Mr. Fong's shop and get some of those red Chinese lanterns."

"Good. And I'll bet some folks here will have Christmas ornaments."

"In Chinatown?" I asked.

With a shrug, Lulu said, "Why not? These folks are smart. They won't not sell something just because they don't believe in what it means."

"I guess you're right," I said as I saw a display of Christmas ornaments in a little trinket shop near Mr. Fong's place. "I like those painted glass pinecones and holly berries. But I want to look around that building first."

"Okay, but if you get me killed, I'll never forgive you, Mercy Allcutt."

"I'm not going to get you killed!"

"Huh."

Nevertheless, in spite of her hesitation, Lulu walked with me down the plaza, turned left at the shops at the end, went past Mr. Fong's place, and strode on until we got to the building across from Chew's Grocery Store.

"It sure smells bad around here," said Lulu, glancing at the grocery store and pursing her lips. "Ew. I don't like seeing those naked ducks hanging there either."

"Every culture has its own customs," I said sententiously. "I'm sure we do things Chinese people think are disgusting."

"I guess," said Lulu doubtfully.

After peering at Chew's store and not seeing Jade, I just walked up to the building of interest and knocked on the boarded-up door. As had happened earlier in the day when Ernie had knocked on it, nothing happened. I knocked harder and succeeded in hurting my knuckles.

"Ow. Well, let's walk around the place and see what we can see. Or hear. I swear I heard what sounded like people talking earlier today, Lulu."

"Great. Just what we want is some big galoot grabbing us for snooping."

"What I heard didn't come from galoots. It came from children or women or little kids," I told her.

"If you say so," said Lulu with a sigh.

"I do say so."

So we walked around the building. I perused it carefully as we did so, looking up at dirty windows, all of which had been boarded over, and trying to determine if there was any way I could get in without breaking something, which would probably only serve to get me arrested. Ernie would love that.

As we stood between "my" building and the one next to it, staring up at a high window, Lulu said, "Wait. I think I hear something."

Standing still as a stone statue, I listened as hard as I could. "Is that someone crying?" I asked, getting worried.

"Don't know," said Lulu. "Oh, it's stopped." We stood still for another few seconds. "It's started again. It sounds like…" Lulu cocked her head. "It sounds like little kids talking in Chinese."

And, by golly, it did. Ever so faintly, I too heard what I believed to be voices.

And then a window in the building next to the one we were scrutinizing opened and a little girl leaned out. "Are you two interested in renting that place? It's a real mess."

The noise of other children behind the little girl floated out to us on the chilly afternoon air.

"Huh," said Lulu. "Guess we did hear something, only it didn't come from this building but that one."

I called to the child, who still leaned out the window. "No, thanks! We were just…looking at the place. Does anybody live in it?"

"No one I know of. It seems empty. We're just moving in here because my parents are opening a shop downstairs."

"Oh. Good luck to your parents," I said, smiling at the girl.

"Thanks," she said with a perky grin.

"This building looks pretty dilapidated," I said. "Hard to imagine anyone living in it."

"You can say that again," said the little girl with a laugh, and she shut her window.

I didn't bother saying it again.

Lulu finally said, "Let's go shopping."

So we did.

I could have *sworn* the sounds I heard came from the supposed-to-be-empty building though. Drat.

NINETEEN

M r. Fong's shop was a wonderland of Chinese beauty. He had furniture and goddesses and jewelry and some absolutely gorgeous vases he told me were "cloisonné." Mr. Fong explained cloisonné items were made of copper filaments glued or soldered to a metal surface. In the items he made, the metal surface was copper. Anyhow, the gluing or soldering process created little compartments he filled with ground glass blended with some kind of oxide—I couldn't remember everything he said—in order to produce the glorious and colorful enamels.

Picking up one that particularly pleased me, I asked, "Do these vases hold water?"

With a gentle smile, Mr. Fong said, "Not many of them actually hold water. They're mainly for display in windows. The sun shining through them can be astonishingly beautiful."

"They're astonishingly beautiful all on their own," I said.

I wanted to buy the vase. It cost more than a hundred dollars, and I was with Lulu. If I bought the vase right then, it might seem as though I were flaunting my wealth in her face, and I didn't want to do that. "I especially love this one," I said wistfully as I gently set the vase back on the table from which I'd lifted it.

"It costs a fortune," muttered Lulu. "Think of all the clothes you could buy with that money."

"Think of all the clothes *you* could buy with it," I said tartly. "I'm not as in love with clothes as you are, Lulu."

"True," said Lulu, gazing at me with what looked an awful lot like despair.

"Oh, come on," I said, laughing. "I'm not all *that* dowdy!"

"Well, you're not too dowdy anymore, for sure," she said, also laughing.

"Oh, look over there, Lulu!" I cried, having spotted some red Chinese paper lanterns on the other side of the shop. "Lanterns."

"Let's get some," said Lulu, instantly taking off for the other side of the store.

Like a flash, I picked up the magnificent cloisonné vase, turned, and whispered to Mr. Fong, "Can you please hold this for me? I'll come back tomorrow and pick it up. Promise. Would you like a down payment?"

Chuckling, Mr. Fong said, "No. I can see you are an honest young woman. I'm particularly pleased you chose this one. It was one of the last cloisonné items my grandfather made. It will give me a pang to give it up." He winked at me. "But I'll console myself with the price it brings."

I smiled back at him. "Good idea. Thank you very much."

"You're very welcome," he said, and took the vase from my hands.

I rushed to catch up with Lulu, who was marveling at a display containing, not merely red Chinese paper lanterns, but some really pretty Christmas decorations, too.

"Look!" she cried, lifting a box full of beautiful glass ornaments that looked as if they'd been hand-painted by a Chinese artist. "These don't look like what I'm used to for Christmas, but they're sure pretty."

"They are," I agreed. "I'll get them. Is there more than one box? These will be gorgeous on our tree."

"You're going to buy them?" asked Lulu. "They're kind of expensive."

"I don't care. If I'm careful, they'll last for the rest of my life." And so would my fantastically expensive cloisonné vase, by golly. I didn't say so to Lulu.

"That's true," said Lulu judiciously, as if my pointing out the salient fact that the delicate glass ornaments would last for years took the sting out of their cost, not to mention the other salient fact that it was my money we were using.

"I think I'll buy two boxes of these. Or— Oh, look! Here's a box of glass ornaments, only they're painted differently. I'll get two of the one and one of the other."

"Good idea," said Lulu, clasping her hands behind her back and looking wistful, as if she wished she could afford to buy all those ornaments. Believe it or not, I knew how she felt; if not about money, about many other things.

We wandered around Mr. Fong's shop for at least another thirty minutes, by the end of which time we'd gathered so many things we couldn't live without for Christmas that we couldn't carry them all. But it was all right. Mr. Fong and I already had a deal about the cloisonné vase I aimed to buy. He said he'd be happy to hold the rest of our purchases until the next day, when I planned to drive my car to work. That way I could then drive it to Chinatown and—I prayed like mad Lulu would go with me—not only pick up everything we'd bought, but get into that building somehow. I'd bring a flashlight and…and…and Mr. Buck! What a brilliant idea!

Anyway, Lulu and I had a good time combing through most of the trinket shops in Chinatown. We ran into Ernie on the other side of Hill Street when we exited a shop selling a ton of Christmas decorations

"Hey, Ern!" Lulu called when we saw him walking toward Hill Street. He looked glum from the back—which was what we could see of him—with his head bowed and his hands in his pockets.

When he heard Lulu's salutation, he turned around and frowned at us. But he started walking our way, so I guess he wasn't displeased to see us.

"Glad you're here. I didn't feel like tramping all over Chinatown again trying to find the two of you," he said grumpily. "Still have to stop by Charley's and pick up Junior's dinner."

"You didn't have much luck?" I asked, feeling guilty for having had so much fun with Lulu while Ernie was attempting to find a murderer and clear Charley Wu's name.

"Actually," said Ernie, still sounding grumpy for some reason, "I got a couple of good tips. Not sure the police will give a rap about them, though."

"Why wouldn't they?" I asked, puzzled.

"Because they don't give a rap about the people in Chinatown, is why."

"Oh, that can't be entirely true, surely!" I said, aghast. "Phil cares, doesn't he?"

"Yeah. Phil's one man in a big, corrupt organization." He heaved an enormous sigh.

"Oh, dear," I said.

"I believe it," said Lulu with more than a hint of bitterness.

"Say, Mercy, do you mind if I invite myself over again tonight? You don't have to feed me, but Charley said Lily can translate those papers, and I want to know what they say."

"Sure," I said. "Happy to have you, and I know Mrs. Buck will be delighted."

"She will, will she?" Ernie sounded skeptical.

"She will. Honest."

"She will," confirmed Lulu.

"Okay then. After I drop off Junior's dinner, why don't I drive us all to your house?" He seemed to notice for the first time that Lulu and I were burdened with abundant paper parcels bound with string. "Here. Let me help you carry those."

"Thanks, Ernie," I said gladly. "Be careful. Some of the things we bought are fragile."

"Great," he said.

But he was cautious with our purchases, which he placed in the back seat of his Studebaker next to Lulu. I had to carry a couple of them on my lap because we'd kind of outdone ourselves in the shopping department. I doubted we'd even have to go to the Broadway to look for more Christmas ornaments, by golly. Well, maybe some that look less Asian and more American, but we'd just have to see after everything was set up in Mercy's Manor.

It didn't take us long to take Junior's dinner into the Figueroa Building. Glennie, who still manned the reception desk, was thrilled.

"Before I take us to your place," said Ernie to me. "I'm going to stop by the loony bin and talk to someone about Mr. Brentwood's vision. If it was a vision. If somebody besides him saw a girl in Chinatown with her hands tied, maybe it was true."

Merciful heavens, I'd forgotten all about poor Mr. Brentwood.

"Good idea," I said.

"Yeah," said Lulu. "I forgot all about that weird guy, too."

At least I wasn't the only one.

Ernie knew precisely where the…Not sure what to call it. Definitely won't call it a loony bin. Think I'll settle on "home." Anyway, Ernie knew precisely where the home was situated on Los Angeles Street. It was a huge white mansion, and he was correct in that it didn't have a sign advertising what it was used for. It did have a tall wrought-iron fence around it and a lovely wrought-iron gate. The gate was locked.

"Nuts," I said.

"No problem," said Ernie, who was wise to the ways of loony bins, I reckon, because he opened a white iron door to a white iron box situated on a pole next to the gate and pressed the button thereby revealed.

After several moments, some sounds came through a speaker tube and then someone inside the home said, "Yes?"

"My name is Ernest Templeton. I'm a private investigator, and Mr. Jerome Brentwood came to see me today. I'd like to speak to someone about what he told me during our appointment if that's possible."

"Our escapee," the person on the other end of the speaking wire said wryly. "Just a minute. Let me ask the matron."

"Thanks," said Ernie.

So we waited there in the bitter wind for what seemed like a century or three before more sounds came from the box and the same voice said, "I'll send out an attendant to unlock the gate. Matron will see you."

"Thank you," said Ernie. He sounded perfectly civil during this entire conversation, by the way. He only spoke sarcastically to me. Sometimes Lulu.

Not long after Ernie and the person in the home finished their conversation, a uniformed man wearing a warm jacket exited the front door of the mansion and hurried to the gate. He unlocked it and said, "Come on inside. It's cold out here."

"Yes," said Ernie, "it is. Thanks for letting us in."

"Matron wants to talk to you," said the man.

Well, this was interesting. Whoever Matron was, it was gratifying to know she wanted to talk to us as much as we wanted to talk to her. Maybe. For all I knew, the man was fibbing.

However, he hadn't fibbed. He led us inside the home and down a few corridors, then stopped at a door sporting a sign with the word "Matron" engraved on it. He knocked once, then opened the door and showed us into the matron's office, which looked quite efficient. I approved.

The woman behind the desk stood and said, "Mr. Templeton? Did I understand your name correctly?"

"Yes, and this is Miss Allcutt, my secretary, and Miss LaBelle, another associate."

Lulu would be pleased to have been called an associate, I'm sure.

"I'm glad you visited," said the matron. "I'm Mrs. Wilkes, and I've been concerned about Mr. Brentwood ever since we had an outing in Chinatown a week and a half ago."

"So this involves Chinatown, does it?" said Ernie, all interest. He withdrew a pad and pencil from his inside coat pocket. I noticed he had to flip the pad's pages more than halfway in order to find a clean sheet. Guess he *had* been busy learning things that day.

"Yes," said Mrs. Wilkes. "We like to take our guests—the ones who are able—to interesting places in and around Los Angeles. We took a group to Chinatown a week and a half ago. Poor Mr. Brentwood became terribly upset by something he saw—or thinks he saw—there." She shook her head as if in frustration. "The problem is, nobody else saw what he said he saw, and his communication skills are such that we can't quite figure out what it was he meant. Something about a girl with black hair and bound hands. He might be confusing bound hands with the old Chinese custom of binding women's feet. I just don't know. And then he managed to get out yesterday and frightened us all. The poor fellow has varied capabilities. He certainly found his way to your office, Mr. Templeton."

"Yes, he did."

"Which sounds enterprising of him," I said in Mr. Brentwood's defense. Poor man. I appreciated Mrs. Wilkes's generosity in calling his abilities "variable." Diplomatic.

"It was enterprising," said Mrs. Wilkes dryly, "but people pay a lot of money to place their unfortunate relations in this institution, and we do our very best to keep them happy and *confined*. They really can't be allowed to roam around the city. Well, you probably found that out for yourself."

"Yes," said Ernie, "we did. But I think Mr. Brentwood really did see something of interest to my investigative service. And, perhaps, the police."

"Oh, dear," said Mrs. Wilkes. "We don't want any police involvement with our guests! That would be terrible."

"I'm sure we can manage to keep Mr. Brentwood's name out of the papers," said Ernie. "But I would like to know approximately where he saw what he believed was a woman with her hands bound."

"Hmm," said Mrs. Wilkes, tapping the end of a pencil on her desk blotter. "Mr. Collins was one of the people who went with the group of guests, and he's here this afternoon. Perhaps he can give you an idea of where the group was when Mr. Brentwood saw whatever it was he saw."

"I'd appreciate it, ma'am," said Ernie.

"Very well. Let me ring the second ward," said Mrs. Wilkes and did so. At least I presume she did, because shortly after she picked up the receiver and dialed a number, she spoke to someone on the telephone. "Yes," she said. "Please have Mr. Collins come to my office. It's regarding the Chinatown trip and Mr. Brentwood's disturbance."

We didn't have long to wait. After a very few minutes, a tap came at Mrs. Wilkes's door, and a uniformed man came in. He removed his cap and gave a nod to Mrs. Wilkes.

And by golly, according to Mr. Collins, Mr. Brentwood saw the bound woman who had so disturbed him not far from Chew's Grocery Store as the "guests" of the home walked from where their small caravan had parked on Yale Street to Chinatown.

TWENTY

When Ernie finally pulled into the drive at Mercy's Manor that evening, I noticed someone had hung a lovely wreath on the front door. Because only Mrs. Buck and Lily were home during the day, I suspected Lily had created the wreath. I hoped she hadn't hung it, which would have exposed her (however briefly) to the outside world. When we lugged everything into the house, my suspicions were proved correct.

"It's beautiful, Lily! You're so artistic," I told her.

Buttercup yipped her approval, too, and I bent to pick her up and lavish kisses upon her curly head.

"I love doing stuff like that. I waited for Mr. Buck to come home so he could hang it on the door because I didn't dare go outside."

"Good for you," said Ernie, who was carrying the last of our packages into the tiled entryway.

I set Buttercup down so Ernie could greet her properly, which he did. However aggravating my employer might be at times, he at least always gave Buttercup her due. I appreciated his consideration. So did Buttercup.

Sue and Caroline must have heard us arrive, because they

showed up in the entryway shortly after we entered the house. Instantly I felt guilty. "I'm really sorry we didn't tell you not to meet us at the Figueroa Building," I said to them both. "I didn't know Ernie was going to haul us all over Chinatown this afternoon."

"Hey!" said Ernie.

Laughing, Sue said, "It's all right. Glynis, the nice girl who sat at the reception desk, told Caroline and me that you had to go out and investigate something."

"Yes, she was correct."

"Huh," said Ernie.

"Very well, so Ernie did most of the investigating. Lulu and I shopped. And we got so many Christmas decorations, too! Most of them are for the tree, but there are a few ornaments to set here and there around the house as well."

"What fun," said Sue, sounding eager.

"At my parents' house," said Caroline, "we use all the ornaments collected over the generations. Some of them aren't worth much, but they're precious to us because they've been loved for so long."

My heart gave a spasm. "That must be so nice," I said, sounding wistful to my own ears. "I wouldn't want anything from my parents' home. My experiences during my childhood weren't especially loving."

"What a shame," said Caroline sympathetically. "According to Lulu, your parents aren't...aren't...well, warm and loveable."

"And *that's* putting it mildly," said Ernie, handing me the last parcel. Lulu, Sue, Caroline and I had been carrying them into the living room and setting them on various tables as Ernie brought them from the Studebaker. "They're kind of like Mr. and Mrs. Grizzly Bear."

"I don't know who they are," said Caroline. She sounded as if she honestly believed there was a couple by that name extant some-where in the U.S.A.

"Ernie's kidding, Caroline," I explained. "Grizzly bears are supposed to be mean and crabby. So are my parents."

"Golly," said Sue. "What a shame."

"But I don't want to think about them," I told everyone. "I'm going to go upstairs and get out of my work clothes. Then, as Mrs. Buck prepares our meal"—I was still full from lunch, but didn't want to explain why to Caroline and Sue—"maybe we can open these packages and decorate the tree and the house."

"Sounds like a good plan to me," said Lulu. "I want to get out of these shoes. I didn't know I'd be walking for miles and miles today when I dressed for work this morning."

I glanced at her footwear and grimaced. "Golly, Lulu, you should have told me to stop dragging you all over the place!"

With a shrug, Lulu said, "Naw. It was worth it. I'll just wear my slippers this evening."

"Am I the one who has to tell Mrs. Buck I'm barging in on another of her dinners?" asked Ernie, sounding peeved.

"Oh, for heaven's sake!" I said. "Mrs. Buck would love it if you did, but if you're afraid of her, I'll tell her."

"I'm not afraid," claimed Ernie, lying through his teeth.

To spare him any mortification, before I went upstairs to change, I walked to the kitchen with a playful Buttercup dancing at my feet.

Mrs. Buck, standing at the range and stirring something that smelled wonderful and which resided in a big pot, turned and grinned at me. "Let me guess," she said. "Mr. Ernie's staying for dinner tonight."

"Right you are," I said. "He had a hard day investigating that murder in Chinatown."

Mrs. Buck's face sobered and she nodded. "Good for him. If anybody can find the real killer of that man, it's Mr. Ernie."

"I suppose so," I said, although I wanted to tell her how helpful I'd been a few times. "It sure smells good in here. What are you fixing us for dinner?"

"They had a good sale on hams at the market, so I picked up a ham big enough for all of us for Christmas dinner."

"It will last that long?" I asked, surprised.

"They're smoked, child, and you have to hang them in order to get the moisture out. Otherwise, they'll get moldy."

Ew. I didn't know that.

Mrs. Buck continued, "Mr. Buck hung it in the cellar, and it'll be just fine come Christmas. The butcher cut me up some smaller ham steaks, so I'm fixing those for tonight's dinner. There will be leftovers, so I'm going to fix up some red beans and rice for tomorrow. I've never fixed red beans and rice for you girls, but I'll bet you'll like it a lot."

"I've never even heard of red beans and rice, but if you fix it, I'm sure we'll love it," I told her. "What's in the big pot?"

"Greens," said Mrs. Buck firmly. "I've never fixed you greens, either, but I figured it's about time to expand your eating tastes. I've got buttered beets to go with the ham, and I cooked up the greens, too. They're in this pot."

"I didn't even know you could cook beet greens," I said, amazed. "You really need to teach me to cook one of these days, Mrs. Buck."

She turned from the range and pierced me with her dark gaze. "You really mean it, don't you, child?"

"Yes," I said passionately. "I mean it! I want to know how to cook. I mean, anything might happen in this old world and if I'm ever left to fend for myself, I want to be able to do it. The good Lord knows, nobody else in my family could fend for him or herself if anything happened to their bags of money."

After a second or two as, I guess, she pondered my words, Mrs. Buck said, "Then I'll be happy to teach you to cook, Miss Mercy. I think you'll be good at it."

"Thank you." I felt my cheeks heat, but that might just have been because the kitchen was warm on that cold December evening.

So I went back to the living room where Caroline and Sue, who had already changed from their work clothes to their at-home duds, were excavating packages. Ernie was throwing a ball for Buttercup, a game she loved. I walked over to him. He looked up from his crouch and said, "Everything jake with Mrs. Buck?"

"As jake as jake can be," I said, eyeing my dog as she bounded across the living room floor and into the dining room. She grabbed her ball and raced back to Ernie. "You've taken over my dog," I told him crossly.

"Hey, I like dogs. I can't have one in my apartment."

"Well, all right then. Play with her. I'm going up to change." I turned to Caroline and Sue, who were exclaiming rapturously over the many trinkets they were unwrapping. "Do you like what we found so far?"

"These are wonderful!" said Sue, holding up a glass ornament with a beautiful poinsettia flower painted on it. "I've never seen anything like these. You say you got them in Chinatown?"

"We did indeed. Mr. Fong's shop. I recommend browsing in his place. He has absolutely beautiful merchandise in there."

"Mr. Fong?" said Caroline.

"Yes. I like his shop best of all the shops we visited in Chinatown."

"Goodness, that's quite an endorsement," said Sue. "And look at this glass pinecone! How do they shape these things anyway?"

"I have no idea. I guess there are glass blowers who can do pretty much anything with glass. Or maybe they're molded. I honestly don't know anything about how Christmas ornaments are made," I said.

I finally made it to the staircase and began walking up. Only then did I truly understand how tiring the day had been. As I trudged up those stairs, I felt as though I'd walked miles. Probably had, actually. I cheered up considerably when Ernie threw Buttercup's ball upstairs and she raced up to get it. What's more, when she picked it up she followed me to my room. It was nice to know I hadn't been abandoned by my dog.

Dinner was a smashing success. Mrs. Buck had made what she called a sweet-potato pie for dessert, too, and had whipped up some cream to dollop on top of it. What with two days of enormous lunches and dinners, I decided I might want to take it easy for the next couple of days or I'd be fat as a pig and unable to fit into my clothes soon.

After dinner, we all retired to the living room. Lulu, Ernie and I were bushed after our busy day of tromping around Chinatown, so we pretty much let Lily, Sue and Caroline decorate the Christmas tree for us. Mr. Buck got out the step ladder, threaded electric lights among the branches—no candles to burn my house down, thank you—and clipped ornaments on the higher boughs.

"I put water in the holder twice today," said Lily.

"Thank you," I said, marveling at the girl. She must miss her family, but she sure didn't complain.

"The tree drinks a lot of water," she said. "Cousin Fung told me to check it often so the needles don't dry up and fall off." She patted a nearby branch. "This is a nice fresh tree, so it should last really well."

"How good of your cousin to give us a fresh tree," I said.

"I told him he'd better or I'd burn down all the trees on his lot," said Lily with a laugh.

"You didn't!" I said, horrified.

"No," she said, still grinning. "I didn't."

"I'm glad." I walked to a chair a few yards from the tree and collapsed into it.

Ernie, who had sat himself on a sofa with his long legs sprawled out before him, and who looked absolutely exhausted, said, "Can we borrow Lily for a bit to go over these notes?"

"Oh, my, I forgot the notes," I said, almost too tired to lift my overstuffed body from my chair. "I'll fetch her from decorating duties."

"And I'll go get the notes in my handbag," said Lulu without enthusiasm. Didn't blame her. She had to climb the stairs again in order to get to her handbag. Ah, well. Nobody ever said life was easy. Actually, I don't know that for a fact, but it makes sense.

As Lulu headed for the staircase, I shoved myself out of my chair—with an embarrassing grunt—and shuffled over to the Christmas tree.

"How does it look?" asked an eager Sue, who had just hooked what looked like a bright red, blown-glass Father Christmas on a middle branch.

"It looks absolutely wonderful," I said, meaning it with all my heart. In actual fact, I had to fight tears. This was the first time in my life I'd had a Christmas tree I cared about, mainly because I could decide what decorations to put on it. No more silver and white "elegance," but multicolored beauty.

My mother would be horrified. Yet one more thing to be happy about.

"Lily," I said as Lily hung a glass ball on the tree, "would you mind talking to Ernie and me for a minute? Maybe you can help us."

Instantly Lily's smile vanished, and it occurred to me she might have merely been putting on a pretense of good cheer. After all, it was her brother who was in jeopardy, and I know Lily cared about him.

"Sure. Be right there."

What a tidy girl she was! She didn't just leave the chair upon which she'd placed a box of ornaments (bought that very day from Mr. Fong's shop), but she was about to move the box and carry the chair back into the dining room when Sue said, "Oh, just leave it there. We'll use those eventually."

"Okay," Lily said, sounding cheerful again.

"Thanks, Lily," I said in a low voice as we walked over to where Ernie continued to sprawl on the sofa.

Lulu joined Ernie at about the same time Lily and I reached the sofa. She held approximately one and a half inches' worth of various sizes and colors of paper.

With a grunt of his own, Ernie pushed himself up and said, "Is there any place private where we can go over this stuff?"

"Sure. My office is private."

"Whatever do you have there?" asked Lily, peering at the stack of paper in Lulu's grip.

"Information your brother gathered from other shopkeepers and businessmen in Chinatown," said Ernie.

"Good old Charley," said Lily, beaming. "I figured if Uncle Hop could bail him out, he'd do his best to discover who killed that awful pig-man."

179

"You were correct," said Ernie. "But a lot of these are in Chinese, and nobody except you can read them for us."

"Happy to," said Lily, and we all retired to my office. Poor Ernie had to lug in another chair, but it probably did his digestion some good.

TWENTY-ONE

E rnie sat behind my desk in my chair, but I didn't object. He had a pocket stuffed full of notebooks and notes of his own. Lulu and I both set our stacks of papers on the desk.

"Mercy, I'll organize these notes I took. Why don't you go through the papers you and Lulu have and sort out the Chinese ones from the English ones. Then maybe you can take notes on whatever we find in all of this paperwork."

"All right," I said, "but I need to get into my top desk drawer for a pad so I can write down the information."

"Right," said Ernie, shoving the chair he occupied back from the desk and opening the drawer. "Shoot, you're neat. Everything's all organized in here."

"Of course, it is," I told him with a sniff. "My desk at my place of employment is equally tidy."

"Well, aren't you just the cat's meow," said a sarcastic Ernie.

"No. I'm an organized professional secretary," I snapped back.

"Right," said Ernie. "Didn't mean to snipe at you, Mercy. I'm just worn out."

"I'm sure we all are," I said, forgiving him, although I didn't tell him so.

Then, as Lily sat as still as a statue of Kwan Yin, whom she somewhat resembled, Lulu, Ernie and I sorted through all the papers Ernie'd gathered during the day, and Ernie read through the notes he'd taken. Lulu and I soon had a stack of Chinese notes higher than the stack of notes written in English.

"Want me just to give them to Lily?" I asked Ernie.

"Yeah. And Lily, you tell Mercy what the notes say. If names are mentioned, give her the names to write down. I might have to talk to some more people tomorrow."

"Very well," said Lily, and she did so.

"My goodness," I muttered after we'd been going through Chinese notes for fifteen minutes or so. "I didn't know Chan Sien Lo had tried to blackmail so many families."

"Neither did I," said Lily grimly. "I'm glad somebody shot him."

"So am I," said Lulu, who had been reading through the notes written in English. "This man seems to have claimed everybody in the entire Chinese community owed him debts of dead relatives, the creepy sneaker."

"Are you writing down the names, too, Lulu?" asked Ernie.

"That's what this"—she held up a pencil—"and this"—she held up a pad of paper—"are for. You think I'm an idiot, Ernie Templeton?"

"No," said a plainly weary Ernie. "Just wanted to be sure."

"Huh," said Lulu.

It took us another forty-five minutes or so, but after comparing all the information gathered from the separate pieces of paper and Ernie's two—he'd filled up *two*—notebooks, we had dozens of names we hadn't had before.

"Sheesh. It's going to take me days to track all of these people down and talk to them."

"Have Uncle Yu take you around. I'll give him a call and tell him not to go to the foothills tomorrow, but to go with you and talk to people about Chan Sien Lo."

"Doesn't your other uncle need the trees?" I asked.

"Hmm. Maybe you're right. Uncle Shen might be better. He

and Uncle Hop have lots of help in the restaurant. I'll give him a call."

"Thanks, Lily," said Ernie. "Will I just ask for him at Hop Luey's?"

"Yeah. I'll tell him to expect you." She gave Ernie a penetrating look up and down. "I'll describe you to him, so he might recognize you."

Ernie slapped a hand across his chest. "Me? He wouldn't recognize *me* if I gave him my name?"

"He might forget your name, although he probably won't. But you whites all look alike to us until we get to know you."

"I've heard that before," I muttered. "This very day, in fact."

"And you thought it was only white people who thought all of us Chinese looked alike, didn't you?" asked Lily with a laugh.

"Pretty much. How silly of me, huh?"

"You just need to know people before you can distinguish them from each other," said Lily. "May I use your telephone?"

"Absolutely," I said, reaching for the candlestick and placing it in front of Lily. Ernie had to pick up a notebook so as not to have it swept to the floor. He frowned at me, but I pretended not to see him.

"Is ten o'clock tomorrow morning a good time to meet?" asked Ernie.

"I don't know, but I'll ask," said Lily.

Lily held the receiver to her ear as she used the dial at the base of the candlestick to call a number. When somebody picked up the wire on the other end, a flood of Cantonese filled the air, some from Lily and some from the various people on the other end. I guess whoever answered the telephone at the restaurant had to holler for Uncle Shen because I heard some shouting. After that, silence reigned for maybe a minute. Then I presume Uncle Shen showed up and took the receiver because the flow of rapid-fire Cantonese resumed. Lily spoke fast and gesticulated quite dramatically. If it was Uncle Shen on the other end, he spoke dramatically. I couldn't understand his words, but they sounded emphatic. Finally Lily said something that might have been "good-bye" and hung the receiver on its cradle.

"Whew!" she said, wiping the back of her hand across her pristine brow. "Uncle Shen sure talks a lot." She turned to Ernie. "Okay, he won't be able to leave the restaurant tomorrow but his son, my cousin Dishi, will be glad to drag you around to see everybody on your list." She pointed at the tablet Ernie held. He'd covered pages with names and notes gleaned from Lulu's, Lily's and my efforts. And his own, too, of course. "And ten o'clock is fine."

"At least we've pretty much discovered that the dead man had intended opening a brothel in Chinatown," I muttered, not even blushing when I said the word "brothel."

"Looks like it, all right," said Ernie.

"Creep," said Lulu.

"Beast," said Lily.

"All right," said Ernie, still sounding and looking weary. "I'd better get going. Thanks for translating, Lily. Thanks for your help, Lulu. And thanks for dinner, Mercy."

"Mrs. Buck's the one to thank for dinner. I just helped eat it. But she promises to teach me to cook."

"Hope you end up as good a cook as she is," said Ernie.

He didn't sound sarcastic. I squinted at him, and he didn't look sarcastic either, so I said, "Thank you. See you at eight tomorrow morning."

"Yeah," he said. "Maybe you will."

Lulu and I laughed. Lily only gazed at us as if we'd lost our minds. She wasn't accustomed to Ernie's work habits, as Lulu and I were.

So we left my office and revisited the living room. Decorating hadn't stopped while the four of us had been busy. Sue and Caroline had adorned the tree gorgeously. There were a few places on it that might be filled in with some more ornaments, but it sure looked pretty.

"Oh, that's so nice!" I cried as soon as I saw it.

"Beautiful!" said Lulu.

"Lovely," said Lily.

"Wow," said Ernie. "It looks really good." He sounded almost stunned.

"It'll look even better in a second," said Mr. Buck. And darned if he didn't bend over and plug in a string of lights that looked like multicolored flowers.

I swear a whole chorus of "Aaahs" went up. Even Mrs. Buck, who stood in the doorway leading to the dining room, aahed. I then decided to get the Bucks a Christmas tree for their own apartment, if they didn't already have one.

Or would that be officious?

Bother. I didn't know. I'd ask Ernie. He'd probably know. But I'd have to do it tomorrow because we were all about to drop dead from exhaustion.

Sue and Caroline had packed everything away after they'd finished decorating the tree and it was a tidy, Christmas-bedecked living room we walked through when we saw Ernie to the door.

"Do you have a tree in your apartment, Ernie?" I asked, sure he'd say he didn't. I was right.

"No. What would I do with a Christmas tree?"

"Put presents under it?"

"You kidding me? All I'd do is bump into it. My apartment's pretty small, kiddo."

I hated when he called me kiddo.

He knew it, so he hurriedly said, "I mean Mercy."

"Don't you get presents from your family in Chicago?" I asked, feeling kind of sorry for Ernie.

"The only member of my family I can stand is my sister, and we exchange gifts at Christmas. That's it except for Pauline." Pauline was Phil Bigelow's lovely wife.

"Do you go to the Bigelows' place for Christmas?" I asked.

"Yeah. Pauline's a good cook, and she fixes a big dinner on Christmas day."

"I see," I said, furiously making plans in my fuddled head. "Well, that's nice."

"Yeah."

We'd made it to the front door, Buttercup leading the way. When I noticed Lily with us, I made her leave the entryway.

"It might be a stupid precaution, but anybody out there might be able to see inside the entryway and on the porch because the lights are on. If anyone *is* snooping, I don't want whoever it is to see you."

"Good idea," said Ernie.

"Okay," said the ever-amiable Lily.

I walked Ernie out to his car. Lulu didn't. I have a feeling her feet were protesting her having walked all over Chinatown in high heels during the day.

"Thanks, Ernie," I said when we reached the Studebaker.

"What for?"

"For helping Charley Wu and going to all this trouble for him and Lily."

"Charley's a pal of mine, and Lily's a nice kid. Thank *you* for giving her a job."

"Well, I guess. Anyway, see you tomorrow."

"Right. Tomorrow."

He leaned over and gave me a quick peck on the cheek. I almost fell over dead in surprise. I couldn't speak but it didn't matter, because he got in his car and backed out of my driveway, gave a tootle on his horn, and sped off back Chinatown-way and to his apartment.

When I went back into my house, it seemed as if everyone except Buttercup had vanished. Guess they'd all gone to bed. Then I saw Lily sitting at the bottom of the staircase. She glanced up at me, and her eyes looked kind of wettish.

"Are you all right, Lily?" I said, sitting next to her. Buttercup leapt upon my lap, and both Lily and I petted her.

"Yes. Thank you. In fact, I can't thank you enough for helping Charley and me the way you're doing. And Mr. Templeton, too. I didn't think there was *one* white person in the City of Los Angeles who cared if a Chinese man got murdered, much less who murdered him. If it weren't for you and Mr. Templeton and Lulu, Charley would have been convicted. I know it."

How disheartening. "I'm sorry, Lily. Human beings have been hating each other for no reason for as long as they've existed, I guess."

"You're right. And we Chinese are no better than you whites. Why, the only reason we're polite to you in Chinatown is because you're there to buy our wares or eat our food. I think most of the Chinese in the area would as soon you all died."

"Good Lord," I said, stunned.

"Not me!" Lily hurried to say. "I know better. So does Charley. That's because he's come to know Mr. Templeton. Why, Mr. Templeton even plays baseball with the Chinatown *Guàn Jūn* team sometimes."

"What does *guàn jūn* mean?" I asked, curious.

"Champion." Lily laughed softly. "So they're the Chinatown Champs, I guess. The other Chinatown team is called the China-town *Shèng Lì Zhě*s. And that means they're the Chinatown Victors. Obviously, sometimes one team wins and the other loses, so their names aren't always appropriate."

"I'll be darned," I said. "Ernie told me he played baseball with Charley sometimes, but I didn't know there were two organized baseball teams in Chinatown."

"Oh, yes. Naturally, no Chinese man would ever be allowed on an American baseball team."

"Right," I said glumly. "Naturally. Nor a Negro or a Mexican man."

"True. So Charley and I already knew not all whites were wicked people, but boy, you couldn't tell that if you just went by the Los Angeles Police Department or half the white people who visit Chinatown."

"I'm sorry, Lily. Honestly, I never much thought about how lucky I was to have been born white until I moved to Los Angeles. But I am lucky. If I were another color, I wouldn't own this lovely house. I wouldn't be working as a secretary for Ernie. I mean, there are all sorts of things I can do and all sorts of places I can go merely because I'm white. I could be the devil incarnate, but if I were white, it wouldn't matter."

"Oh, Mercy, I didn't mean to make you feel bad," said Lily, putting a slender arm around my shoulders.

"It's all right," I said. "The mess the world is in isn't my fault, I guess, but I certainly have come to recognize my good fortune since I moved from Boston to Los Angeles."

"You're one of the good people, Mercy," said Lily, as if she'd already sorted the world's inhabitants into categories.

"Thanks, Lily. So are you."

We grinned at each other. Then I lifted Buttercup off my lap and set her on the staircase. "Come on, Buttercup. Let's go to bed. I'm about to fall asleep on my feet."

"I'm tired, too," said Lily, so we walked up the stairs together, following the much more bumptious Buttercup, who frolicked up the staircase as if she hadn't a care in the world. She probably didn't.

TWENTY-TWO

Buttercup and I slept like a couple of rocks Tuesday night. On Wednesday morning, I not only recalled the gorgeous cloisonné vase waiting for me at Mr. Fong's shop, but I also recalled my intention of getting into that blasted building across from the grocery store in Chinatown. I hoped like heck nobody with a gun would greet me if I managed to do so.

In preparation for my intended adventure, I asked Mrs. Buck if I could borrow a hammer. She looked at me askance. "What you want with a hammer, child?"

"There's some stuff I want to do at the office, and I need to hammer in a couple of nails," I lied.

I didn't like fibbing to Mrs. Buck. For one thing, she was too perceptive and I knew she didn't believe me, although she didn't say so. What she said was, "Huh. All right. Go get a hammer out of the tool cupboard in the utility room."

So I did. While I was gazing around at the neatly arranged tools, I decided I could use a couple of other things. So I grabbed a heavy pry bar and an almost equally heavy wrench. Then I didn't know what to do with them, so I put them and the hammer aside and decided to drive my car to the rear of the house closest to the utility room and put the tools on the floor of the back seat.

"What are you doing?" asked Lulu as I walked into the dining room from the kitchen, where Mrs. Buck was scrambling eggs for our breakfast.

"I'm going to drive the car to work today. I can take all of us."

Rats. One of my tenants might mention the tools on the floor of the back seat. But I'd think of a plausible excuse. I hoped.

"That why you're not dressed yet?" Lulu asked with a yawn.

"You're not dressed, either," I pointed out. In actual fact, Lulu wore one of the Chinese robes she'd bought at one time or another in Chinatown. I was in my own blue chenille robe which was pretty boring.

"Yeah, but you're more organized than I am," said Lulu. Then she squinted at me. "You're not telling me something, Mercy. Are you going to snoop around Chinatown again today? During the day?"

Dang. I grabbed Lulu by a silk-covered arm and whispered, "Come here. If you promise not to tell anyone, I'll let you in on what I'm going to do."

"Okay. I won't tell anybody." She gave me a sudden smile. "Maybe I can help you!"

"Maybe you can, although I don't want you to get hurt."

"Hurt?" Lulu gaped at me. "What're you going to do that might get you hurt? Listen, Mercy, if you're—"

"I'm not going to do anything that might get me hurt!" I barked at her—softly. "But I'm going to get into that building at the end of the street. The one that's supposed to be empty. That's why I'm taking the car. I'm putting some prying and battering tools on the floor of the back seat. In fact, you can *really* help me if you want to. Working together, we can probably pry some of the boards off one of those ground-floor windows and get inside the place."

"Why are you so dead-set on getting into that building?" Lulu asked as if she thought I was a raving lunatic.

"Listen, Lulu. I *know* I heard people in that building. It sounded like girls speaking Chinese. If the rest of us are locked *out* of the place, maybe there are people locked *in* it! Chan's dead, so he can't let them out if they aren't able to get out themselves."

"Why don't you ask Ernie to help you?" said Lulu, calmly and logically.

"I've *asked* Ernie. I even made him walk around the building with me. He thinks I'm nuts."

"So do I," said Lulu.

I heaved a huge sigh. "Very well, maybe I *am* nuts, but I'm not willing to risk leaving people to die in a building if they're in there and can't get out, darn it, Lulu Mullins."

Lulu screwed her face up until she looked like a pale prune. "Don't call me Mullins!"

"Lulu LaBelle, then. Will you help me? If you won't help me, will you at least not tell anyone my plans until I've figured out if anybody's in the building?"

She huffed. "Oh, all right. I'll help you. But what if the dead man has a partner or someone like that in the building? What if he grabs us and forces us into white slavery? What about that?"

"The granddaughter of the man who owns the grocery store across the street from the building says she hasn't seen the dead man's partner since the dead man...well, died. I think he's taken it on the lam or something."

"Why are you so convinced the empty building isn't empty?"

"I already told you!"

"All right, all right. Don't get mad at me. I'll help you. When are we going to do this? Lunch time? After work? It might be dark after work. That would be spooky."

"True, but there wouldn't be many people around. I'll take a flashlight. In fact, I'll take *two* flashlights. One for you and one for me." I cudgeled my brain to think of everything we might need, and added, "I'll bring extra batteries, too. There are some in the tool cupboard."

"I hope you're right about the dead guy's partner being gone," muttered Lulu as she turned away to go back upstairs to dress for work.

"Wear something warm!" I called to her back.

"Right," she said.

Then I wondered if Lulu *owned* anything warm, aside from her coat, scarf and gloves.

Oh, well, Lulu's wardrobe choices weren't my concern. I went outside and moved my 1924 Moon Roadster—which was a lovely blue color, by the way—from beside the front porch to the back of the house. There I made several trips from the tool cupboard to the car, eventually driving the car back to sit beside the front porch again. By then I was nearly frozen solid, and it occurred to me that rather than worrying about Lulu, I'd have been better off wearing my own woolen coat instead of merely my chenille robe. Ah, well.

Shivering, I went back to my bedroom and got into my working clothes. As I aimed to do some manual labor later in the day, I made sure to wear a sensible suit with a gored skirt. That would make moving around easy, and if I had to do any climbing, I wouldn't rip my skirt. Crumb, I hoped I wouldn't have to do any climbing. Ah, well. My course was set.

Naturally, Lulu looked at me askance when we happened to meet in the upstairs hallway to go down to breakfast. She wore a belted pullover sweater over a white blouse. She'd pulled out the blouse's lacy collar to frame the neck of the sweater. The sweater was a vivid red. Her black skirt was relatively full, I was happy to see. Guess she didn't want to rip anything either.

Unfortunately, my own costume was brown and dull. I noticed Lulu's squint and said, "I'm wearing it because it's comfortable, not because it's fashionable."

"Well, that's a good thing anyway," she said.

In other words, I couldn't win.

However, breakfast was delicious. Because of the cold weather, Mrs. Buck had made scrambled eggs and both sausages and bacon, along with toast with butter and three kinds of jam which, I believe, she made herself. The woman was a marvel.

At the table, I told everyone I'd be able to drive them to work, but that Lulu and I had plans to pick up some things in Chinatown after work, so they needn't come to the Figueroa Building, but just walk to Angels Flight by themselves. Unless they wanted to walk up that incredibly steep street instead. Both Caroline and Sue said they didn't mind paying a nickel to avoid the walk in the brisk weather.

"Good thinking," I told them both.

"What do you have to pick up in Chinatown?" asked Sue, always curious, darn it.

"We couldn't fit everything in Ernie's old Studebaker yesterday," I told them. "And I want especially to pick up some things I bought at Mr. Fong's shop, including something quite fragile. I was afraid it would break if I jumbled it with everything else yesterday."

"Among all those fragile Christmas ornaments, you mean?" said Sue skeptically.

"Oh, very well," I said, fumbling for an excuse I should have thought of already but hadn't, "I want to pick up a couple of Christmas presents."

"For you and Caroline," said Lulu, saving my bacon, although she seemed to be dining on a sausage at the moment.

"Oh, how sweet," said Caroline.

"Yes, that's so nice of you, Mercy," said Sue, beaming at me.

"Sure," said I, reminding myself to thank Lulu later.

After breakfast, we all went to our rooms to get our warm coats, scarves, hats and gloves, then said our good-byes to Mrs. Buck and Lily and trooped out to the Roadster. Because I didn't like backing up, I'd pointed the car streetwards when I'd driven it earlier, there being a place for turning around in back of the house.

"What's all this stuff on the floor back here?" asked Sue.

"Some tools I'm taking to Ernie," I said. "He said he and Mr. Buck are going to try to fix his Studebaker so it will last another few months."

"Oh," said Sue. "I think he needs to get another motorcar."

"Motorcars are expensive," said Caroline, the prudent and proper. "He's probably saving up to buy one."

"You're probably right," said Lulu from the front seat.

She then tipped me a wink, and I mouthed "Thank you" at her. She only grinned back at me.

We dropped Sue off at the building housing the dentist for whom she worked, then drove Caroline to Fourth and Broadway and let her out to work at the hosiery counter there. And then we made our way to the Figueroa Building.

Even though it was before eight o'clock in the morning, trying to find a place to park was a nightmare. However, after Mr. Buck hollered at me that he'd unlock the back door, I eventually prevailed by parking in the alleyway behind the building. The alleyway was far from my favorite place, as I'd seen a murder committed there a couple of months back. But one does what one must. Naturally, Mr. Buck had saved Ernie's parking place directly in front of the building. Oddly enough, Lulu and I had seen Ernie's Studebaker parked there when we'd arrived at our workplace.

"Shoot," said Lulu as we exited my Roadster. "Ernie's here already."

"I saw his car too. I guess he's serious about finding the real murderer of Mr. Chan Sien Lo and saving Charley Wu from the electric chair."

"Good for him. I like Charley's mother." Lulu chuckled. "She's a hoot."

"She's also a really good cook," I said.

"Wonder how she and Mrs. Buck would get along."

"Probably like…like red beans and rice," I said for some reason beyond my ken.

"Red beans and rice? What the heck are you talking about, Mercy Allcutt?"

"Mrs. Buck said she's going to prepare red beans and rice for us one of these days. Says it's a delicious dish and we'll all love it."

"Well, then, I guess Mrs. Wu and Mrs. Buck would get along fine," said Lulu.

Mr. Buck opened the back door to the Figueroa building just as we arrived at it. "Thanks, Mr. Buck!" I said cheerily.

"Thanks, Mr. Buck," said Lulu. Her voice was a trifle muffled because she'd drawn her black scarf over her lower face.

"You're more than welcome, ladies," said Mr. Buck. "Happy to do anything to help Miss Mercy and you, Miss Lulu."

Hmmm. For the merest second, I considered asking Mr. Buck to help Lulu and me break into the supposedly empty building in

Chinatown, but I suppressed the urge. Mr. Buck would certainly squeal on us to Ernie. Not on purpose, but because he didn't know we were keeping the evening's agenda from Ernie and didn't want him to know about it.

As Lulu and I walked through various corridors to the front of the building, Lulu said softly, "Do you think we should ask Mr. Buck to help us after work?"

Great minds and all that.

"No. He'd probably tell Ernie."

"Mr. Buck's not a snitch!" said Lulu, offended, unless I miss my guess.

"I know he's not, but he won't like it if we tell him we're keeping our purpose from Ernie. I don't want to put a burden on his conscience, because he probably *would* help us, and he'd feel guilty because I wouldn't let him tell Ernie."

"Huh?" said Lulu.

"Never mind," I said. "Let's just you and me see what we can do."

"Okay, but if we get killed by some crazy Chinaman, I'll never forgive you, Mercy Allcutt."

"I'll risk it," I said, trying not to giggle.

"It's not funny," Lulu announced huffily.

"I appreciate you agreeing to help me, but if you truly don't want to, please don't think you must, Lulu. I don't want both of us to get arrested for breaking and entering."

"Would the police arrest two respectable white ladies for breaking into an old building in Chinatown? I get the impression the Los Angeles Police Department doesn't care about anyone but their white residents. The Negroes, Chinamen and Mexicans can all go rot, is the impression I get from them."

With a miserable sigh, I said, "Yeah. Me, too."

"Huh," said Lulu, reminding me of Ernie.

But we'd made it to the lobby, so I left Lulu at the door. She continued to the reception desk and I turned to walk up the stairs to the third floor. The building was kind of cold that brisk December morning, but I trusted Mr. Buck to get the heater going soon.

The door to Ernest Templeton, P.I.'s office was unlocked when I got to it. Glancing at my wristwatch, I saw it was only five minutes to eight, so I was still early.

"Hey, Ernie," I called as I walked into the outer office. I shucked my hat and coat, stuffed my gloves into my coat pocket, and hung the hat and coat on the rack.

"Morning, Mercy," came Ernie's voice from his office. He sounded distracted, as if he were concentrating on something.

Curious, I stopped at his office door before I got to my desk. Peeping into his room, I saw him madly scribbling on a paper on his desk. The *Los Angeles Times* lay unopened beside the paper upon which he wrote. This was most unlike the Ernest Templeton I knew.

"Whatcha doing?" I asked.

"Trying to figure out who killed that bimbo in Chinatown. I'm trying to create some kind of timeline from the information we gathered yesterday."

How nice of him to say "we." "Are you having any luck?"

Slapping his pencil down on his paper, he growled, "No," and lifted his head to glare at me.

Backing away from his glare, I muttered, "Sorry," and retreated to my desk, where I stuck my handbag into the lower right-hand drawer. I hoped one day the drawer would be full to the brim with client files, even if I had to find another place to store my handbag. I *really* didn't want Ernie to go out of business for lack of work.

I heard rustlings coming from Ernie's office. I expected to hear the newspaper flap open and Ernie's feet hit his desk, but instead, he came to the door of his office. As he continued to glare, I wasn't sure what to do or say.

Finally, he said, "Do you really think there are people in the old building across from Chew's Grocery Store?"

Shocked, I sat up straight. "What?"

"You heard me," Ernie growled. "You do, don't you? And you're going to go down there and prowl around, aren't you?"

My mouth fell open, but nothing came out of it. Shock will do that to a person, I reckon.

"Don't lie to me, Mercy Allcutt. Mr. Buck told me about you gathering pry bars and flashlights this morning."

"He *what*?" I cried, shocked.

"He told me. The only reason I can think for you to be collecting tools is because you aim to go to that building, break in, and find your mythical voices."

"They aren't mythical, and how the heck did Mr. Buck know what I was doing in the utility room this morning?"

"Mrs. Buck called and told him. Because she knows you, she warned him he'd better tell me."

"My own *staff* is conspiring against me?" I bellowed, still shocked.

"Conspiring, hell! They're afraid you're going to get yourself killed, is what."

"Well, I'm not going to get myself killed!" I snarled, standing and bracing my palms on my desk. "If you'd only believe me, I wouldn't have to break into the stupid creepy building alone!"

"No. You'd take me with you, and we'd both get killed."

"Nobody's going to get killed!"

"How do you know that?"

We were both hollering by this time. We both also jumped several feet in the air when Phil Bigelow's voice came at us from the door to the front office.

"Cripes, kids, I could hear you clear down at the elevator," he said.

"What are you sneaking up on us for?" demanded Ernie.

"Yes!" I said. "*You* don't care that Charley Wu didn't kill that man! What do the *police* care if Chinese people get murdered? They'll just grab the nearest Chinese fellow they can find and arrest *him*!"

"That's not fair, Mercy," said Phil, frowning at me.

"The hell it's not," said Ernie, frowning at Phil.

"Yeah," I said, also frowning at Phil. "The hell it's not!"

TWENTY-THREE

I do believe hearing me utter the word "hell" so loudly made all three of us straighten up and shut our mouths. A bunch of glances flew from person to person to person and back again.

Then I cleared my throat and said, "Good morning, Detective Bigelow."

Ernie didn't bother being polite. "What're you doing here, Phil?"

"Cripes, you two don't give a guy a break, do you?"

"Under the circumstances," I said coldly, "no. Why should we?"

"Come on, Mercy. I heard the two of you were questioning people all over Chinatown yesterday, and I wanted to know if you discovered anything. Your friend Wu is out on bail, you know, Ernie. It's not like we're holding him in chains in a dungeon or anything."

"Huh," I said, reminding myself of Lulu.

"How kind and considerate of you," said Ernie. "Listen, Phil, I told you I wasn't going to do your job for you. Yeah, I walked all the hell over Chinatown yesterday, and I talked to about seven thousand Chinese people. I learned a lot. It's a shame the L.A.P.D. doesn't have one or two people who care about the Charley Wus of this world. If they did, they might have learned what I learned."

"That's not fair, Ernie," said Phil.

"It is, too," I said. Shoot, I was sure getting mouthy, wasn't I? "If your precious department gave a rap about people of color, you wouldn't have such a hard time getting information out of them, would you?"

With a huge sigh, Phil admitted, "Probably not."

"Well, then…." I wasn't sure what to say next, so I allowed my words to trail off.

The three of us stood in the office: I behind my desk, Ernie at his office door, and Phil at the front door, staring at each other for what seemed like several hours at least.

Finally, Ernie said, "Why'd you come to my office today?" Abrupt. This was far from Ernie's usual insouciant self. He was noticeably peeved about Charley Wu's problem and the part the police played in it.

"Another Chinese fellow showed up in the French Hospital with a gunshot wound. He let it go too long without treatment, and the doctors don't think he'll make it. Septicemia has already set in."

"So what?" Ernie asked.

"Looks as if this man was shot with the same kind of gun—probably the same gun—that killed the Chan guy. A Colt Positive 32 with a snub-nose barrel. Big hole in his leg. They dug out the bullet. A dumdum. It must have come from the same gun. Those guns are thin on the ground."

Silence filled the office. Tense silence. Silence you could twang like a violin string, if you were feeling poetic. I wasn't. I also wasn't about to speak until Ernie did.

Finally, he did. "You think Charley shot this guy, too?" His tone was sarcastic.

Shoulders slumping, Phil said, "I don't know, Ernie. It doesn't seem likely right now, but who can tell? Unless the fellow regains consciousness and we find an interpreter, we probably won't ever know."

"Huh," said Ernie, reminding me of me. "And you say the man's in the hospital and isn't expected to recover, right?"

"Right," said Phil. "So do you think you can share a little of the information you gathered yesterday?"

Ernie looked at me. I looked back at him. We both frowned, and I shook my head slightly.

The soon-to-be dead Chinese man in the hospital, shot with the same gun and the same kind of bullet used to kill Chan, was probably Chan's lone outrider. When Jade Chew cornered me in that nook in Chinatown, she spoke of seeing only one man besides Chan enter and leave the building across from her grandfather's grocery store. To my mind, this reinforced my notion that people might be trapped in the wretched, dingy Chinatown building, unable to get out. If I was right, whoever was in there must be in a pitiful plight.

At last, Ernie glanced away from me and pinned Phil with a cold glare. "No. No, I don't think I want to share any information we gathered with the L.A.P.D. I don't trust the L.A.P.D.—"

Offended, Phil cried, "You don't trust *me?*"

"You're only one man in a big department, Phil. I might trust you, but you and who else will be privy to my diggings?" Ernie shook his head. "No. Go talk to people yourself. I have more work to do."

"But—"

"Go away, Phil," said Ernie. "Mercy and I have a bunch of letters to write, and I have cases to solve. Why, one rich lady in Hancock Park lost an emerald brooch. You wouldn't want Mrs. High and Mighty to live for the rest of her life without her emerald brooch, would you? Hell, even the L.A.P.D. would probably try to find *her* stolen jewelry. Why try to find out who murdered a Chinese man when you can find an emerald brooch for a rich woman?"

"What?" said Phil. "Now listen here, Ernie—"

Ernie jerked his head at the door and interrupted Phil's protest. "Go away, Phil. I have work to do, and so does Mercy."

"Cripes," said a disgruntled Phil Bigelow. "All right, all right. I'll go. But you're not being fair, Ernie."

"Fair, shmair," said Ernie. "Tell it to the marines."

It only occurred to me later to wonder what the marines had to do with anything. I never did ask Ernie.

Phil said, "Cripes" again and left the office.

As soon as Phil shut the door behind himself, I opened my mouth to talk, but Ernie put his hand up and hushed me. He said softly, "I don't trust him not to listen at the keyhole, so wait until I check." He marched to the front office door and yanked it open, stepped into the hall, and looked both ways. Phil must have been near the elevator because Ernie lifted his hand in a gesture of farewell. It looked to me as if it was a gesture telling Phil not to come back, too, although perhaps I imagined that part.

After making sure Phil either got on the elevator or took the stairs, Ernie came back into the office and closed and locked the front door. "We don't have any appointments scheduled for today, do we?"

"No. I was out of the office almost all day yesterday, so I wasn't here to answer the telephone."

"Slacker," said Ernie. I was about to protest when he went on to say, "Well, you won't be here most of today, either. Get whatever you need to keep warm. Where'd you put all the tools you stole from your house?"

"I didn't steal anything from my house! Those are *my* tools!"

"Bet you've never used one of 'em in your life."

"So what? I bought them!"

"Just teasing you, kid—uh, Mercy. Where are they now?"

"On the floor of the back seat of my Roadster."

"Good. Let's take your Roadster. Most people in the L.A.P.D. recognize my car on sight, and I don't want them to know what I'm doing."

"Most of the citizens of the entire city of Los Angeles probably recognize your car on sight," I muttered. "You drive, okay?"

"Of course, I'll drive. I want to get there and back alive."

"You're the one who taught me to drive, darn it! I'm a good driver!"

"Yeah, yeah, yeah. Give me your key, and let's go to Chinatown. Maybe I can figure out who owns the building and get permission to enter it."

"That's a good idea," I said, never having thought of such a practical course of action. Guess I had some learning to do before I could become an efficient P.I.'s assistant.

"We'll stop by Charley's first. If he's not there, I expect Mr. Fong will know who owns the building." Ernie retreated to his office and came out with his coat, hat and gloves on.

I grabbed my handbag from my desk drawer, hurried to the coat rack next to the front door, and donned my own outerwear. I could pull my brown cloche hat down over my ears and keep them relatively warm. Then I recalled something.

"What about Dishi?"

"What about *what?*" snapped Ernie.

"Dishi. Lily and Charley's cousin or uncle or whoever. He was going to show you around Chinatown today, remember? At ten?"

"Aw, shoot. Well, I'll ask a kid to go to Hop Luey's and tell Dishi not to bother showing me around because I'll be breaking and entering another building."

"Nertz."

"Nertz nothing. Anyhow, maybe we'll be able to find the owner of the building."

"Golly, I hope so." Then I thought about something else. "Oh, dear. I hope Lulu won't be mad at me for going to Chinatown with you instead of her," I said as I all but ran to keep up with my long-legged boss as he scooted down the hallway to the staircase.

"Oh, so you roped her into helping you break and enter, eh?"

I was about to deny his allegation—and hotly too—but he was right so I didn't. "Darn it, Ernie. Nobody believed me when I said I heard people talking in that stupid building. Not even Lulu! But she agreed to help me, which I think was kind of her."

"I think it was stupid of both of you."

"Why? You're going to help me do it now!"

"Only so you won't get arrested and dumped in the clink."

"Nonsense."

"Well, go and tell her she doesn't have to worry," said Ernie. "Tell her I'll be your pigeon today."

"Pigeon, my foot."

When we got to the bottom of the staircase, Ernie stayed at the doorway and I walked over to Lulu, who sat behind the reception desk painting her nails a violent red that went well with her red sweater.

Looking up at me, she said, "'Lo, Mercy. What's up?"

"Ernie agreed to go with me and try to get into that building, so you don't have to go with me after work."

Lulu shot a glance at Ernie, who still lurked at the door of the stairway, and said, "Thank God for small favors."

"Yes. I'm glad he finally saw the light."

"Light, is it?" said Lulu skeptically.

"I think so."

"Well, good luck," she said.

"Thanks."

Ernie began to make his way across the lobby floor, but I caught up with him and stalled his progress. "I had to park in the alleyway because there was nowhere else to park. All the streets nearby were jammed with parked cars."

"Good. Then not so many people will see us, I hope."

"I hope so, too."

When we'd traversed many corridors and reached the back door, Ernie opened it and allowed me to leave the building before him.

"Crumb, it's started drizzling," I said, dismayed.

"Great. Just what we need."

"Maybe if you can find out who owns the building, we can use a key to get in."

"Yeah. That's a thought."

It didn't sound to me as if Ernie considered it to be a *good* thought. Ah well. Grumpy boss. Guess I'd just keep my gob shut so as not to provoke him.

Naturally, I did no such thing. As soon as we were seated in my perky blue Moon Roadster, I posited my theory about the man dying in the hospital being the only other man Jade ever saw with Mr. Chan.

"Who's Jade?"

"Jade Chew. Mr. Chew's granddaughter," I said indignantly.

What was the point of finding things out if he aimed to go and forget them?

"Who's Mr. Chew?"

"Oh, for pity's sake, Ernest Templeton! That grocery store across from the building of interest is Chew's Grocery. Jade is Mr. Chew's granddaughter. She's the one who followed us after you tried to talk to Mr. Chew."

"Ah, okay. I remember. So you say she only saw Chan and one other Chinese man ever use that building?"

"Yes."

"Hmmm."

We didn't speak again until we'd reached Chinatown. It was early enough in the day that Ernie found a parking spot quite easily. Unfortunately, it was too early in the day for any of the Chinatown shops to be open.

"Dammit," said Ernie after his knock at Charley's Noodle Shop drew no response.

"If anyone's open," I said, just having had what I considered a bright, if not brilliant, thought, "it's probably the grocery store. Why don't you drive back there and park?"

"Good idea, Mercy. Yeah. You're probably right."

"Every now and then I have a helpful notion," I told my boss.

"Every now and then," he agreed.

I refrained from punching his arm.

So we got back into my Roadster and Ernie drove farther down Hill, turned right on College, hung another right on Yale, and then turned down the alleyway running behind Chew's Grocery and many of the other shops in Chinatown. He parked next to our building of interest. It didn't smell awfully good when we exited my Roadster. I expect Mr. Chew, and most of the other merchants and residents of that part of Chinatown, used those trash cans in the alley.

By golly, I'd been right! Chew's Grocery was open. It was not only open, it contained Mr. Chew, Charley Wu, and his mother, along with approximately six thousand other Chinese people. They seemed to be gathering supplies for their various homes and businesses.

When Ernie and I walked into the store, past boxes of pigs' trotters and chicken feet, all the happy Chinese chatter in the grocery store stopped abruptly and everyone inside the place turned and looked at us. I'd seldom felt so much like an unwelcome interloper in my life.

Until Mrs. Wu spotted Ernie. Then she squealed. "Mr. Ernie!" and bustled up to us, Charley at her heels.

Speaking of heels, I glanced down at Mrs. Wu's feet, wondering if she might be one of the unfortunate Chinese women whose feet had been bound from infancy. But no. Her feet were small, but they were all there and not bunched up into balls. I was glad. Not, mind you, that I knew for certain there was any pain involved in this particular cultural practice, but I couldn't imagine it being awfully comfy.

"Whatcha doing here, Ernie?" asked Charley.

"Happy to see you, Mr. Ernie," said Mrs. Wu, beaming at him. Both Wus ignored me.

"Do you know who owns the building across the street?" Ernie pointed at the building in question.

Wrinkling his brow, Charley said, "No." Then he lifted his voice and spoke to the other people in the grocery store, I presume asking them Ernie's question. Much muttering among the populace commenced, and at length, a man came forward. He said something to Charley in Cantonese.

Nodding his head, Charley turned to Ernie. "Hú knows."

"Yeah, that's what I want to know too," said Ernie, sounding frustrated.

But I understood. "No, Ernie. He's telling you that Mr. Hú"—I bowed my head at the newcomer—"knows who owns the building."

"Ah," said Ernie.

TWENTY-FOUR

"Can anyone find us a key so we can get into the place?" Ernie asked of both Mr. Hú and Mr. Wu. Goodness, gracious, but I was beginning to love Chinese names. Not sure why, but they kind of tickled me.

Charley and Mr. Hú consulted with each other. Then Mr. Hú said something to Charley and left the store.

To Ernie, Charley said, "He's going to see if Zheng is available. I haven't seen him for a while, so he may be out of town."

"If he isn't here and we can't get a key, will anybody report us if we try to pry the bars off the windows to get into the building?" asked Ernie. "We think there are some people trapped inside it."

I appreciated his use of the word "we."

After thinking about it for a second or three, Charley said, "Naw. In fact, if I didn't have to get ready for the lunch crowd, I'd help you break in. The place is a mess, and I know Chan was using it for something bad."

"After questioning about three hundred people, we think he was going to run an illegal brothel there," said Ernie.

Were there legal brothels in Los Angeles? I didn't ask.

Charley Wu shot me a look as if he didn't approve of Ernie

206

speaking of brothels in the presence of a lady, even if she was white. "Wouldn't surprise me. After I learned he was hitting up most of the other businessmen in Chinatown, but only the ones with daughters, I told him I wasn't going to let my sister marry him. He got really angry."

"That's what you were arguing about the night he was shot?" asked Ernie.

"Yeah. He was furious."

"I'll bet he was," said Ernie. "I'm surprised he didn't shoot *you*."

"Yeah. Me too," said Charley, giving a little shudder. "I didn't know he had a gun, or I might not have yelled so loud."

"Get busy, Chung. You have a restaurant to run," said Mrs. Wu, giving Charley's arm a sharp yank. "Come for lunch today, Mr. Ernie." She glanced at me. "I guess you can come too."

Gee, thanks, is what I wanted to say but didn't. Rather, I smiled and said, "Thank you very much."

Ernie and I left the grocery store and stood under a canopy Mr. Chew had unrolled to protect his buckets of foodstuffs. They didn't smell awfully inviting to my Americanized nose, but I'm sure that's my ignorant bias asserting itself.

Crossing his arms over his chest and stamping his feet in an effort to keep warm, Ernie said, "Stinks here. I don't know how these people turn this junk into food I like to eat, but they seem to."

"I guess," I said, almost glad I wasn't the only prejudiced ignoramus in the vicinity.

Eventually, we saw Mr. Hú hurrying our way. When he saw us looking at him, he shook his head. Ernie stepped out from under the dubious protection of the canopy (the gray sky still drizzled) and greeted him. "No luck?"

"No Zheng. Don't know where he is."

"So there's no key to the building?" Ernie jerked his head at the building in question.

Mr. Hú shook his head again and said, "Bù."

I guess that meant no.

A second later Mr. Hú confirmed my assumption by saying, "No. Can't find Zheng. No key."

"Very well. Thank you for trying," said Ernie.

Mr. Hú nodded and went back into Chew's Grocery Store.

"Okay, I guess that means it's you and me, kid," said Ernie. "Let's get the tools out of your back seat."

So we did. Then we stood before the building, gazing up and around it. Not sure about Ernie, but I was wondering which boarded-over window to tackle first.

Looking down at me, Ernie said, "You're pretty short. Let's find a window close to the ground. Then I'll start prying and you can begin hammering."

"Maybe we should attempt to open the front door first?" I suggested.

Gazing doubtfully at the front door, which had more boards nailed across it than any of the windows, Ernie said, "Hmm. Let me take a look." And he did. Taking off his warm gloves, he shoved them in a pocket in his coat, reached into another pocket, and retrieved a pair of work gloves.

Gazing at my own gloved hands, I berated myself for not thinking to bring work gloves of my own. Depending on what happened from now on, they might be of more use than flashlights and batteries.

At last Ernie said, "Okay. Let's begin here." We both glanced around. Because it was so early on a weekday, we saw no tourists or idle shoppers peering into shop windows. Good.

"How do you want to tackle this?" I asked.

"Some of these boards are kind of loose." Ernie demonstrated by grabbing a board and tugging on it. It wiggled.

"Goodness," I said. "Maybe I can try to take some nails out of the boards with the claw end of the hammer?"

"Doubt it. What I want you to do is bash the door underneath while I use the pry bar to try to get the boards loose. Then maybe we can pull them off. This wood's pretty rickety."

"The whole building looks rickety," I posited.

"Yeah." Rather than have me beat a board with the hammer, he snatched the hammer out of my hand, shoved the pry bar at me, and he gave part of the wooden door over which boards had been nailed a couple of vicious whacks. Sure enough, as the wood began to splinter, the crossed boards stood out more prominently. "Aha," said Ernie. "Good. Give me the pry bar."

I did as he demanded without protest. "What can I do?"

"Stand there and hold the tools," he said.

All that hammering, clobbering, smashing and bashing from Ernie made a lot of noise. Doors and windows around us began to open as people peeked out to see what was going on. Eventually, a couple of Chinese men joined us, bearing tools of their own, and they too gave the front door a beating.

A window of the building next to us opened, and the same girl who'd spoken to me the prior day stuck her head out. "You breaking in?"

"Yes," I said, "but we have permission."

"Good. I think there are some people trapped in there," she said.

Merciful heavens! "I think so too," I told her.

I suspect she was needed elsewhere in the building, because she said, "Well, good luck," shut the window, and disappeared from view.

Prying with all his might, Ernie loosened one board after another until they were all either hanging limply by a nail or two or on the ground. We were left with a battered door. When Ernie tried the knob, he discovered it to be locked.

"Shoot," he said. Actually, he didn't, but I won't repeat the word he used.

Suddenly Mr. Chew appeared among those of us gathered in front of the locked door. In his hands, he carried a whopper of a sledge hammer. Now Mr. Chew was a small man, but boy, he was strong. He lifted that cudgel and gave the doorknob such a powerful blow that it flew off the door and landed with a clank in the street, barely missing a few standees.

"Thanks," said Ernie, gazing at the little man in amazement.

"Thank you, Mr. Chew," I said, smiling at him.

He grunted at us and headed back to his grocery store. Very well then.

"Okay," said Ernie to the gathered crowd. There weren't all that many people standing with us, but we sure had a lot of observers. "Because it's Miss Allcutt here who's sure there are people trapped in this building, why don't you fellows stand aside, and she and I will go in first. Don't want anyone else to get hurt if there's anything amiss in there."

A few muttered Chinese words and a couple of "okays" smote my ears.

I picked up one of the flashlights I'd laid at my feet and handed it to Ernie. As I picked up the other one and turned it on, I said to Ernie, "All right, let's see what's inside."

So, Ernie first, we entered the building. What we discovered immediately was a huge mess. Dirt and grime covered all sorts of boxes looking as if they might have contained foodstuffs. Perhaps they still did, but they were damp and disgusting and covered in filth.

"Crumb," I said. "There's another barred door." I pointed, knowing as I did so that my mother would be furious with me for doing so. Perked me right up.

So Ernie went back outside, retrieved the hammer and pry bar, brought them inside the building, and attacked the barred door. In between the sounds of destruction, I distinctly heard frightened cries behind the door.

"Ernie!" I hollered. "Stop for a minute!"

He stopped, turned, and glowered at me. "What now?"

"There are people behind that door. Listen."

We both listened.

I was correct. We heard female voices speaking in Chinese. They sounded scared, those voices.

"Damnation, you were right," said Ernie, dumbfounded.

I refrained from rolling my eyes. I did walk up to the door and try to speak soothingly through it. I glanced over my shoulder, hoping to find a Chinese person who might help me, but they all seemed to have stayed outside. So, wishing I knew a little Cantonese, I continued to speak soothingly to the people behind the door.

We heard scuttling sounds and more frightened voices, and then

Ernie said, "Well, I guess I'll just have to continue. Wish Chew was here with his sledge hammer."

"You can probably use the wrench or the pry bar," I said. "This doorknob doesn't look as substantial as the one on the outer door."

"Right," said Ernie and resumed whaling away at the door. He managed to pry all the crossed boards from it, tried the knob, found it locked, and hammered a hole next to the knob. Then he reached through the hole and grabbed the doorknob from inside the room. The door swung open.

I hurried inside the room only to stop dead in my tracks. Ernie, behind me, did likewise. Before us, three emaciated Chinese girls huddled behind another young woman, who also looked as if she'd not had a decent meal in days. She stood glaring at us. The glare didn't bother me. What bothered me was the gun she held in her shaking hands—both of them, as her wrists were bound together—aimed at me. *Me*! And I was here on a rescue mission, curse it.

All the pathetic girls behind the armed woman were weeping and wailing in Chinese.

Ernie held up both of his hands and said, "Now wait a minute here. We just want to—"

Boom went the gun. I figured either Ernie or I were dead. But we weren't. The gun-toter's hands were shaking so violently that the bullet went wide. Then the gun fell to the ground, the young woman collapsed, weeping piteously, and Ernie swooped to retrieve the gun. Fortunately, he still wore his work gloves so he didn't get his own fingerprints on the weapon. Knowing the police as I'd come to know them, it wouldn't surprise me if they decided to peg *Ernie* as the villain in this melodrama if they found his fingerprints on the gun.

"Hmm," he said. "A Colt Positive 32 with a snub-nose barrel." He said to me, "Will you please go fetch someone who can speak Cantonese to talk to these women? They look to be in rough shape. Maybe we can finally figure out what the heck happened here."

"Gladly," I said, and scooted through the debris-strewn building. Outside I saw several men standing around chatting and shooting wary glances at the building Ernie and I had just entered. I said to the group in general, "We need someone to translate for us. There are women being held captive inside the building." That was a mere guess on my part, but I figured it was a pretty good one.

A commotion from Chew's Grocery Store drew my attention. Glancing over to it, I saw an irate Mr. Chew trying to catch hold of his granddaughter, who seemed bent on crossing the road to where I stood.

"Jade!" I cried. "Oh, I'm so glad. We need you desperately!"

"Stop it, Grandfather!" she bellowed at her respected forebear. She shook her arm loose and rabbited across the road as fast as she could go. "There are girls in there?" she asked, panting, as she reached me.

"Yes, and they're scared to death. They look like they're almost starved to death, too."

"Chan," said Jade. From her mouth, the name sounded like a curse.

"I expect you're right."

"I figured as much," she grumbled.

Together we walked into the building, across the disgusting floor, and got to where Ernie still stood, peering with consternation at the huddle of girls. He turned, let out a huff of relief, and said, "Oh, good."

TWENTY-FIVE

Jade began her mission of mercy, speaking softly to the poor girls in Cantonese. She stood in the doorway, probably trying to assess their willingness to be approached. They stared at her, frightened beyond bearing if I were any judge, for several moments. Then they all started crying and more or less collapsed on each other. I noticed several of them bore ugly wounds on their wrists as if they'd been bound at one point and had scraped their skin attempting to get their bonds off.

I pointed out this fact to Ernie, who nodded. "Yeah, they've not been treated kindly. I wonder how they ended up trapped in here."

"If they'll stop crying, maybe Jade can get them to tell us," I whispered, as Jade walked gingerly over to the pile of girls, still speaking gently to them. The girls kept crying for a while, but I had a feeling they were so done in by their experience they couldn't keep it up for long.

Jade kept talking, softly and comfortingly. The girl who'd fired the gun at us seemed to be their spokesman. She whispered something to Jade. Not sure if she whispered because she didn't want Ernie and me to hear her, or because she couldn't speak any louder.

Wouldn't have mattered if she'd hollered, as neither Ernie nor I could understand anything she said.

After a few minutes of coaxing the huddled mass, Jade turned to Ernie and me. "You know what we need here is some water and food. Probably something bland. These girls haven't eaten in days, and they've been sucking on dry apples in order to get water."

"Good Lord," I said. "Um, do you know if your grandfather would give us something? I'm kind of afraid to ask him."

With a grimace of understanding, Jade said, "I don't blame you. No. He's not the right person to ask. Crumb. Charley's gone back to his noodle shop, hasn't he?"

"I think so," I told her.

"Darn it." She thought for a second or two and then said, "Can your friend go to Charley's and get some noodles and water for these girls? He and Charley are friends, aren't they?"

"Charley and Ernie? Yes, they're friends." I turned to Ernie. "Can you do that, Ernie? It looks to me as though these girls are starving to death."

"Yeah," said Ernie. "I heard. I don't like leaving you here alone, though."

"I won't be alone," I said, gesturing to the heap of girls and Jade Chew.

"Yeah, but you know what I mean."

"Well, then, maybe you can ask someone outside if he can get these poor girls something to eat and drink," I suggested. "I have a feeling Chan and his henchman are gone for good."

"You may be right," Ernie said. "All right. I'll see if I can convince someone to get these girls some food and water."

"Thanks, Ernie."

"Yes," said Jade. "Thank you. These girls are in bad shape. They probably need medical attention too."

Something occurred to me and I asked Ernie, "Should we call the police?"

"*No!*"

The word came out of Ernie's mouth so emphatically, I jumped. "No?"

"No. Damn the police for incompetent idiots. After we sort out these girls and learn their story, maybe I'll call Phil. Until then, I don't want the police anywhere near here."

"Makes sense to me," I told him.

So, as Jade continued talking to the girls, Ernie left the building and chatted with some of the men gathered outside. I have no idea why nobody else came into the building. I'd be so curious about what Ernie and I were doing, I'd have barged right in. Guess Chinese people are more sedate than I.

"Do you think there's a more comfortable place for these ladies to go close by?" I asked Jade during what seemed like a hiatus in her conversation with the lead woman. Well, I thought of her as the lead woman.

"Probably. My grandfather would pitch a fit if I asked to bring them to him. To him, these poor girls are lost to virtue and good-ness, even though getting kidnapped, held captive, and used by Chan wasn't their fault."

"Good grief, really?"

With a hearty sigh, Jade said, "Really. Anyhow, they're too dirty and stinky and embarrassed to be seen in public."

"Well, they sure can't stay here," I said, stating what I consid-ered the obvious.

"True. But they're all filthy. They haven't bathed in days and days, their hair is dirty, and their clothes are...soiled." Jade wrinkled her nose.

"Oh, dear. I wonder what we can do. I can get them clothing, but I'm not sure about bathing facilities."

Suddenly the girl from next door, of whom I'd only seen a face a couple of times, showed up next to me in the grimy building.

"Mother said you may bring those girls to our home next door. She will see they bathe and eat something."

"Oh, thank you!" I said to the little girl. "What's your name? Mine is Mercy Allcutt, and this"—I pointed again. Take *that*, Moth-er—"is Jade Chew."

Jade said, "Changying and I have met before." She smiled at the girl. "Please thank your mother for us."

A commotion at the front door drew our attention. Darned if Mrs. Wu wasn't marching into the building next to Ernie, who held a bucket full of scrumptious-smelling stuff along with cartons holding several bottles of what looked like soda pop. Coca-Cola, I think it was.

"Mrs. Wu! How kind of you!" I said, smiling at her.

"Mrs. Wu," said Jade. "Changying said her mother will allow these girls to go next door to bathe and eat. Can Mr. Templeton take the food and drink there? It's so…dirty in here."

"*Shì de.*" Mrs. Wu stopped and thought for a second. Then she turned to Ernie and said, "Go next door. Go, go, go." She made shooing motions with her hands.

Ernie turned and said, "I'm going. I'm going."

"You'll have to help me, Mercy," said Jade. "I'm not sure these girls can walk. They've been tied up for days and have injured themselves trying to get unbound."

"Good Lord, what evil people Chan and his crony were."

"I don't know what a crony is, but I think you mean the man helping Chan, and yes, they were both evil. The other guy probably still is."

"Actually," I told her as I walked to the pile of people and bent over to attempt to help a girl to her feet, "he's dead, too, or soon will be. Somebody shot him, but he didn't die instantly. He's in the French Hospital with septicemia and is expected to die any old minute now." Oh, my, those poor things smelled horrible. I tried not to show it.

"Good," said Jade. "I'm happy to hear it." She too gently took a girl's arm and tried to lift her. The girl attempted to rise and stumbled a little bit but eventually got to her feet. By the time she did so, Jade's nose was wrinkling up a storm.

After I got one girl on her feet and leaning against a wall so she wouldn't fall again, I assisted the woman—she was no more than a girl, I realized, when I got closer—who'd tried to shoot us. She stood a little more easily than the other two girls had.

Ernie appeared at my side again. "God. They all stink to high heaven," he said in his most charitable tone of voice.

"Not their fault," snapped Jade. "They've been held captive in this place for a week or more."

"I know it's not their fault," said Ernie, bending over to help yet another girl to her feet. She uttered a small scream and tried to resist. Didn't much blame her, given her experience with men to date, but Ernie persisted and eventually, she gave up and allowed herself to be helped.

The little girl from next door, Changying, walked to the woman leaning against the wall and took her arm. Slowly and draggily, we managed to get all four females into the building next door. Changying's mother met us at the door and tried to hustle the four captives into her home, even though she, too, drew back when the full measure of their filthiness and stench assaulted her. She spoke to her daughter, and Changying said something back. Then she hurried through a door to the back of the house. I heard water running.

Changying's mother and Jade Chew spoke for a few minutes in rapid-fire Cantonese, and Jade nodded. "*Shì de, Shì de.*" Jade turned and translated for Ernie and me. "Changying is filling a big wooden tub in the kitchen for these poor girls to bathe in. After they're clean, they can eat something." To me, she said, "Did you say you could get clothes for them?"

"Yes, if you can suggest a nearby place to find any. Also please tell me what to get."

"Go to the consignment shop at the end of this street." She gestured to the far end of the street upon which the building we were in sat. "Get underwear if they have any, and small-sized dresses or skirts or shirts or whatever you can. We'll worry about proper clothing later."

"Sounds like a good idea to me," I said and hurried out of the building. I knew precisely the consignment shop to which Jade referred because I'd bought an evening dress there once. And my mother hadn't even guessed it wasn't brand new, which just goes to show…something. I'm not sure what.

At any rate, I nearly ran to the shop. It never occurred to me that the place might not be open, but when I tried the knob, it didn't turn. Curses! But what was this? A lovely young woman in a beautiful silk Chinese gown opened the door for me.

"Are you here for those poor girls?" she asked, astonishing me.

"News travels fast," I said, surprised and pleased.

"It does. Here. I've begun to gather some items they can probably use. Do you know who they are yet?"

"I'm sorry. I don't know a thing except that they've been held captive in that wretched building for days and days without food or drink or...sanitary facilities."

The lovely young woman's nose wrinkled. "Oh, dear. That horrid man, Chan, was evil."

"Yes," I said. "He was."

It didn't take more than five minutes for the woman whose name, she said, was Mary, and I to gather enough clothing, undies included, to clothe four emaciated Chinese girls. Mary stuffed everything into a wicker basket, and I hauled it back down the street to Changying's parents' building. When I knocked at the door, Jade opened it immediately.

"That didn't take long," she said.

"No, it didn't. Mary had already begun gathering clothes together. News travels fast around here."

"Telephones are a great invention," said Jade, grinning.

"Aha. I hadn't thought about telephoning."

"Fortunately, Changying's mother, Gladys, thought to telephone Mary."

Gladys? I didn't ask. "I'm glad she did."

Jade carried the wicker basket full of clothes to the back room. I didn't follow her, figuring the poor former captives deserved as much privacy as they could get. I did hear Mrs. Wu's high-pitched voice coming from the back room and figured she was overseeing things properly. An efficient and managing woman, Mrs. Wu.

When Jade returned, I said, "How are the poor girls doing?"

"They're confused and upset, but glad to be getting cleaned up. They're all a mess, and they all have sores of one sort of another on their bodies. I don't even want to think about what Chan and that other man did to them."

"I don't either, but I'm afraid we're going to have to ask. They're going to have to tell us, too, if we want to clear Charley Wu of murder charges. I can't figure out who shot Chan."

"I can," said Jade. "In fact, Yue Wan said she did it."

"What?" I gaped, flabbergasted, at Jade.

"She tried to shoot you, too, didn't she?"

"If she's the one who stood in front of the other girls, yes, she did."

"She was scared to death when you barged in on them."

"We were trying to help!" I said, mortified that anyone would think Ernie and I meant any harm to those wretched girls.

"I know you were," said Jade in a soothing voice. "And now they know I know, too. So everything's jake."

Everything's jake? I swear, slang was everywhere these days.

Jade continued, "Chan was leaning out the ground-floor window, hollering something. Yue Wan picked up the gun he'd laid on a table and shot him in the back. When the other man with Chan tried to tackle her, she shot him, too. Unfortunately, he wasn't killed. He managed to get out the window where Chan fell and hammer boards over it. Those girls were bound hand and foot. It's amazing that Yue Wan managed to pick up the gun and pull the trigger, given her disadvantages."

Fairly stunned, I said, "Good Lord, I should say so." I looked around the front room where we stood. "Where's Ernie?"

"He went across the street to Shu's place to get some slippers for the girls."

"Oh," I said, surprised. "I didn't think about footwear."

"Neither did I until after you left. When I remembered, I asked Mr. Templeton to go buy four pairs of slippers in a small size for the girls."

"Thank you."

"I'm just glad you persisted. When we talked the other day, I didn't know what to do. My grandfather is a great guy, but he wasn't about to go breaking into that building. He's Chinese and sure as heck, he'd have been arrested and tried for something or other."

"Oh, dear. I'm sure you're right. The police are such...I don't know."

"Pigs," said Jade.

"I guess so. Detective Bigelow is a good man, but the department as a whole is pretty corrupt."

With a shrug, Jade said, "It might not even be corruption. It might just mean they don't like Chinese people. Most Chinese people have the same prejudice against whites." She gave me a grin. "I don't."

"I'm glad. And you're probably right." There I went, getting depressed about the human condition again.

At a sharp tap on the front door, Jade went to answer it. And there was Ernie, carrying a paper sack. "Here," he said. "Four pairs of Chinese slippers. Size small. They're all black."

"That's fine," said Jade. "Thank you. I'll take them to the back room."

"Whew," said Ernie. He flopped into a chair in the front room.

I sat in another one. "Thank you, Ernie. I was afraid Lulu and I were going to have to try to break into that building after work. I'm *so* glad you finally believed me."

"Not sure I *did* believe you, but I figured it couldn't hurt to see if you were right. And you were right. Good job, Mercy."

Unaccustomed to being praised by my boss, who was more likely to ridicule and disapprove of my ideas than respect them, I felt my face heat. "Thank you." Recalling what Jade had told me, I asked, "Did Jade tell you about who shot Chan and his henchman?"

"No. Not yet. We'll have to get the girls' statements with a translator. After Jade translates, I'll call Phil and demand he get a legitimate Chinese translator and take down their stories. I guess everyone was right about Chan wanting girls to staff an illegal business."

"Yes, sounds like he was." Don't ask me why, but I'm glad Ernie didn't use the word "brothel." Those poor girls.

We sat in the living room of Changying's parents' house—was her mother's name really Gladys?—for about twenty minutes or so.

Then Mrs. Wu bustled out from the back room and stood in front of Ernie.

"Girls okay," she said. "Eating now. What you going to do with them?"

"Me?" Ernie pointed at his chest. "I'm not sure. We'll have to learn their story. Find out how they got in that building and what Chan and the other man did to them."

Mrs. Wu snorted. "I can tell you that."

"What I mean is, we need to know who shot Chan and his buddy so we can get Charley off the hook for murder."

"Ah," said Mrs. Wu. She nodded sharply. "Well, they'll tell you. It wasn't Chung."

"It was Yue Wan," I said.

Both Ernie and Mrs. Wu looked at me as if I'd lost what was left of my mind.

"Who the devil is…Whoever you said?" said Ernie.

"Yue Wan?" said Mrs. Wu. "Yue Wan? No. Couldn't be."

"You'd rather it be Charley?" I asked, a little irked.

With a frown for me, Mrs. Wu said, "No. Not Chung."

Then it was I explained what Jade had told me. Both Ernie and Mrs. Wu still stared at me, but they changed their minds about me being crazy to judge by their expressions. When I came to the end of my narrative, Mrs. Wu said, "Huh."

Ernie said, "Well, I'll be damned."

"I have no doubt of it," I snapped at him.

TWENTY-SIX

I'm not sure how long we stayed in Changying's parents' house. Mrs. Wu left not long after I'd related the girls' story, probably to spread the news to all of Chinatown about our discovery and the identity of Chan's killer. I doubt even the police would call what Yue Wan did murder. It had been self-defense at the very least.

After what seemed like two or three years, Jade Chew, Changying and Gladys escorted four clean, neatly dressed Chinese girls—I swear, a couple of them weren't more than twelve or thirteen—into the living room. Ernie stood and bowed. Actually, so did I.

"Yue Wan asked me to thank you for rescuing her and the others and to say she's sorry she tried to shoot you. She feared you were going to hurt them."

"I understand," I told her.

"Yeah. No problem," said Ernie.

"Do you know a doctor who can see to the girls' wounds and assess their overall health, Jade?" I asked. "They really should get some medical attention."

"Dr. Fong received a medical degree in England—America wouldn't let him into a medical school here—and he lives not too far away. Why don't I telephone him, explain what happened if he doesn't already know, which he probably does, and ask him if we can bring these girls to him? Or maybe he can come here." She glanced at Gladys, who nodded. "Yes, it's probably better if he comes here."

"We're also going to have to involve the police in order to clear Charley Wu from suspicion of murder."

"They aren't going to arrest Yue Wan, are they?" asked Jade in an accusing tone.

"No," said Ernie. "I'm going to telephone the only honest cop I know and have him and a translator interview the girls. Hmm. Wonder if the police have any Cantonese translators on their staff."

"I doubt it," I said. "Why doesn't Jade translate?" I turned to her. "I mean, if you don't mind. And I'll take notes. I trust myself over any police note-taker."

"Yeah, so do I. Okay. I'll call Phil, and if he doesn't like it our way, he can lump it. If worse comes to worst, we can tell him Chan's buddy shot him. Chan's buddy's probably dead now, so it won't matter, and it'll get Charley off the hook."

Jade and I smiled broadly at Ernie. Gladys said, "Would you like to use our telephone here? We have a party line, but I think I can get everyone to give us privacy."

"Hmm," said Ernie doubtfully. "Might be better if I called Phil from my office. I hate to leave the girls here for fear they might somehow disappear. I mean, they're scared, and I don't blame them, but…"

"Let me call Dr. Fong. If he can come here and see to the girls, you'll probably have plenty of time to go to your office and get back here again," said Jade. "If that's all right with you, Mrs. Sing."

Gladys—so glad to learn her last name—nodded. "Yes, that's a good idea. And you"—she pointed at me—"can stay here, too."

"I'm Mercy Allcutt, Mr. Templeton's secretary," I told everyone who didn't already know it. "Just call me Mercy."

"What a good name for you!" exclaimed Mrs. Sing.

"Yeah. I didn't think Americans gave their children names that suited them, but your parents did."

"Not on purpose," I said, thinking of my mother and father and wishing I hadn't.

"No?" Jade eyed me oddly.

"It's a long story," I told her. "And a boring one. They named my sister Clovilla."

"What does that mean?"

"Nothing, as far as I know. My full first name is Mercedes, so only my friends call me Mercy. My mother never does. She calls me Mercedes Louise Allcutt and generally scolds me after she says my name."

"Oh." Jade didn't seem to know what to say next.

It was all right, though, because Ernie did. "Mercy's a good person, even if her parents stink. Okay, I'll go to the office, and you try to get the doctor here. Please don't allow any of these girls to leave. If they do, things will get even more complicated than they already are. My main goal in all of this is to clear Charley Wu's name."

"I'll see to it that they all stay here," said Mrs. Sing. "And I'll telephone Dr. Fong right now."

"Thank you." Ernie took his hat from the arm of the chair where he'd set it, plopped it on his head, and said, "Mercy, I'm going to pick up your tools from that building and then drive to the office. Be back as soon as I can."

"Good idea about the tools," I said. "Thanks, Ernie."

"No problem, kid. Be back soon."

And he left. As soon as the door shut behind him, I missed him. How silly, huh?

Mrs. Sing had left the room to telephone the doctor. She walked back in, smiling. "Dr. Fong will be here in just a few minutes."

It having occurred to me that doctors might be great guys, but that they worked for money, I said, "I'll be happy to pay the doctor."

Jade, Mrs. Sing and Changying all stared at me. Finally, Mrs. Sing said, "There's no need for that. The community will help these girls."

"Even though Grandfather won't allow them into his home, he'll definitely donate money for their medical care," said Jade.

"Very well," I said, not sure whether or not to be embarrassed by my offer. I'd meant well.

"Thank you for the offer though," said Mrs. Sing.

I only smiled and wished Ernie would come back.

When a knock came at the door, I hoped for a second it would be Ernie standing outside, but it was Dr. Fong. I'm only assuming here, but I expect this Fong was related to all the other Fongs in Los Angeles.

He appeared a dapper, youngish man in a spiffy suit and carrying the requisite doctor's black bag. He smiled at the room in general, and I saw the four former captives draw back and clutch at each other. Now that they'd been cleaned up, I could see all of them had yellowing bruises. Two or three of them bore what looked like bleeding sores, particularly around their wrists and ankles. I almost wished Chan weren't already dead so I could kill him myself.

Jade, continuing her role as translator, spoke softly and gently to the four girls. Her words didn't appreciably lessen their terror, so Mrs. Sing talked to them, too. She was older and, therefore, more of a person to revere, because the girls let go of each other. They were so tense, however, that all four of them looked like sticks about to break in half.

Poor Dr. Fong.

Poor four girls.

Turning and gesturing for the doctor to come closer, Mrs. Sing said some more things to the girls. Dr. Fong stopped a couple of yards away from the sofa upon which all the girls clumped and also said a few words to them.

The girls looked at each other and Yue Wan—I think it was she; it was difficult to tell who was who after their baths and new wardrobes—stood up from the sofa, using its arm to brace herself. She bowed her head as if offering it up to an executioner's axe but remained silent.

Gently, Mrs. Sing took her arm and slowly led her to a door off the living room, opened it, gestured for Dr. Fong to join her, and the three of them left the living room. The three remaining girls clutched each other in panic and gazed, big-eyed, at the closed door through which their leader and the other two people—strangers to them—had gone.

"This is just awful," muttered Jade. She strode up to the sofa and sat next to the leftover former prisoners, all of whom drew away from her in alarm. Jade recommenced talking to them in Cantonese and gradually they relaxed a little bit. Not much.

I swear a millennium passed before the door through which Mrs. Sing and Yue Wan had left the room opened and Yue Wan reentered the living room. The girls on the sofa uttered soft, relieved sighs. Mrs. Sing, Yue Wan and Jade talked to another girl, who stood, still looking scared but not quite so petrified. Mrs. Sing led her to the door and they both vanished behind it.

The two girls began pelting Yue Wan with what I presume were questions and seemed unhappy with her responses. Yue Wan and Jade attempted to reassure them.

I'd be willing to bet, although I didn't have nerve enough to ask, that Dr. Fong had done a relatively thorough examination of Yue Wan, including some of her private places she'd rather not show to a man. However, as at least one and probably two men had already seen and done unspeakable things to those private places, Dr. Fong didn't have much of a choice if he aimed to truly help these girls.

After another millennium crawled by, the door opened and Mrs. Sing led the second girl back to the sofa. There the girl threw herself at Yue Wan and sobbed onto her shoulder. Yue Wan patted her gently, and Mrs. Sing took another girl to see the doctor. What an ordeal those poor things had to go through. And this was their rescue! I could hardly bear to think about what they'd endured whilst being held captive.

At long, long, *long* last another knock came at the door. Jade Chew answered the knock, and there was Ernie. Thank God! Unfortunately—or perhaps not—Phil Bigelow accompanied him. As soon as Jade, Changying and the girls on the sofa saw the suited Phil, they recoiled and clung to each other.

"It's all right," I told Jade and Changying. "Changying, you remember my boss, Mr. Templeton, don't you?"

Changying squinted at Ernie for a year or two, and then slowly nodded. "Yeah. I think I remember him."

"He helped me break into the building where the girls were. We were together the other day when you spoke to us, too."

"Oh, yeah," said Changying slowly. "I recognize him now. Who's the other guy?"

Oh, boy. This should be fun. But I soldiered on, as Ernie seemed to have gone mute. "This is a detective from the police department—"

Various cries from various Chinese people in the room shut me up. It was Jade Chew who saved the day.

"This is the policeman Mr. Templeton said he trusts," she said to Changying. "I think it will be okay."

"It will be okay," said Ernie. He turned to Phil. "Nice to know the L.A.P.D. is held in such high regard, isn't it?"

"Huh," said Phil unhappily.

The doctor's door at the other end of the living room opened once more, and the second-to-last girl was escorted back to the sofa by Mrs. Sing. She glanced at the door and stopped in her tracks.

"This is Mr. Templeton and Detective Bigelow," I hurried to tell her. "If Jade can translate for us, I'll take notes on precisely what happened to the four girls. We'll wait until Dr. Fong has attended to the last girl."

And if Ernie and Phil didn't approve of my management of the situation, they could jolly well lump it.

"Very well," said Mrs. Sing. She gently guided the last girl to the door behind which Dr. Fong and his medical equipment waited.

All of the remaining girls now sported bandages on various parts of their bodies. Well, I could only see their arms and ankles, but I suspected other areas of their persons also bore sticking plasters.

"You might as well sit down," said Jade ungraciously. "Dr. Fong is checking over the last girl, Chu Hua, now. When she comes back, you may question them. You'd better do it, Mr. Templeton. I doubt they'd answer any questions from your policeman friend."

"Will do," said Ernie without looking at Phil. Both men sat in straight-backed chairs they'd lifted from the hallway and brought to the living room.

Silence settled on the room's occupants as we all waited for Dr. Fong to finish examining Chu Hua. I'd never remember all their names. Well, except for Yue Wan, because she'd tried to shoot me, even though she didn't know I was trying to rescue her at the time. I'm sure she felt sorry about it now. Or maybe she didn't. I'd probably never know.

After another three or four centuries dragged past, the doctor's door opened. This time Mrs. Sing brought not only Chu Hua, but Dr. Fong along with her.

Ernie stood respectfully upon Mrs. Sing's entry into the room. So did Phil, although he tried to hide behind Ernie. I acquitted him of cowardice and acknowledged he was being prudent. After all, everyone in the room except Ernie and I hated him already.

Squinting at Ernie and Phil, Dr. Fong said something in Cantonese. Don't know what, but Jade did. "He's Mr. Templeton. He, along with Mercy here, saved the four girls from the building next door. That other man is a policeman." She spoke the last sentence in a truly scathing tone of voice.

"I see. Well, Mr. Templeton and Miss Mercy, thank you. Mr. Policeman, I and the rest of the Chinese citizens of Los Angeles expect you to do your duty properly." He didn't add "for once," but the two words hung in the air like tangible entities.

Phil only nodded. I got the feeling he didn't quite dare open his mouth, much less say anything.

"So," said Ernie, "how will we do this? Miss Chew, can you ask the four women the questions we have of them and translate their answers? Mercy will take down the questions and answers on her secretarial pad."

I didn't have a secretarial pad with me. I had just opened my mouth to say so to Ernie when he reached into his inner coat pocket and withdrew one along with several sharpened pencils.

Walking over to him and taking the pad and pencils, I said, "Thanks, Ernie." I opted not even to look at Phil. I was mad at him and the entire L.A.P.D.

When I was seated and had my pencil poised, Ernie asked Jade, "Is it all right with you if we start asking questions now? This will probably take some time."

"It's all right with me," said Jade. "You're going to be asking these girls to relive some of the most hideous moments of their lives, but I suppose that can't be helped." She stared at Ernie, and I got the impression she was attempting quite hard to be civil to him.

"I know. And I'm sorry. But it's important we know what they endured and by whom, if we want to get Wu Chung out from under suspicion."

Jade eyed him from the corner of her eye. "Yes. Wu Chung. He's important, too, isn't he?"

"He is to me," said Ernie simply.

With a sigh, Jade said, "He is to me, too. In fact, we're going to be married next summer."

"Congratulations," said Ernie, daring a brief smile. I got the oddest impression he'd already been told about Jade and Charley's pending nuptials.

"Right," said Jade. "Chung told you about us so you'd be careful with these poor girls, didn't he?"

"Yes," said Ernie, not waffling even a tiny bit.

"Good. Wu Chung is a good man. He even braved my grandfather to ask if we could marry. It takes a courageous man to deal with my grandfather."

I heard a muffled snort, glanced around the room, and saw Mrs. Sing trying to stifle a giggle.

"All right, then," said Jade. "Let's get this show on the road."

Her use of the idiom surprised me, although I'm not sure why. I should have become accustomed to anything Jade said—or did—by this point.

TWENTY-SEVEN

E rnie started his examination of the girls softly, attempting, I believe, to make them feel less timid. I mentally wished him luck with the effort, which I suspected was doomed from the outset.

He began by asking a totally innocent question: "Where do you girls come from?" Jade interpreted and silence ensued. Jade prodded a little. Silence ensued again. This went on for several frustrating minutes, although I dutifully wrote all the words spoken (in English) in my notepad.

After silence had ensued for about the seventh or eighth time, Jade lost her considerable temper and let loose a barrage of Cantonese on the four refuges. After shrinking back against her anger, Yue Wan again proved herself to be leader of the pack and gave her a soft answer.

"Good," said Jade. Turning to me, she said, "They're all from the Guangdong Province. That's what you people call Canton. They were sold to Chan, who brought them to the United States." Seeing my horrified expression, she went on to say, "Yeah, I know. Sounds terrible, doesn't it? It happens pretty much everywhere. In fact, I wouldn't be surprised if it happened here in the U.S.A. If a harvest is poor, or there's a drought, or there's a flood, or if a herd of marauders overrun your village, sometimes parents are left without the means to support all their children. If that happens in Guangdong, girl children are the first to go."

I didn't even flinch. I just wrote it all down in my secretarial pad.

Ernie resumed his questioning. "Did Chan tell the girls or their parents what he aimed to do with the girls once they got to the United States?"

"No, but they knew. There's only one use for girls who are sold from their families. They become captives. I believe the *romantic* name for them is 'singsong girls'. What that means is they are forced into prostitution."

I'd heard the term "singsong girl," but I didn't say so. The appellation itself sounded so innocent. I was getting an education I didn't much want since I'd forced the issue of that repellant building. My own fault—and not for the first time.

The questioning went on; Ernie asking questions, Jade interpreting, and Yue Wan answering. Occasionally one of the other girls said something, which provoked a small discussion among the four, and then Yue Wan would give Jade the definitive answer, which Jade would translate and I would write down.

As the sorry story unfolded, it turned out to be pretty much what I'd already related to Ernie, with many grim and distasteful details added. At one point I glanced at Phil, who had his head bowed as he stared at the hat on his knees. My gaze didn't linger. I had notes to take.

I'm not sure how long the interview lasted. At least an hour and a half, I guess. Finally, it was Dr. Fong who called an end to it. "I'm sorry, Mr. Templeton. These girls have been through hell, they're exhausted and terrified, and I don't think they can answer any more of your questions. Can we halt this for today? Maybe you can talk to them more another time."

Ernie nodded at Jade and turned to Phil, who still had his head bowed. "Well, Phil? Do you want to set another time for more questions? Personally, I think these women have told you all you need to know, but you're the one who has to decide."

When Phil lifted his head, I was dumbfounded to see tears

standing in his eyes. He quickly wiped them away with his hand. "I've heard enough." His voice was gruff.

"So what will happen now?" asked Jade, who was relentless, bless her.

Phil didn't speak. I got the impression he didn't know what to say *or* do. Therefore, Ernie took over for him.

"Thank you, Miss Chew." He turned to Gladys Sing. "And thank you, Mrs. Sing. And Dr. Fong. We wouldn't have been able to do this without your generosity and assistance."

Mrs. Sing nodded. "These poor girls needed help."

"Yes," Ernie said with a sigh, "they did. Still do. Do you have any idea where they can stay now? They don't have any resources, do they?"

"By resources, do you mean money?" asked Jade.

"Money, family, friends…Anything at all." Glancing at me, Ernie said, "I know Mercy will take them all into her home, but that can't be a permanent solution to their problems."

Jade, Mrs. Sing, Dr. Fong and Changying all turned to stare at me. Jade said, "You can? You actually *would?*"

Darn Ernie! "Well, yes, I could do that. But we're going to have to think of a permanent solution to where they can stay. And maybe find them employment? I don't know." Leaving my notepad and pencils on my lap, I lifted my hands in a gesture of helplessness—or at the very least, incompetence. "I feel totally out of my depth here."

"Oh, I believe I can offer a solution," said Dr. Fong in a musing tone of voice.

So grateful, I nearly burst into tears, I said, "You can?"

"Yes. There's a school for orphans attached to the French Hospital. It's for Chinese orphans and refugees. Because of the Chinese Exclusion Act, no Chinese are legally allowed into the United States, but—as you can see in this case—sometimes people, especially girls, are smuggled in. The orphan asylum is geared to assist such girls. They can learn English and be taught skills sufficient to find employment, at least in the Chinese community."

"Thank you," I said.

"Yes. Thank you, Dr. Fong," said Ernie.

Phil nodded.

"Can we help with transportation or anything?" I asked. "And if, for any reason we need to talk to the girls again, will we be able to do so there? At the orphan asylum?"

"Yes, although I hope you'll leave them alone from now on and let them heal their bodily and emotional wounds. They've been through enough hell, don't you think, without having to retell it over and over? Please never forget that these young women were reared in a culture entirely different from your American way of life. They might have been forced into doing hateful things, but I'm sure they don't want to relive them endlessly."

"I absolutely agree with you," said Ernie. "I'll take the detective here back to my office and we'll discuss the matter. May I have your telephone number, Dr. Fong? And yours, Mrs. Sing?"

"Of course," said Dr. Fong. He reached into a breast pocket and withdrew a small stack of business cards. He peeled one off and handed it to Ernie. "And here's one for you, too, Miss Mercy. You've been of exceptional help to these young women, and I'm sure the entire Chinese community will thank you for it."

"Me?" I squeaked, taking the card and feeling heat creep into my cheeks.

"That's Mercy all over," said Ernie, without too much sarcasm.

"I'll never forget what *you* look like," Jade told me with a cynical twist to her smile.

"Nor I you," I said with no cynicism at all. I do believe that, more than any other emotion churning in my relatively small body, the predominant one was relief. We'd not only saved Charley Wu from the electric chair, but we'd also saved those four miserably abused young women. Girls. Not one of them was older than fifteen, and the only fifteen-year-old was Yue Wan. I couldn't bear to think of myself in a situation like theirs.

I wrote Mrs. Sing's telephone number on the back of Dr. Fong's business card.

Then, after what seemed like four thousand three hundred twenty-five years, eight months, three days, eleven minutes and six

233

seconds, we left Mrs. Sing's home. Dr. Fong accompanied us outside. The street was lined with Chinese people, and it looked to me as if tourists and diners had begun to arrive. Scattered among the Chinese faces were a few white ones.

I heard somebody say something sounding like a salutation in Chinese, and looked to see Mr. Fong of Fong's Toy Shop and Jewelry Store walking briskly toward Ernie, Phil, Dr. Fong and me. Dr. Fong stepped away from Ernie, Phil and me, and walked up to greet the other Fong. They spoke a few words to each other, and Mr. Fong smiled at me. He smiled at *me*, for goodness' sake! I smiled back, feeling kind of like a rag that's been used to scrub filthy floors and then wrung out and hung to dry.

"I'll come to your shop and pick up that vase as soon as I can, Mr. Fong," I assured him.

With a chuckle, Mr. Fong said, "There's no rush, young woman. No rush at all. I'll keep it safe for you."

"Thank you." I nodded and smiled some more, then Ernie tugged on my arm and I turned and stumbled away from Mr. Fong, Dr. Fong and the rest of the denizens of Chinatown. I didn't even know what time it was, and I was too worn out to look at my wristwatch.

My Moon Roadster and Phil's big Hudson were parked nose to tail on Yale Street. When we reached our respective automobiles, Ernie said to Phil, "See you at my office."

"Yeah," said Phil, and he gave us a dispirited almost-wave.

Ernie and I didn't speak until we were pulling into a parking space not too far from the one Mr. Buck always saved for Ernie's dilapidated Studebaker. I don't know where Phil parked, and I didn't much care.

As we walked to the Figueroa Building, Ernie said, "Damn, I'm hungry. What time is it, anyway?"

"I don't know. By golly, I'm hungry too. I didn't even think about food while we were in Chinatown. I hope Mrs. Wu won't be mad at us for not dining at Charley's place."

"Don't worry about Mrs. Wu. I think she'll be able to find people to eat her food even without us."

"I'm sure," I said a little sadly. "She makes the most scrumptious food."

"Yeah, well, let's see if we can find Junior. He can go across the street to the diner and pick us up some sandwiches or something."

"Good idea. Thanks, Ernie."

When we got the front door of the building, Phil joined us, coming from the opposite direction. We didn't bother with greetings, although Ernie was kind enough to ask Phil if he wanted a sandwich.

"Sure." Phil dug into a pocket and came up with a five-dollar bill. "You can use this and get us all something."

Although I didn't much want to, I said, "Thank you."

Ernie took Phil's fiver and said, "Yeah. Thanks."

We walked into the building. Lulu, who had as usual been painting her nails, glanced up and arched back in surprise. "*There* you are! I thought maybe you two got eaten by a dragon or something."

"A dragon?" said Ernie, who sounded as if he'd just returned from a thousand-mile walk.

"Yeah. You know. The Chinese have dragons all over the place in Chinatown." She saw Phil, frowned, and went back to studying her nails, which glistened redly under the building's ceiling lights.

"You know where Junior is, Lulu?" asked Ernie.

"Not sure. Let me call Mr. Buck in the basement. If anyone's seen him, it's probably Mr. Buck."

"There's a telephone in the basement?" I asked, surprised. I hadn't recalled seeing one the last time I'd been down there.

"Mr. Buck asked to have one installed so people can get him if he's down there doing janitorial things."

"Good idea," said Ernie. "Thanks, Lulu. Yeah, please call him. I hope to God somebody can find Junior."

"Whatcha want him for?"

"To get us lunch from the diner across the street," I told her.

"*Lunch*? It's after three o'clock! You mean, you guys haven't had lunch yet?"

"No," said Ernie.

"Lemme call the basement," said Lulu and proceeded to do so. Someone answered the 'phone down there, and Lulu asked for Junior. She replaced the receiver on the cradle and said, "He's down there helping Mr. Buck paint signs. He'll be up in a few minutes."

"Thanks. Will you please send him to my office when he shows up?"

"Sure will," said Lulu.

Ernie, Phil and I walked to the elevator. As I held my handbag, secretarial pad and several pencils, Ernie opened the cage and operated the lever after we entered. The trip to the third floor was accompanied by the sound of the elevator. None of the people in it spoke. Nor did we speak as we walked from the elevator to Ernie's office.

As he unlocked the front door, Ernie said, "Go to my office, you two. I'll leave the door to it open so Junior can find us." He shoved the door open and frowned. "I guess, if the 'phone rings, you should answer it, Mercy, but don't make any appointments for this week, okay?"

"Fine with me," I told him.

As soon as we were all in the outer office, Phil said, "This isn't my fault! I swear to God, that whole mess in Chinatown isn't my fault!"

I wanted to tell him to shut up, but I think it was exhaustion making me cranky. Ernie could deal with his friend. After I hung my coat on the rack, I went to my desk, shoved my handbag into the lower right drawer, realized I hadn't removed my cloche, so I did that and just plopped it on my desk. I noticed it was covered with plaster dust and wood chips. Probably my coat was, too. I hadn't even bothered to look at it as I hung it up.

"I don't give a good God damn whose fault it is, Phil," said Ernie, sounding at least as cross as I felt. "What we need to do now is decide how to fix it."

I stood up from bending over my desk drawer and said, "Without having those poor girls hauled into court to give testimony. They're already terrified, starved, and wounded. If they have to go to court and face a sea of white faces, they'll shatter into bits. They're broken enough already."

"I agree," said Ernie.

Whew! Wasn't sure if Ernie would endorse my plan of action. Still, I shouldn't have doubted him.

"But they're the only ones who know what happened!" said Phil, plainly frustrated.

"No, they aren't. By this time every living soul in Chinatown knows precisely what happened, to whom, how, and who saved them. They aren't going to stand for more manhandling of those four girls. For God's sake, Phil, they're *kids*!"

"Kids their parents sold and who are in this country illegally!"

Ernie stomped into his office, followed by a stomping Phil. I didn't have the energy to stomp, so I just followed both men and sat on a chair before Ernie's desk. "Sit down, Phil," I said to him. At present he stood beside the desk, glaring at a seated Ernie, who didn't bother glaring back. "I know precisely what we can do."

Whirling around to turn his glare on me, Phil said, "What we'll do is tell the truth. The truth is enough to condemn—"

I guess he remembered there was no one extant who could be blamed, unless he wanted to go after another innocent person. "Yes?" I asked sweetly.

"But—" Phil was definitely frustrated.

"Sit *down*, Phil," ordered Ernie. "Mercy's right. The truth is that both of the men who held those girls captive and almost starved and beat them to death are now dead. Who ya gonna pin the crime on? I'll be damned if I'll let you charge that fifteen-year-old girl with murder. Or even manslaughter."

"But—"

Junior appeared at Ernie's door, panting and a trifle paint-splattered, but grinning. He enjoyed working for Ernie.

"What do you want to eat, Mercy?" asked Ernie politely.

I considered the delicatessen across the street and said, "Corned beef on rye. Some potato salad if they have it."

"I'll have the same," said Ernie. "Say, do they have any of those potato chip things over there?"

"Laura Scudder?" said an enthusiastic Junior.

"Who's she?" asked Ernie.

"Laura Scudder's Potato Chips!" said Junior as if everyone in the world should know about them.

"Get us three corned beefs on rye, some potato salad for everybody and get a bag of chips each," said Ernie. He held out the five-dollar bill formerly owned by Phil Bigelow. "Will this cover it? Get a bag of chips for yourself, too."

"That'll be plenty. Thanks, Mr. Ernie!"

"And bring us three bottles of root beer!" I called after Junior.

"Sure will!"

And Junior bounced out of the office a happy boy.

"Keep the change!" Ernie shouted after him.

I expect those words made Junior an even happier boy.

TWENTY-EIGHT

"Pretty free with my money, aren't you?" grumbled Phil.

"Wait here," I said. I rose from my chair, left Ernie's office, went back to my desk, retrieved my handbag, and dug in it for my purse. From my purse, I pulled a five-dollar bill. After putting everything away again, I marched back into Ernie's office, thrust the fiver at Phil, and said, "Here. Now be quiet so we can tell you how to handle the case."

"Mercy!" said Phil. "I didn't mean for you—"

"Shut up, Phil," said Ernie.

I stuffed the fiver into Phil's breast pocket and went back to my chair.

Phil shut up. He retrieved the bill, scowled at it, and held it out to me, but I didn't take it.

"Stuff it, Phil. Mercy's not going to take your money."

I think Phil wanted to protest some more, but a glance at Ernie and then at me dissuaded him. With a sigh, he sat in the other chair before Ernie's desk, stuck his feet out in front of him, jammed his hands into his jacket pockets, and stared at Ernie's desk.

"All right. Mercy, if you can think of anything else to add to my narrative, please do so. What Phil is going to tell his police buddies is that Mr. Chan shot his colleague in the leg. They got into a scuffle, Mr. Chan's colleague got the gun away from him and shot him in the back as Chan tried to escape out the downstairs window. The colleague— What the hell is the guy's name? Does anybody know?" He stared at Phil.

Shaking his head, Phil said, "I don't know if they were able to get his name. From what I've gathered so far, the guy barely made it into the hospital lobby before he collapsed. He'd tried to bandage his wound, but it festered. He was delirious when medical staff got to him. I don't know if he regained consciousness or not. I'll call, but I expect he's dead by this time."

"Did you go to the hospital to see him?"

"Yeah, as soon as I got the call that a gunshot Chinaman had been admitted. He wasn't conscious when I got there and septicemia was well advanced." He shuddered. "A nurse pulled a blanket away from his leg where the wound was, and you could see his leg was red with blood poisoning and swollen clear up to his abdomen. It was...ugly."

"No more than he deserved," I said.

"Maybe not, but you'll have to tell me why I should go with your story instead of the truth," said Phil.

"Because if you tell the truth," barked Ernie, "you're going to have four illegal Chinese girls who have already been through hell testifying in Chinese in a white court where nobody gives a curse about them or their story. Who're you going to pin a crime on? What crime? Crimes were committed against those girls, but they *sure* don't need to testify in front of a bunch of old white men in a foreign-to-them courtroom."

"That's not true," said Phil indignantly. "I heard their story, believed it, and...It was awful. I can't imagine how a judge or jury—"

"What judge? What jury? Why involve a judge and a jury? Unless you're going to charge the fifteen-year-old girl who shot the guy in the hospital with something, why should there be any kind of trial at all? Just convene a coroner's inquest and ask Mercy and me to testify. Maybe Dr. Fong. Mercy took all the notes, so she can type up a summary, leaving out any mention of a girl with a gun, and that will be that. Nobody else needs to get involved, *especially* those girls. The inquest will acquit Charley Wu of any wrongdoing, the bad guys are already dead, and everything will be wrapped up all neat and tidy."

Tidily, I wanted to say but didn't; proving yet again that I can hold my tongue when the stakes are high enough.

"Who saw the guy in the hospital shoot Chan?" asked Phil, who seemed to be going out of his way to play stupid.

"Any one of the girls," said Ernie. "Hell, *all* of them. They were all there, watching."

"And then," I said, continuing the narrative for Ernie, "as he held the gun on them so they were afraid to move or be shot, Mr. Septicemia hammered the window and door shut and took off into the dark. Don't forget that those girls were bound hand and foot, Phil. I don't know how Yue Wan managed to pick up the gun and shoot Septicemia, but she did it. Her hands were *bound*, Phil! That means they were tied together!"

"I know what it means," grumped Phil.

"Well, then, you should be offering her a reward, not threatening to punish her even more. She's been punished enough."

"I'm not threatening to punish anybody," said Phil, still grumpy.

"Also," said Ernie. "In case you suddenly find yourself with a case of warped conscience, if you put the gun into the hands of any one of those girls, Mercy and I can find at least…How many witnesses?" He glanced at me.

"Let me see," I said, thinking hard. "There's Mrs. Sing, Jade Chew, Dr. Fong, Changying and—"

"All right!" cried Phil.

"So there are at least those four witnesses, plus Mercy and me, to say you heard wrong. We can probably find *at least* a hundred more people in Chinatown to corroborate our story, too. You'd feel pretty silly if that happened, wouldn't you?"

"Cripes," muttered Phil. "This is all wrong."

"Not anymore it isn't," I said. "It sounds to me as if everything's going to be all right at last."

"Exactly." Ernie looked at his wristwatch. "Dammit, I'm hungry. I wish Junior'd get here."

"He only left five minutes ago," I reminded him. My stomach growled, and I wished Junior'd get here, too.

"Yeah, yeah, yeah," said Ernie. He'd been leaning over his desk as he spoke to Phil. Now he pushed himself back in his chair, looking worn to a frazzle. "God, I'm bushed. What a day."

As had happened at Mrs. Sing's house several times earlier in the day, silence ensued. Ernie still sat back in his swivel chair. Now he put his hands behind his head. It wouldn't have surprised me if he'd lifted his feet and plunked them on his desk, but he didn't. Phil still sat slumped in his chair, his legs still stuck out in front of him, his hands still shoved in his jacket pockets.

After I don't know how many minutes of that, Phil muttered, "I don't care what you say, I'd never sell my Rosie."

Rose was Phil and Pauline Bigelow's little girl. Not sure how old she was, but she was still a kid. All at once, I remembered some things I'd read about China and the various Chinese provinces. Then I recalled the history of the American West and what I'd read about the Irish potato famine and the concept of Manifest Destiny. It was as if some imp of Satan leaped on my tongue and took it over, because I turned in my chair and stared at Phil.

"You wouldn't, eh? You're just darned lucky you were born in the United States, Phil Bigelow, and some mighty warlord doesn't have his foot on your neck. You're lucky you're not an Apache or a Sioux or, God forbid, one of the Indians our forebears encountered on the eastern shore of this great nation. They're all dead now, you know, because of *us*! You're lucky you're not a poor Irish farmer during the potato famine watching your English overlords eat and drink as you and your entire family starve to death. You're lucky you weren't born a Negro on a Georgia plantation a hundred years ago and got whipped to death for dropping the master's favorite meer-schaum pipe. You're lucky you weren't born in England when the British military went around impressing young men into service on the high seas or as foot soldiers in one of their innumerable wars. You're lucky you haven't had to farm through a deadly drought or live through floods and famine. You're lucky you're not Chinese and living in Los Angeles's Chinatown. You're lucky you're *white*, damn it!"

As had happened once before in this journal, my use of a swear word seemed to make all three of us sitting in Ernie's office jump a little. I shut my mouth, sat up straight in my chair, stared at the window behind Ernie, and cleared my throat. When I dared look at anyone, it was at Ernie. He wore a grin a mile wide on his face. As I continued to gaze at him, I saw him turn to Phil. Only then did I dare a peek at Phil.

Phil, too, had sat up straight in his chair, and he stared at me as if I'd lost my mind. But I hadn't.

"She's right, Phil. You just don't want to admit it."

"I can't believe—"

"Believe it," I demanded. "I read a lot of history books, Phil. Not nice little romantic fantasies, but real books about real history. Human beings are a warlike species, and we treat each other like dirt unless compelled to do otherwise. Why do you think Ernie quit the L.A.P.D.?"

"I know why he quit," Phil mumbled.

"Yeah. You do. And you know they still haven't solved the Taylor murder and why," said Ernie. "It's also probably wise not to say you'd never do something someone else might have had to do in front of Mercy again, because she reads a lot. If that sentence made any sense."

"It did to me," I said.

After a second or two, Phil said, "Yeah, it did to me, too." After another second or two, he added, "I still can't imagine having to sell Rosie."

"I'm sure you can't," I said. "What's more, I'll bet the mothers of those girls—who will never know what's become of them—were pretty upset about them being sold, too. I understand girls aren't valued in China as boys are." I shot a glare at both men in the room. "And don't either of you *dare* say you don't blame them. Did you tell Pauline you were sorry she'd given birth to a girl rather than a boy, Phil Bigelow?"

"What?" Phil gaped at me.

"Well, *did* you?"

"No, of course not!"

"Good."

We all heard the front office door open and the sprightly sound of Junior whistling. I heard Phil's sigh of relief and Ernie's wicked chuckle. I'm almost certain he was as gleeful that I'd actually used a swear word as that Junior was there with the food.

"Here you go!" Junior said as he carried a big paper sack and a smaller, clinking one, into Ernie's office. "Three root beers, three corned beefs on rye, three potato salads wrapped in waxed paper, and three bags of Laura Scudder's potato chips. Well, four, if you count mine." He grinned, plainly not noticing any tension remaining in the room.

"Thanks, Junior. Do you have enough left for a decent tip for yourself?" I asked. I also rose and took the paper sacks from him. Feeding men was women's work, after all. I gave a small snarl, startling Junior, who looked at me oddly. "Sorry," I said. "Just my stomach growling."

"I thought it was *you* growling," said Junior.

"Well," I admitted, "Maybe just a little."

"Golly," said Junior. Probably because he feared I'd snarl again, he hurried to say, "Oh, yeah, there was plenty left over for a tip. Thanks, Miss Mercy!"

"Thank you for fetching the food and drinks," I told Junior.

"Here," said Junior. "Lemme put the bottles on the table." He did so, pulling them out of the paper sack and placing one in front of each place at the desk.

"Thanks, Junior," I said.

"Yeah," said Ernie. "Thanks, Junior."

"Thanks," muttered Phil. He looked as though he'd rather not hear me snarl again, too.

"Happy to help," said Junior, who was unmistakably telling the truth. He resumed whistling whilst jingling the change in his paint-stained trousers as soon as he'd cleared Ernie's office door.

"You tipped him too much," grunted Phil.

Being sure I didn't knock over any root-beer bottles, I carefully moved the paper sack full of food closer to me on Ernie's desk, opened it, and asked Ernie, "Can you eat a sandwich and a half? Maybe two sandwiches? It seems that Mr. Bigelow doesn't care to dine with us this afternoon."

"Hey!" said Phil.

"You'd probably just better shut up for the rest of this day, Phil," advised Ernie. "Mercy's feeling the full force of her power as a female."

"Yes," I said. "I am." Turning to Phil, I asked, "So are you going to shut up and eat, or shall I give Ernie your sandwich, salad and chips? I guess you can have the root beer."

"I'll be quiet," mumbled Phil.

"Good." I handed Ernie a waxed-paper-wrapped sandwich, a wrinkled wad of waxed paper full of potato salad, and a very cunning bag made of waxed paper that was filled with potato chips and fastened with two staples at the folded-over tops. Frowning, I peered into the almost-empty paper sack that had held the food. "Oh, good, they included some napkins—goodness! They're made of paper! Oh, and there are three little spoons." I lifted out the spoons. "Why, I think they're made of cardboard or something like it. I've never seen anything like them before."

"People are inventing all sorts of interesting things these days," said Ernie, ripping open his sandwich bag and reaching for a spoon, which he promptly dipped into the opening he'd made in his waxed-paper bundle of potato salad.

I shoved Phil's food and drink at him. He caught it before it could slide off the edge of the desk, but he didn't speak. He did, however, make a little tray for himself out of his handkerchief and set his lunch out before him.

"Glad you thought about getting us root beers," said Ernie, reaching into a pocket and withdrawing one of those multi-purpose knives. From it, he found the bottle opener and opened all the bottles, which fizzed over slightly. I mopped up the fizz with the napkin I had been going to give to Phil. He could jolly well use his hanky if he wanted to wipe mustard off his chin.

"You're welcome," said I. And I, too, made myself a little luncheon spot on Ernie's desk.

Boy, that was probably the best corned beef on rye I'd ever had. The only thing that would have made it better was if Mother had been there to see me eat it. The potato salad and chips were good, too. Root beer isn't my favorite beverage, but it sure washed down my lunch in an admirable fashion.

The two men finished dining—eating, I mean—before I did. In fact, I had to wrap up the second half of my sandwich because I couldn't eat it and everything else, too. "Want my other half-sandwich, Ernie?"

"Thanks, Mercy. Don't mind if I do." He took it, unwrapped it, and commenced eating it as I finished my potato salad and chips.

Phil rolled his empty wrappers in a big sheet of waxed paper and held it in his lap. If the atmosphere in Ernie's office had been jollier, he'd probably have risen and taken his trash to Ernie's waste-paper basket. In order to do that, however, I'd have had to move, and I don't think Phil quite dared ask me to move on his account, which was all right with me.

"Here," I said to Ernie, shoving my almost-empty waxy bag of potato salad at him. "Eat this, too, will you? If I eat any more food, I'll burst. As it is, Mrs. Buck will probably scold me for not having much appetite for dinner."

"Tomorrow do you think you can go over your notes and type up a summary, Mercy?" asked Ernie, licking his cardboard spoon. "I'll read it over before we take it to Charley's. I want him and his mother and maybe Dr. Fong and Jade Chew to hear it, too, if they can't read it."

"Hey!" said Phil.

Ernie and I both turned to glare at him. After opening his mouth to protest some more, Phil gave up. He even lifted his hands in an I-give-up gesture. "Sure. Go ahead. There's no way I'm going to hear any story other than the one you're going to give me, is there?"

"No," said Ernie and I together. Ernie added, "Not unless you understand Cantonese or Mr. Septicemia, as Mercy calls him, makes a miraculous recovery."

With a shudder, Phil said, "He's not going to do that. Guaranteed."

"Good. Then everything's jake," said Ernie.

"Yup," I agreed. "Everything's jake."

I think my use of a slang word so soon after I'd uttered a swear word proved too much for Phil to bear. He rose from his chair, said, "Excuse me," to me and, after I'd made room for him to do so, he walked out of Ernie's office.

Ernie and I heard the hall door close not long afterward.

Stepping silently through Ernie's office door, I checked to make sure the outer office door was closed and that Phil was on its other side. He was, so I walked to the front door and locked it so he couldn't sneak back in.

Ernie finally plopped his feet on his desk, but not until he'd gathered all the paper goods remaining thereon, stuffed them into the big paper food sack, and dumped them into his waste-paper basket.

"God, what a day," he said with an enormous sigh.

"Yes," I agreed. "It was."

For the record, when I drove my Moon Roadster up to the porch of my house that evening, Lily ran outside, tore to the driver's side of the car, opened the door, flung it wide, and gave me the biggest bear hug I'd ever received in my life. Evidently Charley or one of her other relations had telephoned her at my house to tell her the news. Lily cried all over my coat, but it didn't matter as it was already dirty with plaster dust and wood chips.

TWENTY-NINE

I arose early the next morning in order to get to work smack on time so I could go through my notes and create a coherent and cohesive summary of what Ernie and I thought should be said about the events in question. According to me, I'd done a great job by ten-thirty.

According to Ernie, I'd done a great job, too, although he had me change one or two things. When I asked him why he wanted them changed, he said, "Never underestimate the stupidity of the people who'll be reading this report. I want things spelled out in mind-numbing detail so there can be no possibility of a misunderstanding on anyone's part."

"I thought I'd done that pretty well already," I said a trifle stiffly.

"You did, but some things bear repeating. Also, I want to add a few names as witnesses, but we'll have to get those in Chinatown. I don't want to include anyone's name if they don't want their name mentioned. It's probably a good idea only to mention men's names, too."

"But that's not fair to Jade! She did all the translating!"

"I know it, and you know it, and everyone else who was there knows it. But you're going to get more people to believe all this if you say a man did it rather than a woman. Or a girl."

"Jade's not a girl. She's twenty-one!"

"And she's engaged to marry Charley, don't forget. She has a big stake in the outcome of this fiasco."

"Hmm. You're right about that, I guess."

"You know I am. And don't forget it's not just the Chinese who think most women are half-wits. A few years ago, people were saying riding in cars would make women's guts fall out," said Ernie.

He was right. Specifically, women's wombs were mentioned as the "guts" that would fall out. "How could I ever have forgotten that?"

"Dunno." He crossed out Jade's name and inserted Dr. Fong's. "I'll ask him if he minds having his name used as translator before I use it. If he objects, maybe he can suggest the name of another man."

"Stupid men," I groused.

"Precisely what I just said," acknowledged Ernie, grinning. He made a few other changes—I refuse to call them corrections, because he mainly lied by making them—and handed the document, which was several pages long, back to me. "Will you please retype this? Make a couple of carbon copies, please."

"I will. The carbon copies get paler, the more of them I make."

"I know, but after we get back from Chinatown today, you'll certainly have to type it again. We'll have the department make mimeos of the report eventually. Or even take it to a printer. What the hell, I'll *pay* to have the story told the way we want it told."

"I can pay for the printing," I said.

"I know you can," said Ernie, sounding a trifle curt. "But I can, too, and I'll do it if it needs to be done."

"Very well," I said, understanding it wasn't merely masculine prejudice at work here, but…well, I guess it was masculine prejudice, but it wasn't Ernie's. He wanted to make absolutely *certain* no man could read my report and declare it was written by an incompetent *female*. In fact, if I had to, I'd tell everyone that Ernie had dictated it to me, I'd taken it down on my secretarial pad, and then transcribed it. The last sentence was true, even it hadn't been Ernie who'd dictated it.

I could even show them my secretarial pad. I was almost, if not quite, positive that nobody who would be given the report could read Pitman Shorthand. Anyhow, I'd leave my pad in the office, so nobody could make the attempt if a Pitman user could be found.

So there.

At any rate, I retyped the report and gave it to Ernie. He said, "Good. Let's go to Chinatown and have lunch at Charley's. We can take Lulu if she wants to come with us."

"Sounds good to me," I said, and it did. Besides, I wanted to pick up my cloisonné vase from Mr. Fong's shop.

Lulu wanted to come with us, so we all trooped out to Ernie's crumbling Studebaker. I told Lulu about yesterday's doings as Ernie drove down Hill Street to Chinatown.

"Good Lord," cried Lulu. "I can hardly believe it!"

"I can't either, but it's all true."

"My word, so there *were* girls trapped inside that building!"

"Yes, and they were about starving to death, too, poor things."

"I'm glad you and Ernie rescued them."

"So am I."

"Yeah," said Ernie grudgingly, "so am I, curse it."

"Don't be such a grouch," I told him. "You saved those girls' lives. I wish we could get word to their parents, but there's probably no way to do it."

"Doubt it," agreed Ernie.

"But I'll ask Jade," I said after thinking over the matter for a second. "You never know about these things."

Ernie took his gaze away from traffic for a split-second to look at me. Then he returned his attention to driving and shook his head. "If anybody can do it, it'll be you." His words didn't sound significantly laudatory.

In spite of his tone, I said, "Thank you."

Lulu laughed at both of us.

Ernie found a parking space right there on Hill Street close to Charley's noodle shop, which made me happy, mainly because I was still tired from the day before. *And* from struggling with my notes in order to make them say what Ernie and I wanted them to say and not what they *did* say.

As soon as we got out of Ernie's car, Chinese people stopped what they were doing and turned to stare at us. A couple of them even came up to us, ignored Lulu and me, bowed at Ernie and said something that sounded like, "*Shye-shye.*"

To each "*shye-shye*," Ernie replied, "You're welcome," so I figured out what the Chinese words meant.

Lulu leaned over and whispered, "Why aren't they thanking you?"

"Because they think only men can do anything. Same as with white people."

"But you *did* help rescue those girls!" said Lulu indignantly. "In fact, if it wasn't for you, those poor things would still be trapped in that building."

"I know that, you know that, Ernie knows that, Mrs. Sing, Jade Chew, Dr. Fong—in fact, *everyone* knows that, but it's only men who get thanked."

"That doesn't make any sense," said Lulu.

"It's the way of the world," I said, feeling misused and weary.

"Nertz," said Lulu.

"I agree."

"All right, ladies, let's get some noodles." Ernie pulled the door to Charley's place open, and we walked in.

The chatter in the room stopped instantly, and all the denizens therein turned to stare at us. Charley Wu shouted something at the kitchen in Chinese and came tearing around the counter to shake Ernie's hand.

"Thank you, Ernie! Thank you! According to Dr. Fong, you found out who really killed that devil Chan!"

"Mercy and I did," said Ernie. "Mercy took all the notes."

Although I sensed he didn't much want to, Charley took my hand and said, "Thank you," to me too.

"You're welcome," I said back.

And then Mrs. Wu burst through the swinging kitchen door,

talking a mile a minute in Chinese, ran over to Ernie and me, and gave Ernie a big hug. Then she gave *me* one, by golly!

"You two saved my son!" she exclaimed—I think. She had a heavy accent. Whatever she said, I know she included me in her appreciation, and I appreciated her for it.

Eventually, we got to sit at the counter and have lunch. Mrs. Wu fed us something other than our regular pork and noodles, although I'm not sure what it was. It had almonds, chicken, and noodles, and it was hotter than heck. But scrumptious. *Quite* scrumptious.

Ernie ascertained that Charley could read English, so he left a copy of the report with him. "Look this over. If you have any questions, let me know. Show it to anyone else you want, and let me know if any of them have questions or suggestions. Do it quickly because we want to get it to the police department tomorrow at the latest."

"Will do," said Charley. "Thanks again. I'll show it to Dr. Fong and Mr. Chew. And my uncles, too."

"Good. Give me a call when you're through. We'll get this thing to the L.A.P.D., and your problems should be solved."

After we'd eaten and climbed down from our stools, we had to walk the gamut of Chinatown citizens who'd heard we were in Charley's shop and rushed inside to stare at us. They all thanked us and shook our hands—yes, even mine a time or two—and we eventually made it out the door.

"Whew!" said Lulu. "What a mob."

"Yeah," said Ernie. "And now we have to visit Mrs. Sing."

"Because Mr. Fong's shop is on the way, may I pop in there and pick up my vase?" I asked.

"Sure."

"You mean you bought one of those fabulous vases?" Lulu asked, agog.

Dang. I forgot I hadn't meant Lulu to know, because the vase was so expensive. Too bad, Mercy Allcutt. Deception is never the answer. Well, not too often, anyway. Sometimes it was about the only way to get anything done.

"Yes. I asked him to hold it for me because we had so much

other stuff to carry and I was afraid I'd drop it." That wasn't even much of a fib.

"Oh, I'm so glad you bought one of them. They're *so* pretty!"

So much for attempting to spare Lulu's feelings. I should have known better. Lulu isn't a petty person.

"I'll go in with you," said Ernie. "I want to see Mrs. Sing and Miss Chew, and I don't want you dawdling and oohing and aahing over all the pretty things."

"We won't dawdle," I said, feeling insulted.

Ernie was correct to go with us, however, because as I gazed around at all the gorgeous merchandise for sale in Mr. Fong's shop, I was mightily tempted to dawdle and even ooh and aah a few times. Ernie wouldn't allow me to do that, of course.

Mr. Fong saw us coming, smiled, and walked over to greet us. He carried a wrapped parcel. "Miss Allcutt, this is for you," he said, and handed me the package.

"Thank you!" I said, taking the parcel, surprised.

"It's the vase you wanted to purchase," went on Mr. Fong. "You performed heroically yesterday along with you, Mr. Templeton"—Mr. Fong bowed to Ernie, who bowed back—"and I want you to have it. I have something for you, too, Mr. Templeton."

"Thanks," said a definitely startled Ernie.

"I remember you from when you bought one of my cinnabar bracelets for your sister and thought you could use a tie clasp."

"Thanks!" said Ernie again. I could tell he meant his thanks.

It took us a little longer than Ernie wanted it to for us to conclude our business in Chinatown that day, but the time was well spent. Even grumpy Mr. Chew, Jade's grandfather, thanked us for saving the girls and clearing Charley Wu's name.

Jade was overjoyed to see us and gave Ernie and me both a wrapped package. "For Christmas," she said, smiling up a storm.

"Thank you!" I said, surprised and gratified.

"Thank *you*," said Jade.

And so it went. We finally finished our business—Dr. Fong said he'd get together with Charley and one of them would call Ernie if they wanted any changes made to our report—and we got back to the Figueroa Building not too long after our technical lunch hour was over.

True to Dr. Fong's word, Charley telephoned Ernie's office with suggestions for the report we aimed to turn in to the police. Ernie asked me to take notes as he and Charley talked, so I locked the front office door, grabbed my secretarial pad and several pencils, and went to Ernie's office. There I plunked myself down on a visitor's chair in front of Ernie's desk and poised my pencil over my pad.

It took darned near *forever* to get that wretched document polished so everyone involved—and even a few people who weren't—was pleased with it. My fingers cramped a couple of times, and I had to shake out my hand. Ernie frowned a little but didn't mind. Eventually, Ernie and Charley concluded they had created the result they desired.

Then I had to type the whole blasted thing again. I made three carbon copies. Good thing I'm a quick and neat typist—for which skill I can thank the Boston Y.W.C.A.—because it didn't take me more than thirty or forty minutes to get the whole report typed for what I hoped was the last time and take it in to Ernie's office. As I'd been typing, Ernie'd been lounging in his swivel chair, his feet on his desk, reading the *Los Angeles Times*. I acquitted him of being lazy, because he'd been anything *but* ever since the idiotic L.A.P.D. had arrested Charley Wu for a murder he didn't commit. In fact, Ernie had been a real hero, by golly!

I didn't tell him so. "Here," I said, handing the thick report to him when he lowered his newspaper.

With a sigh, Ernie said, "Thanks. I hope this is the last time I'll ever have to see the damn thing."

"I hope so, too. I sure don't want to have to type it again."

"Don't blame you. Okay, go write your book while I read through this monster report again."

"Thanks, Ernie. My fingers hurt, so I think I'll just read and leave the writing for another day." I didn't tell him that after this week, I was considering switching my novelistic pursuits from mysteries to historical romances. Real-life mysteries could be dreadful and grubby and disgusting. Of course, novelists never wrote about the icky stuff. It was probably just as well.

The report passed muster, thank God!

"I'm taking this to the print shop up the street to get it printed. Think I'll have a hundred copies made. That should ensure that everyone who needs one gets one, whether they want it or not."

"Sounds good to me," I said as I watched Ernie plop his hat on his head and shrug himself into his warm overcoat. He unlocked the front office door and slouched off. He came back about two hours later with an armload of newly printed reports.

"I'll take a dozen or so of these to Phil tomorrow," he told me.

I was just packing up to go home. "Good. He'll be delighted." And then I paused, thinking of something we needed to do before we could call the case completely closed. "Um, Ernie?"

He squinted at me. "Yeah?"

"We need to do one last thing before we call this case closed."

"Cripes. What?"

"Call the home where Mr. Brentwood lives and tell the matron Mr. Brentwood was absolutely correct, and he played a part in solving a tricky problem."

After looking at me for approximately a year and a half, Ernie expelled a gigantic sigh and said, "You're right." So he picked up the receiver from the telephone's cradle, dialed the reception desk, and asked Lulu to get in touch with whatever the name of the home was where Mr. Brentwood lived.

When he hung up the receiver after speaking to the matron, Ernie said, "Glad you thought about poor old Brentwood. Mrs. Wilkes said he's been worried about seeing a bound woman ever since the home took those inmates, or whatever they call 'em, to Chinatown."

"I'm so glad." Another thought occurred to me. "Say, want to come to dinner tonight? We can regale the ladies with our derring-do in Chinatown. We can leave out the disgusting parts."

"Happy to eat another one of Mrs. Buck's meals, but I really don't want to talk about the case again in this lifetime. Maybe the next, too."

"Don't much blame you."

So we left the office together, Ernie locking the stack of reports in his office, handing me one, and taking three or four with him. "Just in case," he said, and we walked to the elevator together.

When we reached the lobby, Caroline and Sue had already arrived, and Lulu was ready to head for home.

"You gals want a ride to Mercy's house?" asked Ernie.

"Can we all fit in that rattletrap of yours?" asked Lulu.

"We've done it before," Sue reminded her.

"Yes. Thank you, Mr. Templeton," said Caroline. "It's quite cold outside. A ride would be most appreciated."

So Ernie drove us all home. Lulu, Sue and Caroline were squished in the back seat. I had the honor of sitting in the front seat.

Mrs. Buck was delighted to feed Ernie again. And Lily nearly knocked him over when she ran to give him a hug for saving her brother. She gave me one, too, so I didn't mind.

THIRTY

After Phil Bigelow turned in his report about the Chan murder to his superiors, they didn't even think a coroner's inquest was necessary. They just did whatever it was they had to do to remove any stain from Charley Wu's character, deleted any mention of him from their books, and closed the case. I don't think anyone even thought to ask what had become of the girls we'd rescued, which was fine with Ernie and me. I know because I asked him.

During the week and a half that remained before Christmas after everything I just related happened, Lulu and I pretty much denuded the shelves of all the ten-cent stores in town and the Broadway Department of Christmas funnery. I don't think that's a word, and I don't care.

By then, I was so relieved to have cleared Charley's name and rescued those poor girls, I didn't much care about anything except having a wonderful Christmas celebration in my new-to-me home. I didn't even care about my mother, who telephoned several times to demand I spend Christmas Eve and Christmas Day in Pasadena with her and my father. I didn't hesitate a single second before saying "No." I didn't feel faint afterward, what's more. Well, not after the first telephonic refusal, at any rate.

Christmas Eve at Mercy's Manor was a happy affair, and the attendees were an eclectic group.

Sue Krekeler and Caroline Terry went, respectively, to San Bernardino and Alhambra to spend the holiday with their families. Lulu and her brother Rupert came to my house, as did Ernie, Lily Wu, Mrs. Wu, Charley Wu, Jade Chew, Mr. and Mrs. Buck and their son Calvin.

I had invited their daughter, Loretta, too, but she was teaching school in Mississippi and couldn't get to Los Angeles. I wished she could get out of Mississippi. I'd read too much in recent weeks about how colored people were treated in our southern states to feel comfortable with her there. I even went so far as to tell Mrs. Buck so.

"Bless your sweet heart, child, that's the only place she could find to teach! She wouldn't be allowed to teach most other places, because of her color."

I felt my mouth pinch up and was about to say something when Mrs. Buck went on. "Child, I pray for the day when everyone is like you and doesn't care about a person's color, but I'm afraid that day's a long way off right now. If it will ease your heart, I can tell you that Loretta is looking at teaching at a couple of private all-Negro schools here in California."

"I didn't know there were schools like that," I said, displaying my ignorance again. I was used to it.

"Oh, laws, yes, child. I expect the same is true for the children in Chinatown."

"I expect you're right," I said, my feeling of Christmas merriment dimming for a minute.

"But you're a light in Mr. Buck's and my life, child. And Calvin's, too. If it wasn't for Mr. Ernie, he'd have gone to the electric chair by this time. Same with that Chinese fellow out there."

Mrs. Wu brought a large white cardboard container filled with what Jade told me was a special Chinese treat. Charley carried a smaller container which, Jade said, was to dip the contents of the large container in. When Ernie and I carried both containers to the kitchen, I was a trifle trepidatious—I don't think that's a word, either—fearing Mrs. Buck might object to her ham-centered dinner plans being altered.

Ernie set the large container on a spare bit of kitchen counter, and I set the smaller one beside it. When she opened the large container, Mrs. Buck threw up her arms, and I feared a rebellion was about to transpire. Then she lowered her arms and said, "Well, I don't know what those things are, but what the heck."

Peering into the large container, Ernie smiled broadly. "They're dumplings! And I'll bet the small container contains the sauce to dip them in. Be careful. I see chili flakes floating in there."

"What are chili flakes?" I asked weakly.

"Some kind of ground-up dried chili peppers. I suspect the sauce is made with soy and hoisin sauce, and some sesame oil and chili flakes. I'm no cook."

I wanted to ask what hoisin sauce was but didn't.

"Let's ask Charley!" Ernie said. "He'll know. All I know is that the dipping stuff and the dumplings are delicious together."

"Huh," said Mrs. Buck. "If you say so, Mr. Ernie, I'll serve it all up, but you'll have to tell me how to do it."

"Oh," said Ernie, sounding and looking as if he were at a loss.

But I had one of my brilliant ideas. "I know! Let's serve them along with the appetizers!" I'd had the Bucks and Lily set out a corner table in the living room to hold appetizers. "We can put the dumplings on a platter and put the sauce in a bowl in the middle of the dumplings. You know, the dumplings can kind of rest around the bowl of sauce."

"Good thinking," said Ernie.

"Yes. That should work," said Mrs. Buck doubtfully.

"But," I added, sensing what might become her next objection. "You hadn't anticipated these, so let me get a platter and a bowl to use, and Ernie and I can set the dumplings and sauce on the appetizer table."

"Thank you, child," said Mrs. Buck, sounding relieved.

"I love those dumplings," said Lily wistfully. "You won't regret this, Mrs. Buck."

Shaking her head, Mrs. Buck said, "If you say so, child."

So I dashed up to my room, found the glorious Chinese platter I'd aimed to give to Chloe the next time I saw her—I'd hoped it would be that night, but she and Harvey gave in and went to our parents' house in Pasadena—and brought it downstairs. It couldn't quite hold all the dumplings with the white bowl into which Ernie dumped most of the sauce, but that was all right. We could either refill the platters or eat the dumplings left over the next morning. The Bucks would be having their own Christmas celebration on Christmas Day, and they weren't expected to work.

The dumplings were heavenly. We all thanked Mrs. Wu, who seemed pleased with herself, her son, her daughter, her soon-to-be daughter-in-law, and life in general.

It was a darned good thing I had so many leaves to put into the dining room table, because we required a huge table to hold all the foodstuffs and seat all the people. But we managed nicely. I made Ernie sit at the head of the table, which he didn't want to do.

"I don't know how to carve a ham!" he cried, horrified.

"I'll slice it in the kitchen," said Mrs. Buck, laughing at him. So she did.

We all sat at the table, including the Bucks and Calvin and the Chinese contingent. My rule as of the preceding week was that nobody would ever be excluded from my home based merely on the color of their skin.

Mrs. Buck's steamed persimmon pudding with hard sauce was fabulous. It contained currants, but I didn't mind currants as long as I didn't have to eat candied orange peels along with them.

After dinner, stuffed and happy, we brought tea and coffee to the living room. Mr. Buck plugged in the Christmas tree lights and turned off the overhead lights, and my eyes got all misty. My very first Christmas in my very first home.

"Can anybody play the piano?" Lulu asked after we'd been staring at the Christmas tree for what seemed like an hour or two.

After a several-second pause, Ernie said, "I took piano lessons when I was a kid. I still like to play sometimes."

"Really?" I was astounded. Unfortunately, I sounded like it.

"Really," he said snappishly. "I'm not just a good detective, you know."

"I'm impressed," I said. "There are music sheets in the piano bench, but I don't know if there are any Christmas carols among them."

"Why do you have a piano if you can't play the thing?" he asked.

With a shrug I said, "I always wanted to take piano lessons. I'm hoping I can still take them one of these days."

"I'm surprised your mother didn't make you take lessons," he said as he rose from the sofa with something of a grunt.

"So am I," I told him, surprised she hadn't until I realized something. "She only made me do stuff I didn't want to do," I said as Ernie made his way to the piano, switched on the light over the music stand, and sat on the bench.

"Hope this thing has been tuned recently," he muttered as he placed his hands on the keys.

"I keep it tuned," I told him.

By the way, in case you believed I'd allowed the Bucks and Lily to languish in the kitchen to clean everything up, you'd be wrong. I'd had the foresight to hire three Spanish-speaking women to clean up after our meal. I also told them to join in the festivities when they were finished cleaning, but I'm not sure they understood me. Ernie solved the problem by telling them in Spanish what I just told them in English.

"I didn't know you could speak Spanish *and* Cantonese," I said, impressed.

"I'm not as dumb as I look," he told me.

"Good thing," I told him back.

So we sang Christmas carols—at least the ones Ernie could remember how to play—and had a good old time. I noticed Jade knew a few of the carols we sang, too. And the Bucks sang a duet of a song I'd never heard before. They both had fabulous voices. Calvin accompanied them on the piano. After that, Ernie ceded piano-playing duties to Calvin Buck, who was an excellent pianist.

When I asked him where he'd learned, he looked kind of bashful and merely said, "Oh, here and there."

Ernie told me later that Calvin had been taught by a piano player in a Los Angeles saloon that catered to colored people. Learn something new every day. The place was now an ice-cream parlor, according to Ernie, and nobody played the piano there any longer. When I said Calvin must have been a very small child when he'd begun his lessons, Ernie only smiled and said, "He was."

After we'd been singing, talking, and laughing for I don't know how long, I noticed the Spanish-speaking ladies had joined us. They were kind of squished up against a far wall, but they seemed to be enjoying the music and the general jollity.

Along about midnight, folks began drifting off. I wished everyone goodnight at my front door—Lulu and I had asked Mr. Buck to hang our red paper Chinese lanterns in the black-and-white tiled entryway, and they were glorious.

The Chinese contingent left in a clump, followed shortly by the Spanish-speakers. That left Lulu, Ernie, the Bucks and me. We were all bushed.

"I'm going to bed," said Lulu, yawning. "Great Christmas Eve, Mercy."

"It was, wasn't it? Thanks, Lulu. You made it special."

"Aw, shucks," said Lulu, teasing me. But I'd meant it.

"We're going to turn in, too, Miss Mercy," said Mr. Buck. He and Mrs. Buck and Calvin thanked me for a wonderful evening, too.

"You did all the work!" I said, meaning it.

They only smiled, shook Ernie's and my hands, and walked through the living room to the hall, through the kitchen, and to their apartment off the kitchen.

That left Ernie and me.

"Best Christmas Eve I've ever spent," said Ernie when we were alone.

"I'm so glad."

Never mind what happened next, but Ernie eventually left my place for his cold, lonely apartment on Yale Street near Chinatown in downtown Los Angeles.

HOLLYWOOD ANGELS

MERCY ALLCUTT NOVEL, BOOK #8

"Lulu, you can't go alone!" I gaped at my friend and tenant, Lulu LaBelle, with horror.

"Nertz, Mercy. This is just for an interview and to talk about my career goals. I've talked to him several times in his office. He took me to dine and dance at the Club Parisienne. You know he did!"

"I know, but this seems different somehow." What's more, I didn't like it. Lulu was probably my best friend, and I didn't want her to get hurt by a devious Lothario.

"It is different. He wants to take a few still photos of me to see if he thinks I'll look good on the screen." Lulu plucked at a violent red sleeve of her violent red dress with fingers the nails of which were painted a violent red matching the dress. She was truly blink-worthy that evening.

"But Lulu, it's night! You're the one who told me these talent scouts, directors and producers are often up to no good and try to take advantage of the young women who are longing to be stars."

"Yes, I know, but this fellow is the goods, all right. Look here, he even has a card!" She handed me a thickish piece of oblong card-board, upon which was printed in florid print Elbert R. Smedley,

Agent-Producer-Director. Printed on the card, too, were Smedley's address and telephone number.

"Anybody can get cards printed, Lulu," I told her, doubt clear to hear in my voice.

"Nertz, Mercy! Like I said, I've been to his office, and I've been out to dinner with him. His office is in a good part of town. I've been to his office three times!"

"Yes, so you said."

"Well, then! He's legit! He's helped lots of girls get their start."

"What are their names?" I asked.

Lulu tossed her head. "I can't remember. Anyhow, he's had bad luck with them backing out at the last minute after he did all the groundwork for them, but he said he's sure I won't be like that. He's going to take photos of me this evening and show them around as soon as he gets them developed. He knows some casting directors will want me!"

"But I thought you said this appointment tonight isn't in his office," I said, still attempting to make Lulu see reason. I'd known for months she wanted to be a big star on the silver screen, but she mostly just sat around all day fiddling with her fingernails behind the reception desk at the Figueroa Building where we both worked.

"Of course, it isn't," said Lulu as if it made sense for him to be seeing her in a different address than where his office lay. "Other talent scouts and producers are always trying to snitch the people he's promoting. He doesn't want them to get a look at me, for fear someone will steal me before he can get me established. They're all jealous of him!"

Oh, dear. This really didn't sound right to me.

"May I please just drive you to his location, Lulu? I'll sit in the car and wait for you. I won't get in your way, I promise."

"It's the middle of January, Mercy! You'll freeze to death if you wait in your car."

"I don't mind," I said, which was the truest test of friendship I could think of. Lulu was right. We might live in Los Angeles and not the frozen North, but the night air was cold.

"Nonsense. He's sending a car for me. See?"

"It's nice he's sending a car for you," I said. "As long as he aims to bring you home early and in one piece."

"What do you mean? Mercy Allcutt! Do you think I'm an idiot? I've heard all the bad stories! I know what goes on. Mr. Smedley won't do anything awful to me. He just won't."

"I guess there's no use arguing with you anymore, right?"

"Right." Lulu clapped her black cloche hat with the violent red silk flowers on it on her bottle-blond hair and stuck a pretty Chinese pin with a red whatchamacallit at its end to hold the hat in place. Then she twirled in front of the Cheval glass mirror in my room, my room being the only room in Mercy's Manor to have a full-length mirror.

"Well, good luck," I said doubtfully.

"Thanks, Mercy. Stop worrying!"

"I'll try." I also tried to sound cheerful.

And Lulu left for her appointment with the talent scout who was going to make her a huge star in the Hollywood firmament.

It took me a long time to get to sleep that night. Buttercup, my adorable apricot miniature poodle, finally got disgusted with my tossing and turning and leapt off my bed and curled up on the rug.

I don't know how long I'd been asleep when I awoke again to a sleepy "Woof" from Buttercup and a gentle shaking of my shoulder.

"M-Mercy?"

Blinking in surprise, I leaned over and pulled the chain on my bedside table's lamp. My eyes grew wide and my mouth fell open when I saw a disheveled Lulu, her lipstick smeared, her mascara running down her cheeks, her dress torn and the red roses on her hat dragging around her shoulders. "Lulu! You look like you've been in the Battle of the Somme! What did that beast do to you? What in the world happened!"

"I-I'll tell you. But later, okay? I h-h-had to take a t-t-taxicab home, but I don't have any m-m-money! Will you please lend me enough m-money for the cab fare?"

"Lulu! Of course, I'll pay for your cab fare. Stay here. Don't move. I want to know what that horrible, cheating, louse of a bounder did to you! I'll kill him with my bare hands! I knew you shouldn't have gone to see him!"

It was, probably, the stupidest and wrongest (I'm sure that's not a word) sentence I could say to the poor girl, who knew better than I that she shouldn't have met Mr. Smedley at night. She collapsed onto my bed, sobbing as if her heart and several bones were broken.

Available in Paperback and eBook from Your Favorite Bookstore or Online Retailer

ACKNOWLEDGMENTS

Diana Jackson has become the hero of my life. She's my plot partner, editor, and overall best influence over my writing life I've ever had. Thank you, Diana! I'll never be able to thank you enough. By the way, Diana lives in the U.K., and I live in the U.S.A., but that hasn't mattered so far.

Thank you, too, to Sue Krekeler and Margaret Cronk for their excellent beta reading. I don't know why they want to do this, but I'm *so* glad they do!

The Chinatown depicted in my Mercy Allcutt books isn't the one that was there in Mercy's day; however, I know and love it so well that I use it. Today's Chinatown wasn't around until the late 1930s. So I cheat occasionally. I do *so much* research for these books, I figure a cheat every now and then is fair.

If you enjoy this book, please tell people and leave a review somewhere online. Thank you! Authors rely on word-of-mouth. We can't survive without readers!

ABOUT THE AUTHOR

Award-winning author Alice Duncan lives with a herd of wild dachshunds (enriched from time to time with fosterees from New Mexico Dachshund Rescue) in Roswell, New Mexico. She's not a UFO enthusiast; she's in Roswell because her mother's family settled there fifty years before the aliens crashed (and living in Roswell, NM, is cheaper than living in Pasadena, CA, unfortunately). Alice would love to hear from you at alice@aliceduncan.net

www.aliceduncan.net

CPSIA information can be obtained
at www.ICGtesting.com
Printed in the USA
BVHW051309131022
649382BV00005B/97